DEATH WISH

Or-tis had Juana partially upon a table and with one hairy hand he was choking her. When he saw me he went white and whipped a pistol from its holster. Juana dragged his arm down as he pulled the trigger so the bullet went into the floor.

Before he could shake her off I had wrenched the weapon from his grasp. I asked Juana if he had wronged her.

"Not yet," she said. "He just came in."

He commenced to plead and then to whimper. He promised me freedom if I let him live. He promised never to bother Juana again. He would have promised me the sun and the moon and all the little stars, had he thought I wished them, but I wished only one thing just then—to see him die.

By Edgar Rice Burroughs
Published by Ballantine Books:

THE MOON MAID
THE MOON MEN

The *Tarzan* series
    24 books

The *Mars* series
    11 books

The *Pellucidar* series
    6 books

The *Venus* series
    5 books

THE LAND THAT TIME FORGOT
THE PEOPLE THAT TIME FORGOT
OUT OF TIME'S ABYSS

ALL COMPLETE AND UNABRIDGED!

THE
MOON
MEN

Edgar Rice Burroughs

A Del Rey Book

BALLANTINE BOOKS • NEW YORK

A Del Rey Book
Published by Ballantine Books

ISBN 0-345-37406-1

This edition published by arrangement with Edgar Rice Burroughs, Inc.

Manufactured in the United States of America

First Ballantine Books Edition: June 1992

Cover Art by Lawrence Schwinger. Copyright © 1992 by Edgar Rice Burroughs, Inc.

Contents

THE MOON MEN

1.	A Strange Meeting	3
2.	Soor, the Tax Collector	15
3.	The Hellhounds	25
4.	Brother General Or-tis	38
5.	The Fight on Market Day	50
6.	The Court Martial	61
7.	Betrayed	71
8.	The Arrest of Julian 8th	83
9.	I Horsewhip an Officer	94
10.	Revolution	103
11.	The Butcher	113

THE RED HAWK

1.	The Flag	125
2.	Exodus	137
3.	Armageddon	148
4.	The Capitol	158
5.	The Sea	171
6.	Saku the Nipon	182
7.	Bethelda	193
8.	Raban	204
9.	Reunion	217
10.	Peace	226

THE MOON MEN

1

A Strange Meeting

IT WAS EARLY in March, 1969, that I set out from my bleak camp on the desolate shore some fifty miles southeast of Herschel Island after polar bear. I had come into the Arctic the year before to enjoy the first real vacation that I had ever had. The definite close of the Great War, in April two years before, had left an exhausted world at peace—a condition that had never before existed and with which we did not know how to cope.

I think that we all felt lost without war—I know that I did; but I managed to keep pretty busy with the changes that peace brought to my bureau, the Bureau of Communications, readjusting its activities to the necessities of world trade uninfluenced by war. During my entire official life I had had to combine the two—communications for war and communications for commerce, so the adjustment was really not a Herculean task. It took a little time, that was all, and after it was a fairly well accomplished fact I asked for an indefinite leave, which was granted.

My companions of the hunt were three Eskimos, the youngest of whom, a boy of nineteen, had never before seen a white man, so absolutely had the last twenty years of the Great War annihilated the meager trade that had formerly been carried on between their scattered settlements and the more favored lands of so-called civilization.

But this is not a story of my thrilling experiences in the rediscovery of the Arctic regions. It is, rather, merely in way of explanation as to how I came to meet *him* again after a lapse of some two years.

We had ventured some little distance from shore when I, who was in the lead, sighted a bear far ahead. I had scaled a hummock of rough and jagged ice when I made the discovery and, motioning to my companion to follow me, I slid and stumbled to the comparatively level stretch of a broad floe beyond, across which I ran toward another icy barrier that shut off my view of the bear. As I reached it I turned to look back for my companions, but they were not yet in sight. As a matter of fact I never saw them again.

The whole mass of ice was in movement, grinding and cracking; but I was so accustomed to this that I gave the matter little heed until I had reached the summit of the second ridge, from which I had another view of the bear which I could see was moving directly toward me, though still at a considerable distance. Then I looked back again for my fellows. They were no where in sight, but I saw something else that filled me with consternation—the floe had split directly at the first hummock and I was now separated from the mainland by an ever widening lane of icy water. What became of the three Eskimos I never knew, unless the floe parted directly beneath their feet and engulfed them. It scarcely seems credible to me, even with my limited experience in the Arctics, but if it was not that which snatched them forever from my sight, what was it?

I now turned my attention once more to the bear. He had evidently seen me and assumed that I was prey for he was coming straight toward me at a rather rapid gait. The ominous cracking and groaning of the ice increased, and to my dismay I saw that it was rapidly breaking up all about me and as far as I could see in all directions great floes and little floes were rising and falling as upon the bosom of a long, rolling swell.

Presently a lane of water opened between the bear and me, but the great fellow never paused. Slipping into the water he swam the gap and clambered out upon the huge floe upon which I tossed. He was over two hundred yards away, but I covered his left shoulder with the top of my sight and fired. I hit him and he let out an awful roar and came for me on a run. Just as I was about to fire again the floe split once more directly in front of him and he went into the water clear out of sight for a moment.

When he reappeared I fired again and missed. Then he started to crawl out on my diminished floe once more. Again I fired. This time I broke his shoulder, yet still he managed to clamber onto my floe and advance toward me. I thought that he would never die until he had reached me and wreaked his vengeance upon me, for though I pumped bullet after bullet into him he continued to advance, though at last he barely dragged himself forward, growling and grimacing horribly. He wasn't ten feet from me when once more my floe split directly between me and the bear and at the foot of the ridge upon which I stood, which now turned completely over, precipitating me into the water a few feet from the great, growling beast. I turned and tried to scramble back onto the floe from which I had been thrown, but its sides were far too precipitous and there was no other that I could possibly reach, except that upon which the bear lay grimacing at me. I had clung to my rifle and without more ado I struck out for a side of the floe, a few yards from the spot where the beast lay apparently waiting for me.

He never moved while I scrambled up on it, except to turn his head so that he was always glaring at me. He did not come toward me and I determined not to fire at him again until he did, for I had discovered that my bullets seemed only to infuriate him. The art of big game hunting had been practically dead for years as only rifles and ammunition for the killing of men had been manufactured. Being in the government service I had found no difficulty in obtaining a permit to bear arms for hunting purposes, but the government owned all the firearms and when they came to issue me what I required, there was nothing to be had but the ordinary service rifle as perfected at the time of the close of the Great War, in 1967. It was a great mankiller, but it was not heavy enough for big game.

The water lanes about us were now opening up at an appalling rate, and there was a decided movement of the ice toward the open sea, and there I was alone, soaked to the skin, in a temperature around zero, bobbing about in the Arctic Ocean marooned on a half acre of ice, with a wounded and infuriated polar bear, which appeared to me at this close range to be about the size of the First Presbyterian Church at home.

I don't know how long it was after that that I lost consciousness. When I opened my eyes again I found myself in a nice, white iron cot in the sick bay of a cruiser of the newly formed International Peace Fleet which patroled and policed the world. A hospital steward and a medical officer were standing at one side of my cot looking down at me, while at the foot was a fine looking man in the uniform of an admiral. I recognized him at once.

"Ah," I said, in what could have been little more than a whisper, "you have come to tell me the story of Julian 9th. You promised, you know, and I shall hold you to it."

He smiled. "You have a good memory. When you are out of this I'll keep my promise."

I lapsed immediately into unconsciousness again, they told me afterward, but the next morning I awoke refreshed and except for having been slightly frosted about the nose and cheeks, none the worse for my experience. That evening I was seated in the admiral's cabin, a Scotch highball, the principal ingredients of which were made in Kansas, at my elbow, and the admiral opposite me.

"It was certainly a fortuitous circumstance for me that you chanced to be cruising about over the Arctic just when you were," I had remarked. "Captain Drake tells me that when the lookout sighted me the bear was crawling toward me; but that when you finally dropped low enough to land a man on the floe the beast was dead less than a foot from me. It was a close shave, and I am mighty thankful to you and to the cause, whatever it may have been, that brought you to the spot."

"That is the first thing that I must speak to you about,"

he replied. "I was searching for you. Washington knew, of course, about where you expected to camp, for you had explained your plans quite in detail to your secretary before you left, and so when the President wanted you I was dispatched immediately to find you. In fact, I requested the assignment when I received instructions to dispatch a ship in search of you. In the first place I wished to renew our acquaintance and also to cruise to this part of the world, where I had never before chanced to be."

"The President wanted me!" I repeated.

"Yes, Secretary of Commerce White died on the fifteenth and the President desires that you accept the portfolio."

"Interesting, indeed," I replied; "but not half so interesting as the story of Julian 9th, I am sure."

He laughed good naturedly. "Very well," he exclaimed; "here goes!"

Let me preface this story, as I did the other that I told you on board the liner Harding two years ago, with the urgent request that you attempt to keep constantly in mind the theory that there is no such thing as time—that there is no past and no future—that there is only *now*, there never has been anything but *now* and there never will be anything but *now*. It is a theory analogous to that which stipulates that there is no such thing as space. There may be those who think that they understand it, but I am not one of them. I simply know what I know—I do not try to account for it. As easily as I recall events in this incarnation do I recall events in previous incarnations; but, far more remarkable, similarly do I recall, or should I say *foresee*? events in incarnations of the future. No, I do not foresee them—I have lived them.

I have told you of the attempt made to reach Mars in the Barsoom and of how it was thwarted by Lieutenant-Commander Orthis. That was in the year 2026. You will recall that Orthis, through hatred and jealousy of Julian 5th, wrecked the engines of the Barsoom, necessitating a landing upon the moon, and of how the ship was drawn into the mouth of a great lunar crater and through the crust of our satellite to the world within.

After being captured by the Va-gas, human quadrupeds of the moon's interior, Julian 5th escaped with Nah-ee-lah, Princess of Laythe, daughter of a race of lunar mortals similar to ourselves, while Orthis made friends of the Kalkars, or Thinkers, another lunar human race. Orthis taught the Kalkars, who were enemies of the people of Laythe, to manufacture gunpowder, shells and cannon, and with these attacked and destroyed Laythe.

Julian 5th and Nah-ee-lah, the moon maid, escaped from the burning city and later were picked up by the Barsoom which had been repaired by Norton, a young ensign, who with two other officers had remained aboard. Ten years after they had landed upon the inner surface of the moon Julian 5th and his companions brought the Barsoom to dock safely at the city of Washington, leaving Lieutenant-Commander Orthis in the moon.

Julian 5th and the Princess Nah-ee-lah were married and in that same year, 2036, a son was born to them and was called Julian 6th. He was the great-grandfather of Julian 9th for whose story you have asked me, and in whom I lived again in the twenty-second century.

For some reason no further attempts were made to reach Mars, with whom we had been in radio communication for years. Possibly it was due to the rise of a religious cult which preached against all forms of scientific progress and which by political pressure was able to mold and influence several successive weak administrations of a notoriously weak party that had had its origin nearly a century before in a group of peace-at-any-price men.

It was they who advocated the total disarmament of the world, which would have meant disbanding the International Peace Fleet forces, the scrapping of all arms and ammunition, and the destruction of the few munition plants operated by the governments of the United States and Great Britain, who now jointly ruled the world. It was England's king who saved us from the full disaster of this mad policy, though the weaklings of this country aided and abetted by the weaklings of Great Britain succeeded in cutting the peace fleet in two, one half of it being turned over to the merchant marine, in reducing the number of munition factories and in scrapping half the armament of the world.

And then in the year 2050 the blow fell. Lieutenant-Commander Orthis, after twenty-four years upon the moon, returned to Earth with one hundred thousand Kalkars and a thousand Va-gas. In a thousand great ships they came bearing arms and ammunition and strange, new engines of destruction fashioned by the brilliant mind of the arch villain of the universe.

No one but Orthis could have done it. No one but Orthis would have done it. It had been he who had perfected the engines that had made the Barsoom possible. After he had become the dominant force among the Kalkars of the moon he had aroused their imaginations with tales of the great, rich world lying ready and unarmed within easy striking distance of them. It had been an easy thing to enlist their labor in the building of the ships and the manufacture of the countless accessories necessary to the successful accomplishment of the great adventure.

The moon furnished all the needed materials, the Kalkars furnished the labor and Orthis the knowledge, the brains and the leadership. Ten years had been devoted to the spreading of his propaganda and the winning over of the Thinkers, and then fourteen years were required to build and outfit the fleet.

Five days before they arrived astronomers detected the fleet as minute specks upon the eyepieces of their telescopes. There was much speculation, but it was Julian 5th alone who guessed the truth. He warned the governments at London and Washington, but though he was then in command of the International Peace Fleet his appeals were treated with levity and ridicule. He knew Orthis and so he knew that it was easily within the man's ability to construct a fleet, and he also knew that only for one purpose would Orthis return to Earth with so great a number of ships. It meant war, and the earth had nothing but a handful of cruisers wherewith to defend herself—there were not available in the world twenty-

five thousand organized fighting men, nor equipment for
more than half again that number.

The inevitable occurred. Orthis seized London and Washington simultaneously. His well armed forces met with practically no resistance. Their could be no resistance for there
was nothing wherewith to resist. It was a criminal offense to
possess firearms. Even edged weapons with blades over six
inches long were barred by law. Military training, except for
the chosen few of the International Peace Fleet, had been
banned for years. And against this pitiable state of disarmament and unpreparedness was brought a force of a hundred
thousand well armed, seasoned warriors with engines of destruction that were unknown to earth men. A description of
one alone will suffice to explain the utter hopelessness of the
cause of the earth men.

This instrument, of which the invaders brought but one,
was mounted upon the deck of their flag ship and operated
by Orthis in person. It was an invention of his own which no
Kalkar understood or could operate. Briefly, it was a device
for the generation of radio-activity at any desired vibratory
rate and for the directing of the resultant emanations upon
any given object within its effective range. We do not know
what Orthis called it, but the earth men of that day knew it
was an electronic rifle.

It was quite evidently a recent invention and, therefore, in
some respects crude, but be that as it may its effects were
sufficiently deadly to permit Orthis to practically wipe out
the entire International Peace Fleet in less than thirty days as
rapidly as the various ships came within range of the electronic rifle. To the layman the visual effects induced by this
weird weapon were appalling and nerve shattering. A mighty
cruiser vibrant with life and power might fly majestically to
engage the flagship of the Kalkars, when as by magic every
aluminum part of the cruiser would vanish as mist before the
sun, and as nearly ninety per cent of a peace fleet cruiser,
including the hull, was constructed of aluminum, the result
may be imagined—one moment there was a great ship forg-
ing through the air, her flags and pennants flying in the wind,

her band playing, her officers and men at their quarters; the next a mass of engines, polished wood, cordage, flags and human beings hurtling earthward to extinction.

It was Julian 5th who discovered the secret of this deadly weapon and that it accomplished its destruction by projecting upon the ships of the Peace Fleet the vibratory rate of radioactivity identical with that of aluminum, with the result that, thus excited, the electrons of the attacked substance increased their own vibratory rate to a point that they became dissipated again into their elemental and invisible state—in other words aluminum was transmuted into something else that was as invisible and intangible as ether. Perhaps it was ether.

Assured of the correctness of his theory, Julian 5th withdrew in his own flagship to a remote part of the world, taking with him the few remaining cruisers of the fleet. Orthis searched for them for months, but it was not until the close of the year 2050 that the two fleets met again and for the last time. Julian 5th had, by this time, perfected the plan for which he had gone into hiding, and he now faced the Kalkar fleet and his old enemy, Orthis, with some assurance of success. His flagship moved at the head of the short column that contained the remaining hope of a world and Julian 5th stood upon her deck beside a small and innocent looking box mounted upon a stout tripod.

Orthis moved to meet him—he would destroy the ships one by one as he approached them. He gloated at the easy victory that lay before him. He directed the electronic rifle at the flagship of his enemy and touched a button. Suddenly his brows knitted. What was this? He examined the rifle. He held a piece of aluminum before its muzzle and saw the metal disappear. The mechanism was operating, but the ships of the enemy did not disappear. Then he guessed the truth, for his own ship was now but a short distance from that of Julian 5th and he could see that the hull of the latter was entirely coated with a grayish substance that he sensed at once for what it was—an insulating material that rendered the aluminum parts of the enemy's fleet immune from the invisible fire of his rifle.

Orthis's scowl changed to a grim smile. He turned two dials upon a control box connected with the weapon and again pressed the button. Instantly the bronze propellers of the earth man's flagship vanished in thin air together with numerous fittings and parts above decks. Similarly went the exposed bronze parts of the balance of the International Peace Fleet, leaving a squadron of drifting derelicts at the mercy of the foe.

Julian 5th's flagship was at that time but a few fathoms from that of Orthis. The two men could plainly see each other's features. Orthis's expression was savage and gloating, that of Julian 5th sober and dignified.

"You thought to beat me, then!" jeered Orthis. "God, but I have waited and labored and sweated for this day. I have wrecked a world to best you, Julian 5th. To best you and to kill you, but to let you know first that I am going to kill you— to kill you in such a way as man was never before killed, as no other brain than mine could conceive of killing. You insulated your aluminum parts thinking thus to thwart me, but you did not know—your feeble intellect could not know— that as easily as I destroyed aluminum I can, by the simplest of adjustments, attune this weapon to destroy any one of a hundred different substances and among them human flesh or human bone.

"That is what I am going to do now, Julian 5th. First I am going to dissipate the bony structure of your frame. It will be done painlessly—it may not even result in instant death, and I am hoping that it will not. For I want you to know the power of a real intellect—the intellect from which you stole the fruits of its efforts for a lifetime; but not again, Julian 5th, for to-day you die—first your bones, then your flesh, and after you, your men and after them your spawn, the son that the woman I loved bore you; but she—she shall belong to me! Take that memory to hell with you!" and he turned toward the dials beside his lethal weapon.

But Julian 5th placed a hand upon the little box resting

upon the strong tripod before him, and he, it was, who touched a button before Orthis had touched his. Instantly the electronic rifle vanished beneath the very eyes of Orthis and at the same time the two ships touched and Julian 5th had leaped the rail to the enemy deck and was running toward his arch enemy.

Orthis stood gazing, horrified, at the spot where the greatest invention of his giant intellect had stood but an instant before, and then he looked up at Julian 5th approaching him and cried out horribly.

"Stop!" he screamed. "Always all our lives you have robbed me of the fruits of my efforts. Somehow you have stolen the secret of this, my greatest invention, and now you have destroyed it. May God in Heaven—"

"Yes," cried Julian 5th, "and I am going to destroy you, unless you surrender to me with all your force."

"Never!" almost screamed the man, who seemed veritably demented, so hideous was his rage. "Never! This is the end, Julian 5th, for both of us," and even as he uttered the last word he threw a lever mounted upon a control board before him. There was a terrific explosion and both ships, bursting into flame, plunged meteorlike into the ocean beneath.

Thus went Julian 5th and Orthis to their deaths, carrying with them the secret of the terrible destructive force that the latter had brought with him from the moon; but the earth was already undone. It lay helpless before its conquerors. What the outcome might have been had Orthis lived can only remain conjecture. Possibly he would have brought order out of the chaos he had created and instituted a reign of reason. Earth men would at least have had the advantage of his wonderful intellect and his power to rule the ignorant Kalkars that he had transported from the moon.

There might even have been some hope had the earth men banded together against the common enemy, but this they did not do. Elements which had been discontented with this or that phase of government joined issues with the invaders. The lazy, the inefficient, the defective, who ever placed the blame for their failures upon the shoulders of the successful, swarmed to the banners of the Kalkars, in whom they sensed kindred souls.

Political factions, labor and capital saw, or thought they saw, an opportunity for advantage to themselves in one way or another that was inimical to the interests of the others. The Kalkar fleets returned to the moon for more Kalkars until it was estimated that seven million of them were being transported to earth each year.

Julian 6th, with Nah-ee-lah, his mother, lived, as did Ortis, the son of Orthis and a Kalkar woman, but my story is not to be of them, but of Julian 9th, who was born just a century after the birth of Julian 5th.

Julian 9th will tell his own story.

2

Soor, the Tax Collector

I was born in the Teivos of Chicago on January 1st, 2100, to Julian 8th and Elizabeth James. My father and mother were not married as marriages had long since become illegal. I was called Julian 9th. My parents were of the rapidly diminishing intellectual class and could both read and write. This learning they imparted to me, although it was very useless learning—it was their religion. Printing was a lost art and the last of the public libraries had been destroyed almost a hundred years before I reached maturity, so there was little or nothing to read, while to have a book in one's possession was to brand one as of the hated intellectuals, arousing the scorn and derision of the Kalkar rabble and the suspicion and persecution of the lunar authorities who ruled.

The first twenty years of my life were uneventful. As a boy I played among the crumbling ruins of what must once have been a magnificent city. Pillaged, looted and burned half a hundred times Chicago still reared the skeletons of some mighty edifices above the ashes of her former greatness. As a youth I regretted the departed romance of the long gone days of my fore-fathers when the earth men still retained sufficient strength to battle for existence. I deplored the quiet stagnation of my own time with only an occasional murder to break the monotony of our bleak existence. Even the Kalkar Guard stationed on the shore of the great lake seldom harassed us, unless there came an urgent call from higher authorities for an additional tax collection, for we fed them well and they had the pick of our women and young girls—almost, but not quite, as you shall see.

The commander of the guard had been stationed here for years and we considered ourselves very fortunate in that he was too lazy and indolent to be cruel or oppressive. His tax collectors were always with us on market day; but they did not exact so much that we had nothing left for ourselves as refugees from Milwaukee told us was the case there.

I recall one poor devil from Milwaukee who staggered into our market place on a Saturday. He was nothing more than a bag of bones and he told us that fully ten thousand people had died of starvation the preceding month in his Teivos. The word Teivos is applied impartially to a district and to the administrative body that misadministers its affairs. No one knows what the word really means, though my mother has told me that her grandfather said that it came from another world, the moon, like Kash Guard, which also means nothing in particular—one soldier is a Kash Guard, ten thousand soldiers are a Kash Guard. If a man comes with a piece of paper upon which something is written that you are not supposed to be able to read and kills your grandmother or carries off your sister you say: "The Kash Guard did it."

That was one of the many inconsistencies of our form of government that aroused my indignation even in youth—I refer to the fact that the Twenty-Four issued written proclamations and commands to a people it did not allow to learn to read and write. I said, I believe, that printing was a lost art. This is not quite true except as it refers to the mass of the people, for the Twenty-Four still maintained a printing department, where it issued money and manifestos. The money was used in lieu of taxation—that is, when we had been so overburdened by taxation that murmurings were heard even among the Kalkar class, the authorities would send agents among us to buy our wares, paying us with money that had no value and which we could not use except to kindle our fires.

Taxes could not be paid in money as the Twenty-Four would only accept gold and silver, or produce and manufactures, and as all the gold and silver had disappeared from circulation while my father was in his teens we had to pay with what we raised or manufactured.

Three Saturdays a month the tax collectors were in the market places appraising our wares and on the last Saturday they collected one per cent of all we had bought or sold during the month. Nothing had any fixed value—to-day you might haggle half an hour in trading a pint of beans for a goat skin and next week if you wanted beans the chances were more than excellent that you would have to give four or five goat skins for a pint, and the tax collectors took advantage of that—they appraised on the basis of the highest market values for the month.

My father had a few long haired goats—they were called Montana goats, but he said they really were Angoras, and my mother used to make cloth from their fleece. With the cloth, the milk and the flesh from our goats we lived very well, having also a small vegetable garden beside our house; but there were some necessities that we had to purchase in the market place. It was against the law to barter in private, as the tax collectors would then have known nothing about a man's income. Well, one winter my mother was ill and we were in sore need of coal to heat the room in which she lay, so father went to the commander of the Kash Guard and asked permission to purchase some coal before market day. A soldier was sent with him to Hoffmeyer, the agent of the Kalkar, Pthav, who had the coal concession for our district— the Kalkars have everything—and when Hoffmeyer discovered how badly we needed coal he said that for five milk goats father could have half his weight in coal.

My father protested, but it was of no avail and as he knew how badly my mother needed heat he took the five goats to Hoffmeyer and brought back the coal. On the following market day he paid one goat for a sack of beans equal to his weight and when the tax collector came for his tithe he said to father: "You paid five goats for half your weight in beans, and as everyone knows that beans are worth twenty times as much as coal, the coal you bought must be worth one hundred goats by now, and as beans are worth twenty times as much as coal and you have twice as much beans as coal your beans are now worth two hundred goats, which makes your trades for this month amount to three hundred goats. Bring me, therefore, three of your best goats.''

He was a new tax collector—the old one would not have done such a thing; but it was about that time that everything began to change. Father said he would not have thought that things could be much worse; but he found out differently later. The change commenced in 2017, right after Jarth became Jemadar of the United Teivos of America. Of course, it did not all happen at once. Washington is a long way from Chicago and there is no continuous railroad between them. The Twenty-Four keeps up a few disconnected lines; but it is hard to operate them as there are no longer any trained mechanics to maintain them. It never takes less than a week to travel from Washington to Gary, the western terminus.

Father said that most of the railways were destroyed during the wars after the Kalkars overran the country and that as workmen were then permitted to labor only four hours a day, when they felt like it, and even then most of them were busy making new laws so much of the time that they had no chance to work, there was not enough labor to operate or maintain the roads that were left, but that was not the worst of it. Practically all the men who understood the technical details of operation and maintenance, of engineering and mechanics, belonged to the more intelligent class of earthmen and were, consequently, immediately thrown out of employment and later killed.

For seventy-five years there had been no new locomotives built and but few repairs made on those in existence. The Twenty-Four had sought to delay the inevitable by operating a few trains only for their own requirements—for government officials and troops; but it could now be but a question of a short time before railroad operation must cease—forever. It didn't mean much to me as I had never ridden on a train— never even seen one, in fact, other than the rusted remnants, twisted and tortured by fire, that lay scattered about various localities of our city; but father and mother considered it a calamity—the passing of the last link between the old civilization and the new barbarism.

Airships, automobiles, steamships, and even the telephone had gone before their time; but they had heard their fathers tell of these and other wonders. The telegraph was still in operation, though the service was poor and there were only a few lines between Chicago and the Atlantic seaboard. To the west of us was neither railroad nor telegraph. I saw a man when I was about ten years old who had come on horseback from a Teivos in Missouri. He started out with forty others to get in touch with the east and learn what had transpired there in the past fifty years; but between bandits and Kash Guards all had been killed but himself during the long and adventurous journey.

I shall never forget how I hung about picking up every scrap of the exciting narrative that fell from his lips nor how my imagination worked overtime for many weeks thereafter as I tried to picture myself the hero of similar adventures in the mysterious and unknown west. He told us that conditions were pretty bad in all the country he had passed through; but that in the agricultural districts living was easier because the Kash Guard came less often and the people could gain a fair living from the land. He thought our conditions were worse than those in Missouri and he would not remain, preferring to face the dangers of the return trip rather than live so comparatively close to the seat of the Twenty-Four.

Father was very angry when he came home from market after the new tax collector had levied a tax of three goats on him. Mother was up again and the cold snap had departed leaving the mildness of spring in the late March air. The ice had gone off the river on the banks of which we lived and I was already looking forward to my first swim of the year. The goat skins were drawn back from the windows of our little home and the fresh, sun-laden air was blowing through our three rooms.

"Bad times are coming, Elizabeth," said father, after he had told her of the injustice. "They have been bad enough in the past; but now that the swine have put the king of swine in as Jemadar—''

''S-s-sh!'' cautioned my mother, nodding her head toward the open window.

Father remained silent, listening. We heard footsteps passing around the house toward the front and a moment later the form of a man darkened the door. Father breathed a sigh of relief.

''Ah!'' he exclaimed, ''it is only our good brother Johansen. Come in, Brother Peter and tell us the news.''

''And there is news enough,'' exclaimed the visitor. ''The old commandant has been replaced by a new one, a fellow by the name of Or-tis—one of Jarth's cronies. What do you think of that?''

Brother Peter was standing between father and mother with his back toward the latter, so he did not see mother place her finger quickly to her lips in a sign to father to guard his speech. I saw a slight frown cross my father's brow, as though he resented my mother's warning; but when he spoke his words were such as those of our class have learned through suffering are the safest.

''It is not for me to think,'' he said, ''or to question in any way what the Twenty-Four does.''

''Nor for me,'' spoke Johansen quickly; ''but among friends—a man cannot help but think and sometimes it is good to speak your mind—eh?''

Father shrugged his shoulders and turned away. I could see that he was boiling over with a desire to unburden himself of some of his loathing for the degraded beasts that Fate had placed in power nearly a century before. His childhood had still been close enough to the glorious past of his country's proudest days to have been impressed through the tales of his elders with a poignant realization of all that had been lost and of how it had been lost. This he and mother had tried to impart to me as others of the dying intellectuals attempted to nurse the spark of a waning culture in the breasts of their offspring against that always hoped for, yet seemingly hopeless, day when the world should start to emerge from the slough of slime and ignorance into which the cruelties of the Kalkars had dragged it.

"Now, Brother Peter," said father, at last, "I must go and take my three goats to the tax collector, or he will charge me another one for a fine." I saw that he tried to speak naturally; but he could not keep the bitterness out of his voice.

Peter pricked up his ears. "Yes," he said, "I had heard of that piece of business. This new tax collector was laughing about it to Hoffmeyer. He thinks it a fine joke and Hoffmeyer says that now that you got the coal for so much less than it was worth he is going before the Twenty-Four and ask that you be compelled to pay him the other ninety-five goats that the tax collector says the coal is really worth."

"Oh!" exclaimed mother, "they would not really do such a wicked thing—I am sure they would not."

Peter shrugged. "Perhaps they only joked," he said; "these Kalkars are great jokers."

"Yes," said father, "they are great jokers; but some day I shall have my little joke," and he walked out toward the pens where the goats were kept when not on pasture.

Mother looked after him with a troubled light in her eyes and I saw her shoot a quick glance at Peter, who presently followed father from the house and went his way.

Father and I took the goats to the tax collector. He was a small man with a mass of red hair, a thin nose and two small, close-set eyes. His name was Soor. As soon as he saw father he commenced to fume.

"What is your name, man?" he demanded insolently.

"Julian 8th," replied father. "Here are the three goats in payment of my income tax for this month—shall I put them in the pen?"

"What did you say your name is?" snapped the fellow.

"Julian 8th," father repeated.

"Julian 8th!" shouted Soor. "Julian 8th! I suppose you are too fine a gentleman to be brother to such as me, eh?"

"Brother Julian 8th," said father sullenly.

"Go put your goats in the pen and hereafter remember

that all men are brothers who are good citizens and loyal to our great Jemader.''

When father had put the goats away we started for home; but as we were passing Soor he shouted: ''Well?''

Father turned a questioning look toward him.

''Well?'' repeated the man.

''I do not understand,'' said father; ''have I not done all that the law requires?''

''What's the matter with you pigs out here?'' Soor fairly screamed. ''Back in the eastern Teivos a tax collector doesn't have to starve to death on his miserable pay—his people bring him little presents.''

''Very well,'' said father quietly, ''I will bring you something next time I come to market.''

''See that you do,'' snapped Soor.

Father did not speak all the way home, nor did he say a word until after we had finished our dinner of cheese, goat's milk and corn cakes. I was so angry that I could scarce contain myself; but I had been brought up in an atmosphere of repression and terrorism that early taught me to keep a still tongue in my head.

When father had finished his meal he rose suddenly—so suddenly that his chair flew across the room to the opposite wall—and squaring his shoulders he struck his chest a terrible blow.

''Coward! Dog!'' he cried. ''My God! I cannot stand it. I shall go mad if I must submit longer to such humiliation. I am no longer a man. There are no men! We are worms that the swine grind into the earth with their polluted hoofs. And I dared say nothing. I stood there while that offspring of generations of menials and servants insulted me and spat upon me and I dared say nothing but meekly to propitiate him. It is disgusting.

''In a few generations they have sapped the manhood from American men. My ancestors fought at Bunker Hill, at Gettysburg, at San Juan, at Chateau Thierry. And I? I bend the knee to every degraded creature that wears the authority of the beasts at Washington—and not one of them is an American—scarce one of them an earth man. To the scum of the moon I bow my head—I who am one of the few survivors of the most powerful people the world ever knew.''

"Julian!'' cried my mother, "be careful, dear. Some one may be listening.'' I could see her tremble.

"And you are an American woman!'' he growled.

"Julian, don't!'' she pleaded. "It is not on my account— you know that it is not—but for you and our boy. I do not care what becomes of me; but I cannot see you torn from us as we have seen others taken from their families, who dared speak their minds.''

"I know, dear heart,'' he said after a brief silence. "I know—it is the way with each of us. I dare not on your account and Julian's, you dare not on ours, and so it goes. Ah, if there were only more of us. If I could but find a thousand men who dared!''

"S-s-sh!'' cautioned mother. "There are so many spies. One never knows. That is why I cautioned you when Brother Peter was here to-day. One never knows.''

"You suspect Peter?'' asked father.

"I know nothing,'' replied mother; "I am afraid of every one. It is a frightful existence and though I have lived it thus all my life, and my mother before me and her mother before that, I never became hardened to it.''

"The American spirit has been bent, but not broken,'' said father. "Let us hope that it will never break.''

"If we have the hearts to suffer always it will not break,'' said mother, "but it is hard, so hard—when one even hates to bring a child into the world,'' and she glanced at me, "because of the misery and suffering to which it is doomed for life. I yearned for children, always; but I feared to have them—mostly I feared that they might be girls. To be a girl in this world to-day—Oh, it is frightful!''

After supper father and I went out and milked the goats and saw that the sheds were secured for the night against the dogs. It seemed as though they became more numerous and more bold each year. They ran in packs where there were only individuals when I was a little boy and it was scarce safe for a grown man to travel an unfrequented locality at night. We were not permitted to have firearms in our possession, nor even bows and arrows, so we could not exterminate them and they seemed to realize our weakness, coming close in among the houses and pens at night.

They were large brutes—fearless and powerful. There was one pack more formidable than the others which father said appeared to carry a strong strain of collie and airedale blood—the members of this pack were large, cunning and ferocious and were becoming a terror to the city—we called them the Hellhounds.

3

The Hellhounds

AFTER WE RETURNED to the house with the milk Jim Thompson and his woman, Mollie Sheehan, came over. They lived up the river about half a mile, on the next farm, and were our best friends. They were the only people that father and mother really trusted, so when we were all together alone we spoke our minds very freely. It seemed strange to me, even as a boy, that such, big strong men as father and Jim should be afraid to express their real views to any one, and though I was born and reared in an atmosphere of suspicion and terror I could never quite reconcile myself to the attitude of servility and cowardice which marked us all.

And yet I knew that my father was no coward. He was a fine-looking man, too—tall and wonderfully muscled—and I have seen him fight with men and with dogs and once he defended mother against a Kash Guard and with his bare hands he killed the armed soldier. He lies in the center of the goat pen now, his rifle, bayonet and ammunition wrapped in many thicknesses of oiled cloth beside him. We left no trace and were never even suspected; but we know where there is a rifle, a bayonet and ammunition.

Jim had had trouble with Soor, the new tax collector, too, and was very angry. Jim was a big man and, like father, was always smooth shaven as were nearly all Americans, as we called those whose people had lived here long before the Great War. The others—the true Kalkars—grew no beards. Their ancestors had come from the moon many years before.

25

They had come in strange ships year after year, but finally, one by one, their ships had been lost and as none of them knew how to build others or the engines that operated them the time came when no more Kalkars could come from the moon to earth.

That was good for us, but it came too late, for the Kalkars already here bred like flies in a shady stable. The pure Kalkars were the worst, but there were millions of half-breeds and they were bad, too, and I think they really hated us pure bred earth men worse than the true Kalkars, or moon men, did.

Jim was terribly mad. He said that he couldn't stand it much longer—that he would rather be dead than live in such an awful world; but I was accustomed to such talk—I had heard it since infancy. Life was a hard thing—just work, work, work, for a scant existence over and above the income tax. No pleasures—few conveniences or comforts; absolutely no luxuries—and, worst of all, no hope. It was seldom that any one smiled—any one in our class—and the grown-ups never laughed. As children we laughed—a little; not much. It is hard to kill the spirit of childhood; but the brotherhood of man had almost done it.

"It's your own fault, Jim," said father. He was always blaming our troubles on Jim, for Jim's people had been American workmen before the Great War—mechanics and skilled artisans in various trades. "Your people never took a stand against the invaders. They flirted with the new theory of brotherhood the Kalkars brought with them from the moon. They listened to the emissaries of the malcontents and, afterward, when Kalkars sent their disciples among us they 'first endured, then pitied, then embraced.' They had the numbers and the power to combat successfully the wave of insanity that started with the lunar catastrophe and overran the world—they could have kept it out of America; but they didn't—instead they listened to false prophets and placed their great strength in the hands of the corrupt leaders."

"And how about your class?" countered Jim, "too rich

and lazy and indifferent even to vote. They tried to grind us
down while they waxed fat off of our labor.''

''The ancient sophistry!'' snapped father. ''There was
never a more prosperous or independent class of human beings in the world than the American laboring man of the
twentieth century.

''You talk about us! We were the first to fight it—my people fought and bled and died to keep Old Glory above the
capitol at Washington; but we were too few and now the Kash
flag of the Kalkars floats in its place and for nearly a century
it has been a crime punishable by death to have the Stars and
Stripes in your possession.''

He walked quickly across the room to the fireplace and
removed a stone above the rough, wooden mantel. Reaching
his hand into the aperture behind he turned toward us.

''But cowed and degraded as I have become,'' he cried,
''thank God I still have a spark of manhood left—I have had
the strength to defy them as my fathers defied them—I have
kept this that has been handed down to me—kept it for my
son to hand down to his son—and I have taught him to die
for it as his forefathers died for it and as I would die for it,
gladly.''

He drew forth a small bundle of fabric and holding the
upper corners between the fingers of his two hands he let it
unfold before us—an oblong cloth of alternate red and white
stripes with a blue square in one corner, upon which were
sewn many little white stars.

Jim and Mollie and mother rose to their feet and I saw
mother cast an apprehensive glance toward the doorway. For
a moment they stood thus in silence, looking with wide eyes
upon the thing that father held and then Jim walked slowly
toward it and, kneeling, took the edge of it in his great, horny
fingers and pressed it to his lips and the candle upon the
rough table, sputtering in the spring wind that waved the goat
skin at the window, cast its feeble rays upon them.

''It is the Flag, my son,'' said father to me. ''It is Old
Glory—the flag of your fathers—the flag that made the world
a decent place to live in. It is death to possess it; but when I

am gone take it and guard it as our family has guarded it since the regiment that carried it came back from the Argonne.''

I felt tears filling my eyes—why, I could not have told them—and I turned away to hide them—turned toward the window and there, beyond the waving goat skin, I saw a face in the outer darkness. I have always been quick of thought and of action; but I never thought or moved more quickly in my life than I did in the instant following my discovery of the face in the window. With a single movement I swept the candle from the table, plunging the room into utter darkness, and leaping to my father's side I tore the Flag from his hands and thrust it back into the aperture above the mantel. The stone lay upon the mantel itself, nor did it take me but a moment to grope for it and find it in the dark—an instant more and it was replaced in its niche.

So ingrained were apprehension and suspicion in the human mind that the four in the room with me sensed intuitively something of the cause of my act and when I had hunted for the candle, found it and relighted it they were standing, tense and motionless where I had last seen them. They did not ask me a question. Father was the first to speak.

''You were very careless and clumsy, Julian,'' he said. ''If you wanted the candle why did you not pick it up carefully instead of rushing at it so? But that is always your way—you are constantly knocking things over.''

He raised his voice a trifle as he spoke; but it was a lame attempt at deception and he knew it, as did we. If the man who owned the face in the dark heard his words he must have known it as well.

As soon as I had relighted the candle I went into the kitchen and out the back door and then, keeping close in the black shadow of the house, I crept around toward the front, for I wanted to learn, if I could, who it was who had looked in upon that scene of high treason. The night was moonless but clear, and I could see quite a distance in every direction, as our house stood in a fair size clearing close to the river. Southeast of us the path wound upward across the approach to an ancient bridge, long since destroyed by raging mobs or rotting away—I do not know which—and presently I saw the figure of a man silhouetted against the starlit sky as he topped the approach. The man carried a laden sack upon his back. This fact was, to some extent, reassuring as it suggested that the eavesdropper was himself upon some illegal mission and that he could ill afford to be too particular of the actions of others. I have seen many men carrying sacks and bundles at night—I have carried them myself. It is the only way, often, in which a man may save enough from the tax collector on which to live and support his family.

This nocturnal traffic is common enough and under our old tax collector and the indolent commandant of former times not so hazardous as it might seem when one realizes that it is punishable by imprisonment for ten years at hard labor in the coal mines and, in aggravated cases, by death. The aggravated cases are those in which a man is discovered trading something by night that the tax collector or the commandant had wanted for himself.

I did not follow the man, being sure that he was one of our own class, but turned back toward the house where I found the four talking in low whispers, nor did any of us raise his voice again that evening.

Father and Jim were talking, as they usually did, of the West. They seemed to feel that somewhere, far away toward the setting sun, there must be a little corner of America where men could live in peace and freedom—where there were no Kash Guards, tax collectors or Kalkars.

It must have been three quarters of an hour later, as Jim and Mollie were preparing to leave, that there came a knock upon the door which immediately swung open before an invitation to enter could be given. We looked up to see Peter Johansen smiling at us. I never liked Peter. He was a long, lanky man who smiled with his mouth; but never with his eyes. I didn't like the way he used to look at mother when he thought no one was observing him, nor his habit of changing women every year or two—that was too much like the Kalkars. I always felt toward Peter as I had as a child when, barefooted, I stepped unknowingly upon a snake in the deep grass.

Father greeted the newcomer with a pleasant "Welcome, Brother Johansen;" but Jim only nodded his head and scowled, for Peter had a habit of looking at Mollie as he did at mother, and both women were beautiful. I think I never saw a more beautiful woman than my mother and as I grew older and learned more of men and the world I marveled that father had been able to keep her and, too, I understood why she never went abroad; but stayed always closely about the house and farm. I never knew her to go to the market place as did most of the other women. But I was twenty now and worldly wise.

"What brings you out so late, Brother Johansen?" I asked. We always used the prescribed "Brother" to those of whom we were not sure. I hate the word—to me a brother meant an enemy as it did to all our class and I guess to every class—even the Kalkars.

"I followed a stray pig," replied Peter to my question. "He went in that direction," and he waved a hand toward the market place. As he did so something tumbled from beneath his coat—something that his arm had held there. It was an empty sack. Immediately I knew who it was owned the face in the dark beyond our goatskin hanging. Peter snatched the sack from the floor in ill-concealed confusion and then I saw the expression of his cunning face change as he held it toward father.

"Is this yours, Brother Julian?" he asked. "I found it just before your door and thought that I would stop and ask."

"No," said I, not waiting for father to speak, "it is not ours—it must belong to the man whom I saw carrying it, full, a short time since. He went by the path beside the old bridge." I looked straight into Peter's eyes. He flushed and then went white.

"I did not see him," he said presently: "but if the sack is not yours I will keep it—*at least it is not high treason to have it in my possession*." Then, without another word, he turned and left the house.

We all knew then that Peter had seen the episode of the Flag. Father said that we need not fear, that Peter was all right; but Jim thought differently and so did Mollie and mother. I agreed with them. I did not like Peter. Jim and Mollie went home shortly after Peter left and we prepared for bed. Mother and Father occupied the one bedroom. I slept on some goat skins in the big room we called the living room. The other room was a kitchen. We ate there also.

Mother had always made me take off my clothes and put on a mohair garment for sleeping. The other young men I knew slept in the same clothes they wore during the day; but mother was particular about this and insisted that I have my sleeping garments and also that I bathe often—once a week in the winter. In the summer I was in the river so much that I had a bath once or twice a day. Father was also particular about his personal cleanliness. The Kalkars were very different.

My underclothing was of fine mohair, in winter. In summer I wore none: I had a heavy mohair shirt and breeches, tight at waist and knees and baggy between, a goatskin tunic and boots of goatskin. I do not know what we would have done without the goats—they furnished us food and raiment. The boots were loose and fastened just above the calf of the leg with a strap—to keep them from falling down. I wore nothing on my head, summer or winter; but my hair was heavy. I wore it brushed straight back, always, and cut off square behind just below my ears. To keep it from getting in my eyes I always tied a goatskin thong about my head.

I had just slipped off my tunic when I heard the baying of the Hellhounds close by. I thought they might be getting into the goat pen, so I waited a moment, listening and then I heard a scream—the scream of a woman in terror. It sounded down by the river near the goat pens, and mingled with it was the vicious growling and barking of the Hellhounds. I did not wait to listen longer, but seized my knife and a long staff. We were permitted to have no edged weapon with a blade over six inches long. Such as it was, it was the best weapon I had and much better than nothing.

I ran out the front door, which was closest, and turned toward the pens in the direction of the Hellhounds' deep growling and the screams of the woman.

As I neared the pens and my eyes became accustomed to the outer darkness I made out what appeared to be a human figure resting partially upon the top of one of the sheds that formed a portion of the pen wall. The legs and lower body dangled over the edge of the roof and I could see three or four Hellhounds leaping for it, while another, that had evidently gotten a hold, was hanging to one leg and attempting to drag the figure down.

As I ran forward I shouted at the beasts and those that were leaping for the figure stopped and turned toward me. I knew something of the temper of these animals and that I might expect them to charge, for they were quite fearless of man ordinarily; but I ran forward toward them so swiftly and with such determination that they turned growling and ran off.

The one that had hold of the figure succeeded in dragging it to earth just before I reached them and then it discovered me and turned, standing over its prey, with wide jaws and terrific fangs menacing me. It was a huge beast, almost as large as a full grown goat, and easily a match for several men as poorly armed as I. Under ordinary circumstances I should have given it plenty of room; but what was I to do when the life of a woman was at stake?

I was an American, not a Kalkar—those swine would throw a woman to the Hellhounds to save their own skins—and I had been brought up to revere woman in a world that considered her on a par with the cow, the nanny and the sow, only less valuable since the latter were not the common property of the state.

I knew then that death stood very near as I faced that frightful beast and from the corner of an eye I could see its mates creeping closer. There was no time to think, even, and so I rushed in upon the Hellhound with my staff and blade. As I did so I saw the wide and terrified eyes of a young girl looking up at me from beneath the beast of prey. I had not thought to desert her to her fate before; but after that single glance I could not have done so had a thousand deaths confronted me.

As I was almost upon the beast it sprang for my throat, rising high upon its hind feet and leaping straight as an arrow. My staff was useless and so I dropped it, meeting the charge with my knife and a bare hand. By luck the fingers of my left hand found the creature's throat at the first clutch; but the impact of his body against mine hurled me to the ground beneath him and there, growling and struggling, he sought to close those snapping fangs upon me. Holding his jaws at arm's length I struck at his breast with my blade, nor did I miss him once. The pain of the wounds turned him crazy and yet, to my utter surprise found I still could hold him and not that alone; but that I could also struggle to my knees and then to my feet—still holding him at arm's length in my left hand.

I had always known that I was muscular; but until that moment I had never dreamed of the great strength that Nature had given me, for never before had I occasion to exert the full measure of my powerful thews. It was like a revelation from above and of a sudden I found myself smiling and in the instant a miracle occurred—all fear of these hideous beasts dissolved from my brain like thin air and with it fear of man as well. I, who had been brought out of a womb of fear into a world of terror, who had been suckled and nurtured upon apprehension and timidity—I, Julian 9th, at the age of twenty years, became in the fraction of a second utterly fearless of man or beast. It was the knowledge of my great power that did it—that and, perhaps, those two liquid eyes that I knew to be watching me.

The other hounds were closing in upon me when the creature in my grasp went suddenly limp. My blade must have found its heart. And then the others charged and I saw the girl upon her feet beside me, my staff in her hands, ready to battle with them.

"To the roof!" I shouted at her; but she did not heed.

Instead she stood her ground, striking a vicious blow at the leader as he came within range.

Swinging the dead beast above my head I hurled the carcass at the others so that they scattered and retreated again and then I turned to the girl and without more parley lifted her in my arms and tossed her lightly to the roof of the goat shed. I could easily have followed to her side and safety had not something filled my brain with an effect similar to that which I imagined must be produced by the vile concoction brewed by the Kalkars and which they drank to excess, while it would have meant imprisonment for us to be apprehended with it in our possession. At least, I know that I felt a sudden exhilaration—a strange desire to accomplish wonders before the eyes of this stranger, and so I turned upon the four remaining Hellhounds who had now bunched to renew the attack and without waiting for them I rushed toward them.

They did not flee; but stood their ground, growling hideously, their hair bristling upon their necks and along their spines, their great fangs bared and slavering; but among them I tore and by the very impetuosity of my attack I overthrew them. The first sprang to meet me and him I seized by the neck and clamping his body between my knees I twisted his head entirely around until I heard the vertebrae snap. The other three were upon me then, leaping and tearing; but I felt no fear. One by one I took them in my mighty hands and lifting them high above my head hurled them violently from me. Two only returned to the attack and these I vanquished with my bare hands disdaining to use my blade upon such carrion.

It was then that I saw a man running toward me from up the river and another from our house. The first was Jim, who had heard commotion and the girl's screams and the other was my father. Both had seen the last part of the battle and neither could believe that it was I, Julian, who had done this thing. Father was very proud of me and Jim was, too, for he had always said that having no son of his own father must share me with him.

And then I turned toward the girl who had slipped from

the roof and was approaching us. She moved with the same graceful dignity that was mother's—not at all like the clumsy clods that belonged to the Kalkars, and she came straight to me and laid a hand upon my arm.

"Thank you!" she said; "and God bless you. Only a very brave and powerful man could have done what you have done."

And then, all of a sudden, I did not feel brave at all; but very weak and silly, for all I could do was finger my blade and look at the ground. It was father who spoke and the interruption helped to dispel my embarrassment.

"Who are you?" he asked, "and from where do you come? It is strange to find a young woman wandering about alone at night; but stranger still to hear one who dares invoke the forbidden deity."

I had not realized until then that she had used His name; but when I did recall it, I could not but glance apprehensively about to see if any others might be around who could have heard. Father and Jim I knew to be safe; for there was a common tie between our families that lay in the secret religious rites we held once each week. Since that hideous day that had befallen even before my father's birth—that day, which none dared mention above a whisper, when the clergy of every denomination, to the last man, had been murdered by order of the Twenty-Four, it had been a capital crime to worship God in any form whatsoever.

Some madman at Washington, filled, doubtless, with the fumes of the awful drink that made them more bestial even than Nature designed them, issued the frightful order on the ground that the church was attempting to usurp the functions of the state and that also the clergy were inciting the people to rebellion—nor do I doubt but that the latter was true. Too bad, indeed, that they were not given more time to bring their divine plan to fruition.

We took the girl to the house and when my mother saw her and how young and beautiful she was and took her in her arms, the child broke down and sobbed and clung to mother, nor could either speak for some time. In the light of the candle I saw that the stranger was of wondrous beauty. I have said that my mother was the most beautiful woman I had ever seen, and such is the truth; but this girl who had come so suddenly among us was the most beautiful girl.

She was about nineteen, delicately molded and yet without weakness. There were strength and vitality apparent in every move she made as well as in the expression of her face, her gestures and her manner of speech. She was girlish and at the same time filled one with an impression of great reserve strength of mind and character. She was very brown, showing exposure to the sun, yet her skin was clear—almost translucent.

Her garb was similar to mine—the common attire of people of our class, both men and women. She wore the tunic and breeches and boots just as mother and Mollie and the rest of us did; but somehow there was a difference—I had never before realized what a really beautiful costume it was. The band about her forehead was wider than was generally worn and upon it were sewn numerous tiny shells, set close together and forming a pattern. It was her only attempt at ornamentation; but even so it was quite noticeable in a world where women strove to make themselves plain rather than beautiful—some going even so far as to permanently disfigure their faces and those of their female offspring, while others, many, many others, killed the latter in infancy. Mollie had done so with two. No wonder that grown-ups never laughed and seldom smiled!

When the girl had quieted her sobs on mother's breast father renewed his questioning; but mother said to wait until morning, that the girl was tired and unstrung and needed sleep. Then came the question of where she was to sleep. Father said that he would sleep in the living room with me and that the stranger could sleep with mother; but Jim suggested that she come home with him as he and Mollie had three rooms, as did we, and no one to occupy his living room. And so it was arranged, although I would rather have had her remain with us.

At first she rather shrank from going, until mother told her that Jim and Mollie were good, kind-hearted people and that she would be as safe with them as with her own father and mother. At mention of her parents the tears came to her eyes and she turned impulsively toward my mother and kissed her, after which she told Jim that she was ready to accompany him.

She started to say good-by to me and to thank me again; but, having found my tongue at last, I told her that I would go with them as far as Jim's house. This appeared to please her and so we set forth. Jim walked ahead and I followed with the girl and on the way I discovered a very strange thing. Father had shown me a piece of iron once that pulled smaller bits of iron to it. He said that it was a magnet.

This slender, stranger girl was certainly no piece of iron, nor was I a smaller bit of anything; but nevertheless I could not keep away from her. I cannot explain it—however wide the way was I was always drawn over close to her, so that our arms touched and once our hands swung together and the strangest and most delicious thrill ran through me that I had ever experienced.

I used to think that Jim's house was a long way from ours—when I had to carry things over there as a boy; but that night it was far too close—just a step or two and we were there.

Mollie heard us coming and was at the door, full of questionings, and when she saw the girl and heard a part of our story she reached out and took the girl to her bosom, just as mother had. Before they took her in the stranger turned and held out her hand to me.

"Good night!" she said, "and thank you again, and, once more, may God, our Father, bless and preserve you."

And I heard Mollie murmur: "The Saints be praised!" and then they went in and the door closed and I turned homeward, treading on air.

4

Brother General Or-tis

THE NEXT DAY I set out as usual to peddle goat's milk. We were permitted to trade in perishable things on other than market days, though we had to make a strict accounting of all such bartering. I usually left Mollie until the last as Jim had a deep, cold well on his place where I liked to quench my thirst after my morning trip; but that day Mollie got her milk fresh and first and early—about half an hour earlier than I was wont to start out.

When I knocked and she bid me enter she looked surprised at first, for just an instant, and then a strange expression came into her eyes—half amusement, half pity—and she rose and went into the kitchen for the milk jar. I saw her wipe the corners of her eyes with the back of one finger; but I did not understand why—not then.

The stranger girl had been in the kitchen helping Mollie and the latter must have told her I was there, for she came right in and greeted me. It was the first good look I had had of her, for candle light is not brilliant at best. If I had been enthralled the evening before there is no word in my limited vocabulary to express the effect she had on me by daylight. She—but it is useless. I cannot describe her!

It took Mollie a long time to find the milk jar—bless her!—though it seemed short enough to me, and while she was finding it the stranger girl and I were getting acquainted. First she asked after father and mother and then she asked our names. When I told her mine she repeated it several times.

"Julian 9th," she said; "Julian 9th!" and then she smiled up at me. "It is a nice name, I like it."

"And what is your name?" I asked.

"Juana," she said—she pronounced it Whanna; "Juana St. John."

"I am glad," I said, "that you like my name; but I like yours better." It was a very foolish speech and it made me feel silly; but she did not seem to think it foolish, or if she did she was too nice to let me know it. I have known many girls; but mostly they were homely and stupid. The pretty girls were seldom allowed in the market place—that is, the pretty girls of our class. The Kalkars permitted their girls to go abroad, for they did not care who got them, as long as some one got them; but American fathers and mothers would rather slay their girls than send them to the market place, and the former often was done. The Kalkar girls, even those born of American mothers, were coarse and brutal in appearance—low-browed, vulgar, bovine. No stock can be improved, or even kept to its normal plane, unless high grade males are used.

This girl was so entirely different from any other that I had ever seen that I marvelled that such a glorious creature could exist. I wanted to know all about her. It seemed to me that in some way I had been robbed of my right for many years that she should have lived and breathed and talked and gone her way without my ever knowing it, or her. I wanted to make up for lost time and so I asked her many questions.

She told me that she had been born and raised in the Teivos just west of Chicago, which extended along the Desplaines River and embraced a considerable area of unpopulated country and scattered farms.

"My father's home is in a district called Oak Park," she said, "and our house was one of the few that remained from ancient times. It was of solid concrete and stood upon the corner of two roads—once it must have been a very beautiful place, and even time and war have been unable entirely to erase its charm. Three great poplar trees rose to the north of it beside the ruins of what my father said was once a place

where motor cars were kept by the long dead owner. To the
south of the house were many roses, growing wild and lux-
uriant, while the concrete walls, from which the plaster had
fallen in great patches, were almost entirely concealed by the
clinging ivy that reached to the very eaves.

"It was my home and so I loved it; but now it is lost to
me forever. The Kash Guard and the tax collector came seldom—we were too far from the station and the market place,
which lay southwest of us, on Salt Creek. But recently the
new Jemadar, Jarth, appointed another commandant and a
new tax collector. They did not like the station at Salt Creek
and so they sought for a better location and after inspecting
the district they chose Oak Park, and my father's home being
the most comfortable and substantial, they ordered him to
sell it to the Twenty-Four.

"You know what that means. They appraised it at a high
figure—fifty thousand dollars it was, and paid him in paper
money. There was nothing to do and so we prepared to move.
Whenever they had come to look at the house my mother
had hidden me in a little cubby-hole on the landing between
the second and third floors, placing a pile of rubbish in front
of me, but the day that we were leaving to take a place on
the banks of the Desplaines, where father thought that we
might live without being disturbed, the new commandant
came unexpectedly and saw me.

"How old is the girl?" he asked my mother.

"Fifteen," she replied sullenly.

" 'You lie, you sow!' he cried angrily; 'she is eighteen if
she is a day!'

"Father was standing there beside us and when the commandant spoke as he did to mother I saw father go very white
and then, without a word, he hurled himself upon the swine
and before the Kash Guard who accompanied him could prevent, father had almost killed the commandant with his bare
hands.

"You know what happened—I do not need to tell you.
They killed my father before my eyes. Then the commandant
offered my mother to one of the Kash Guard, but she snatched

his bayonet from his belt and ran it through her heart before they could prevent her. I tried to follow her example, but they seized me.

"I was carried to my own bedroom on the second floor of my father's house and locked there. The commandant said that he would come and see me in the evening and that everything would be all right with me. I knew what he meant and I made up my mind that he would find me dead.

"My heart was breaking for the loss of my father and mother, and yet the desire to live was strong within me. I did not want to die—something urged me to live, and in addition there was the teaching of my father and mother. They were both from Quaker stock and very religious. They educated me to fear God and to do no wrong by thought or violence to another, and yet I had seen my father attempt to kill a man, and I had seen my mother slay herself. My world was all upset. I was almost crazed by grief and fear and uncertainty as to what was right for me to do.

"And then darkness came and I heard some one ascending the stairway. The windows of the second story are too far from the ground for one to risk a leap; but the ivy is old and strong. The commandant was not sufficiently familiar with the place to have taken the ivy into consideration and before the footsteps reached my door I had swung out of the window and, clinging to the ivy, made my way to the ground down the rough and strong old stem.

"That was three days ago. I hid and wandered—I did not know in what direction I went. Once an old woman took me in overnight and fed me and gave me food to carry for the next day. I think that I must have been almost mad, for mostly the happenings of the past three days are only indistinct and jumbled fragments of memory in my mind. And then the Hellhounds! Oh, how frightened I was! And then—you!"

I don't know what there was about the way she said it; but it seemed to me as though it meant a great deal more than she knew herself. Almost like a prayer of thanksgiving, it was, that she had at last found a safe haven of refuge—safe and permanent. Anyway, I liked the idea.

And then Mollie came in, and as I was leaving she asked me if I would come that evening, and Juana cried: "Oh, yes, do!" and I said that I would.

When I had finished delivering the goats' milk I started for home, and on the way I met old Moses Samuels, the Jew. He made his living, and a scant one it was, by tanning hides. He was a most excellent tanner, but as nearly every one else knew how to tan there were not many customers; but some of the Kalkars used to bring him hides to tan. They knew nothing of how to do any useful thing, for they were descended from a long line of the most ignorant and illiterate people in the moon and the moment they obtained a little power they would not even work at what small trades their fathers once had learned, so that after a generation or two they were able to live only off the labor of others. They created nothing, they produced nothing, they became the most burdensome class of parasites the world ever has endured.

The rich nonproducers of olden times were a blessing to the world by comparison with these, for the former at least had intelligence and imagination—they could direct others and they could transmit to their offspring the qualities of mind that are essential to any culture, progress or happiness that the world ever may hope to attain.

So the Kalkars patronized Samuels for their tanned hides, and if they had paid him for them the old Jew would have waxed rich; but they either did not pay him at all or else mostly in paper money. That did not even burn well, as Samuels used to say.

"Good morning, Julian," he called as we met. "I shall be needing some hides soon, for the new commander of the Kash Guard has heard of old Samuels and has sent for me and ordered five hides tanned the finest that can be. Have you seen this Or-tis, Julian?" He lowered his voice.

I shook my head negatively.

"Heaven help us!" whispered the old man. "Heaven help us!"

"Is he as bad as that, Moses?" I asked.

The old man wrung his hands. "Bad times are ahead, my son," he said. "Old Samuels knows his kind. He is not lazy like the last one and he is more cruel and more lustful; but about the hides. I have not paid you for the last—they paid me in paper money; but that I would not offer to a friend in payment for a last year's bird's nest. Maybe that I shall not be able to pay you for these new hides for a long time; it depends upon how Or-tis pays me. Sometimes they are liberal—as they can afford to be with the property of others; but if he is a half-breed, as I hear he is, he will hate a Jew, and I shall get nothing. However, if he is pure Kalkar it may be different—the pure Kalkars do not hate a Jew more than they hate other Earthmen, though there is one Jew who hates a Kalkar."

That night we had our first introduction to Or-tis. He came in person; but I will tell how it all happened. After supper I went over to Jim's. Juana was standing in the little doorway as I came up the path. She looked rested now and almost happy. The hunted expression had left her eyes and she smiled as I approached. It was almost dusk, for the spring evenings were still short; but the air was balmy, and so we stood on the outside talking.

I recited the little gossip of our district that I had picked up during my day's work—the Twenty-Four had raised the local tax on farm products—Andrew Wright's woman had given birth to twins, a boy and a girl; but the girl had died; no need of comment here as most girl babies die—Soor had said that he would tax this district until we all died of starvation—pleasant fellow, Soor—one of the Kash Guard had taken Nellie Levy—Hoffmeyer had said that next winter we would have to pay more for coal—Dennis Corrigan had been sent to the mines for ten years because he had been caught reading at night. It was all alike, this gossip of ours—all sordid, or sad, or tragic; but then life was a tragedy with us.

"How stupid of them to raise the tax on farm products," remarked Juana; "their fathers stamped out manufactures and commerce and now they will stamp out what little agriculture is left.''

"The sooner they do it the better it will be for the world," I replied. "When they have starved all the farmers to death they themselves will starve."

And then, suddenly, she reverted to Dennis Corrigan. "It would have been kinder to have killed him," she said.

"That is why they did not do so," I replied.

"Do you ever trade at night?" she asked, and then before I could reply: "Do not tell me. I should not have asked; but I hope that you do not—it is so dangerous; nearly always are they caught."

I laughed. "Not nearly always," I said, "or most of us would have been in the mines long since. We could not live otherwise. The accursed income tax is unfair—it has always been unfair, for it falls hardest on those least able to support it."

"But the mines are so terrible!" she exclaimed, shuddering.

"Yes," I replied, "the mines are terrible. I would rather die than go there."

After a while I took Juana over to our house to see my mother. She liked the house very much. My father's father built it with his own hands. It is constructed of stone taken from the ruins of the old city—stone and brick. Father says that he thinks the bricks are from an old pavement, as we still see patches of these ancient bricks in various localities. Nearly all our houses are of this construction, for timber is scarce. The foundation walls and above the ground for about three feet are of rough stones of various sizes and above this are the bricks. The stones are laid so that some project farther than others and the effect is odd and rather nice. The eaves are low and over-hanging and the roof is thatched. It is a nice house and mother keeps it scrupulously clean within.

We had been talking for perhaps an hour, sitting in our living room—father, mother, Juana, and I—when the door was suddenly thrust open without warning and we looked up to see a man in the uniform of a Kash Guard confronting us.

Behind him were others. We all rose and stood in silence. Two entered and took posts on either side of the doorway and then a third came in—a tall, dark man in the uniform of a commander, and we knew at once that it was Or-tis. At his heels were six more.

Or-tis looked at each of us and then, singling out father, he said: "You are Brother Julian 8th."

Father nodded. Or-tis eyed him for a moment and then his gaze wandered to mother and Juana, and I saw a new expression lessen the fierce scowl that had clouded his face from the moment of his entry. He was a large man; but not of the heavy type which is most common among his class. His nose was thin and rather fine, his eyes cold, gray, and piercing. He was very different from the fat swine that had preceded him—very different and more dangerous; even I could see that. I could see a thin, cruel upper lip and a full and sensuous lower. If the other had been a pig this one was a wolf and he had the nervous restlessness of the wolf—and the vitality to carry out any wolfish designs he might entertain.

This visit to our home was typical of the man. The former commander had never accompanied his men on any excursion of the sort; but the teivos was to see much of Or-tis. He trusted no one—he must see to everything himself and he was not lazy, which was bad for us.

"So you are Brother Julian 8th!" he repeated. "I do not have good reports of you. I have come for two reasons tonight. One is to warn you that the Kash Guard is commanded by a different sort of man from whom I relieved. I will stand no trifling and no treason. There must be unquestioned loyalty to the Jemadar at Washington—every national and local law will be enforced. Trouble makers and traitors will get short shrift. A manifesto will be read in each market place Saturday—a manifesto that I have just received from Washington. Our great Jemadar has conferred greater powers upon the commanders of the Kash Guard. You will come to me with all your grievances. Where justice miscarries I shall be the court of last resort. The judgment of any court may be appealed to me.

"On the other hand, let wrongdoers beware as under the new law any cause may be tried before a summary military court over which the commander of the Kash Guard must preside."

We saw what it meant—it didn't require much intelligence to see the infamy and horror of it. It meant nothing more nor less than that our lives and liberty were in the hands of a single man and that Jarth had struck the greatest blow of all at human happiness in a land where we had thought such a state no longer existed—taken from us the last mocking remnant of our already lost freedom, that he might build for his own aggrandizement a powerful political military machine.

"And," continued Or-tis, "I have come for another reason—a reason that looks bad for you, Brother Julian; but we shall see what we shall see," and turning to the men behind him he issued a curt command: "Search the place!" That was all; but I saw, in memory, another man standing in this same living room—a man from beneath whose coat fell an empty sack when he raised an arm.

For an hour they searched that little three room house. For an hour they tumbled our few belongings over and over; but mostly they searched the living room and especially about the fireplace did they hunt for a hidden nook. A dozen times my heart stood still as I saw them feeling of the stones above the mantel.

We all knew what they sought—all but Juana—and we knew what it would mean if they found it. Death for father and for me, too, perhaps, and worse for mother and the girl. And to think that Johansen had done this awful thing to curry favor for himself with the new commander! I knew it was he—I knew it as surely as though Or-tis had told me. To curry favor with the commander! I thought that that was the reason then. God, had I but known his real reason!

And while they searched, Or-tis talked with us. Mostly he talked with mother and Juana. I hated the way that he looked at them, especially Juana; but his words were fair enough. He seemed to be trying to get an expression from them of their political ideas—he, who was of the class that had ruthlessly stolen from women the recognition they had won in the twentieth century after ages of slavery and trials, attempting to sound them on their political faiths! They had none—no women have any—they only know that they hate and loathe the oppressors who have hurled them back into virtual slavery. That is their politics; that is their religion. Hate. But then the world is all hate—hate and misery.

Father says that it was not always so; but that once the world was happy—at least, our part of the world; but the people didn't know when they were well off. They came from all other parts of the world to share our happiness and when they had won it they sought to overthrow it, and when the Kalkars came they helped them.

Well, they searched for an hour and found nothing; but I knew that Or-tis was not satisfied that the thing he sought was not there and toward the end of the search I could see that he was losing patience. He took direct charge at last and then when they had no better success under his direction he became very angry.

"Yankee swine!" he cried suddenly, turning upon father. "You will find you cannot fool a descendant of the great Jemadar Orthis as you have fooled the others—not for long. I have a nose for traitors—I can smell a Yank farther than most men can see one. Take a warning, take a warning to your kind. It will be death or the mines for every traitor in the teivos."

He stood then in silence for a moment, glaring at father and then his gaze moved to Juana.

"Who are you, girl?" he demanded. "Where do you live and what do you do that adds to the prosperity of the community?"

"Adds to the prosperity of the community!" It was a phrase often on their lips and it was always directed at us—a meaningless phrase, as there was no prosperity. We supported the Kalkars and that was their idea of prosperity. I suppose ours was to get barely sufficient to sustain life and strength to enable us to continue slaving for them.

"I live with Mollie Sheehan," replied Juana, "and help her care for the chickens and the little pigs; also I help with the housework."

"H-m!" ejaculated Or-tis. "Housework! That is good—I shall be needing some one to keep my quarters tidy. How about it, my girl? It will be easy work, and I will pay you well—no pigs or chickens to slave for. Eh?"

"But I love the little pigs and chickens," she pleaded, "and I am happy with Mollie—I do not wish to change."

"Do not wish to change, eh?" he mimicked her. She had drawn farther behind me now, as though for protection, and closer—I could feel her body touching mine. "Mollie can doubtless take care of her own pigs and chickens without help. If she has so many she cannot do it alone, then she has too many, and we will see why it is that she is more prosperous than the rest of us—probably she should pay a larger income tax—we shall see."

"Oh, no!" cried Juana, frightened now on Mollie's account. "Please, she has only a few, scarcely enough that she and her man may live after the taxes are paid."

"Then she does not need you to help her," said Or-tis with finality, a nasty sneer upon his lip. "You will come and work for me, girl!"

And then Juana surprised me—she surprised us all, and particularly Or-tis. Before she had been rather pleading and seemingly a little frightened; but now she drew herself to her full height and with her chin in air looked Or-tis straight in the eye.

"I will not come," she said, haughtily; "I do not wish to." That was all.

Or-tis looked surprised; his soldiers, shocked. For a moment no one spoke. I glanced at mother. She was not trembling as I had expected. Her head was up, too, and she was openly looking her scorn of the Kalkar. Father stood as he usually did before them, with his head bowed; but I saw that he was watching Or-tis out of the corners of his eyes and that his fingers were moving as might the fingers of hands fixed upon a hated throat.

"You will come," said Or-tis, a little red in the face now at this defiance. "There are ways," and he looked straight at me—and then he turned upon his heel and, followed by his Kash Guard, left the house.

5

The Fight on Market Day

WHEN THE DOOR had closed upon them Juana buried her face in her hands.

"Oh, what misery I bring everywhere," she sobbed. "To my father and mother I brought death, and now to you all and to Jim and Mollie I am bringing ruin and perhaps death also. But it shall not be—you shall not suffer for me! He looked straight at you, Julian, when he made his threat. What could he mean to do? You have done nothing. But you need not fear. I know how I may undo the harm I have so innocently done."

We tried to assure her that we did not care—that we would protect her as best we could and that she must not feel that she had brought any greater burden upon us than we already carried; but she only shook her head and at last asked me to take her home to Mollie's.

She was very quiet all the way back, though I did my best to cheer her up.

"He cannot make you work for him," I insisted. "Even the Twenty-Four, rotten as it is, would never dare enforce such an order. We are not yet entirely slaves."

"But I am afraid that he will find a way," she replied, "through you, my friend. I saw him look at you and it was a very ugly look."

"I do not fear," I said.

"I fear for you. No, it shall not be!" She spoke with such vehement finality that she almost startled me and then she bid me good night and went into Mollie's house and closed the door.

All the way back home I was much worried about her, for I did not like to see her unhappy. I felt that her fears were exaggerated, for even such a powerful man as the commandant could not make her work for him if she did not wish to. Later he might take her as his woman if she had no man, but even then she had some choice in the matter—a month in which to choose some one else if she did not care to bear his children. That was the law.

Of course, they found ways to circumvent the law when they wanted a girl badly enough—the man of her choice might be apprehended upon some trumped-up charge, or even be found some morning mysteriously murdered. It must be a heroic woman who stood out against them for long, and a man must love a girl very deeply to sacrifice his life for her—and then not save her. There was but one way and by the time I reached my cot I was almost frantic with fear lest she might seize upon it.

For a few minutes I paced the floor and with every minute the conviction grew that the worst was about to happen. It became an obsession. I could see her even as plainly as with my physical eyesight and then I could stand it no longer.

Bolting for the doorway I ran as fast as my legs would carry me in the direction of Jim's house. Just before I reached it I saw a shadowy figure moving in the direction of the river. I could not make out who it was; but I knew and redoubled my speed.

A low bluff overhangs the stream at this point and upon its edge I saw the figure pause for a moment and then disappear. There was a splash in the water below just as I reached the rim of the bluff—a splash and circling rings spreading outward on the surface of the river in the starlight.

I saw these things—the whole picture—in the fraction of a moment, for I scarcely paused upon the bluff's edge; but dove headlong for the rippling water close to the center of those diverging circles.

We came up together, side by side, and I reached out and

seized her tunic, and thus, holding her at arm's length, I swam ashore with her, keeping her chin above water. She did not struggle and when at last we stood upon the bank she turned upon me, tearless, yet sobbing.

"Why did you do it?" she moaned. "Oh, why did you do it? It was the only way—the only way."

She looked so forlorn and unhappy and so altogether beautiful that I could scarcely keep from taking her in my arms, for then, quite unexpectedly, I realized what I had been too stupid to realize before—that I loved her.

But I only took her hands in mine and pressed them very tightly and begged her to promise me that she would not attempt this thing again. I told her that she might never hear from Or-tis again and that it was wicked to destroy herself until there was no other way.

"It is not that I fear myself," she said. "I can always find this way out at the last minute; but I fear for you who have been kind to me. If I go now you will no longer be in danger."

"I would rather be in danger than have you go," I said simply. "I do not fear."

And she promised me before I left her that she would not try it again until there was no other way.

As I walked slowly homeward my thoughts were filled with bitterness and sorrow. My soul was in revolt against this cruel social order that even robbed youth of happiness and love. Although I had seen but little of either something within me—some inherent instinct I suspect—cried aloud that these were my birthright and that I was being robbed of them by the spawn of lunar interlopers. My Americanism was very strong in me—stronger, perhaps, because of the century old effort of our oppressors to crush it and because always we must suppress any outward evidence of it. They called us Yanks in contempt; but the appellation was our pride. And we, in turn, often spoke of them as kaisers; but not to their faces. Father says that in ancient times the word had the loftiest of meanings; but now it has the lowest.

As I approached the house I saw that the candle was still

burning in the living room. I had left so hurriedly that I had given it no thought, and as I came closer I saw something else, too. I was walking very slowly and in the soft dust of the pathway my soft boots made no sound, or I might not have seen what I did see—two figures, close in the shadow of the wall, peering through one of our little windows into the living room.

I crept stealthily forward until I was close enough to see that one was in the uniform of a Kash Guard while the other was clothed as are those of my class. In the latter I recognized the stoop shouldered, lanky figure of Peter Johansen. I was not at all surprised at this confirmation of my suspicions.

I knew what they were there for—hoping to learn the secret hiding place of the Flag—but I also knew that unless they already knew it there was no danger of their discovering it from the outside, since it had been removed from its hiding place but once in my lifetime that I knew of and might never again be, especially since we knew that we were suspected. So I hid and watched them for a while and then circled the house and entered from the front as though I did not know that they were there, for it would never do to let them know that they had been discovered.

Taking off my clothes I went to bed, after putting out the candle. I do not know how long they remained—it was enough to know that we were being watched, and though it was not pleasant I was glad that we were forewarned. In the morning I told father and mother what I had seen. Mother sighed and shook her head.

"It is coming," she said. "I always knew that sooner or later it would come. One by one they get us—now it is our turn."

Father said nothing. He finished his breakfast in silence and when he left the house he walked with his eyes upon the ground, his shoulders stooped and his chin upon his breast—slowly, almost unsteadily, he walked, like a man whose heart and spirit are both broken.

I saw mother choke back a sob as she watched him go and I went and put my arm about her.

"I fear for him, Julian," she said. "A spirit such as his suffers terribly the stings of injustice and degradation. Some of the others do not seem to take it so to heart as he; but he is a proud man of a proud line. I am afraid—" she paused as though fearing even to voice her fears—"I am afraid that he will do away with himself."

"No," I said, "he is too brave a man for that. This will all blow over—they only suspect—they do not know, and we shall be careful and then all will be right again—as right as anything ever is in this world."

"But Or-tis?" she questioned. "It will not be right until he has his will."

I knew that she meant Juana.

"He will never have his will," I said. "Am I not here?"

She smiled indulgently. "You are very strong, my boy," she said; "but what are two brawny arms against the Kash Guard?"

"They would be enough for Or-tis," I replied.

"You would kill him?" she whispered. "They would tear you to pieces!"

"They can tear me to pieces but once."

It was market day and I went in with a few wethers, some hides and cheese. Father did not come along—in fact, I advised him not to as Soor would be there and also Hoffmeyer. One cheese I took as tribute to Soor. God, how I hated to do it! But both mother and father thought it best to propitiate the fellow, and I suppose they were right. A lifetime of suffering does not incline one to seek further trouble.

The market place was full, for I was a little late. There were many Kash Guards in evidence—more than usual. It was a warm day—the first really warm day we had had—and a number of men were sitting beneath a canopy at one side of the market place in front of Hoffmeyer's office. As I approached I saw that Or-tis was there, as well as Pthav, the coal baron, and Hoffmeyer, of course, with several others including some Kalkar women and children.

I recognized Pthav's woman—a renegade Yank who had gone to him willingly—and their little child, a girl of about six. The latter was playing in the dust in front of the canopy some hundred feet from the group, and I had scarcely recognized her when I saw that which made my heart almost stop beating for an instant.

Two men were driving a small bunch of cattle into the market place upon the other side of the canopy, when suddenly I saw one of the creatures, a great bull, break away from the herd and with lowered head charge toward the tiny figure playing, unconscious of danger in the dust. The men tried to head the beast off, but their efforts were futile. Those under the canopy saw the child's danger at the same time that I did and they rose and cried aloud in warning. Pthav's woman shrieked and Or-tis yelled lustily for the Kash Guard; but none hastened in the path of the infuriated beast to the rescue of the child.

I was the closest to her and the moment that I saw her danger I started forward; but even as I ran there passed through my brain some terrible thoughts. She is Kalkar! She is the spawn of the beast Pthav and of the woman who turned traitor to her kind to win ease and comfort and safety! Many a little life has been snuffed out because of her father and his class! Would they save a sister or a daughter of mine?

I thought all these things as I ran; but I did not stop running—something within impelled me to her aid. It must have been simply that she was a little child and I the descendant of American gentlemen. No, I kept right on in the face of the fact that my sense of justice cried out that I let the child die.

I reached her just a moment before the bull did and when he saw me there between him and the child he stopped and with his head down he pawed the earth, throwing clouds of dust about, and bellowed—and then he came for me; but I met him half way, determined to hold him off until the child escaped if it were humanly possible for me to do so. He was a huge beast and quite evidently a vicious one, which possibly explained the reason for bringing him to market, and altogether it seemed to me that he would make short work of me; but I meant to die fighting.

I called to the little girl to run and then the bull and I came together. I seized his horns as he attempted to toss me, and I exerted all the strength in my young body. I had thought that I had let the Hellhounds feel it all that other night; but now I knew that I had yet had more in reserve, for to my astonishment I held that great beast and slowly, very slowly, I commenced to twist his head to the left.

He struggled and fought and bellowed—I could feel the muscles of my back and arms and legs hardening to the strain that was put upon them; but almost from the first instant I knew that I was master. The Kash Guards were coming now on the run, and I could hear Or-tis shouting to them to shoot the bull; but before they reached me I gave the animal a final mighty wrench so that he went first down upon one knee and then over on his side and there I held him until a sergeant came and put a bullet through his head.

When he was quite dead Or-tis and Pthav and the others approached. I saw them coming as I was returning to my wethers, my skins and my cheese. Or-tis called to me and I turned and stood looking at him as I had no mind to have any business with any of them that I could avoid.

"Come here, my man," he called.

I moved sullenly toward him a few paces and stopped again.

"What do you want of me?" I asked.

"Who are you?" He was eyeing me closely now. "I never saw such strength in any man. You should be in the Kash Guard. How would you like that?"

"I would not like it," I replied. It was about then, I guess, that he recognized me, for his eyes hardened. "No," he said, "we do not want such as you among loyal men." He turned upon his heel; but immediately wheeled toward me again.

"See to it, young man," he snapped, "that you use that strength of yours wisely and in good causes."

"I shall use it wisely," I replied, "and in the best of causes."

I think Pthav's woman had intended to thank me for saving her child, and perhaps Pthav had, too, for they had both come toward me; but when they saw Or-tis's evident hostility toward me they turned away, for which I was thankful. I saw Soor looking on with a sneer on his lips and Hoffmeyer eyeing me with that cunning expression of his.

I gathered up my produce and proceeded to that part of the market place where we habitually showed that which we had to sell, only to find that a man named Vonbulen was there ahead of me. Now there is an unwritten law that each family has its own place in the market. I was the third generation of Julians who had brought produce to this spot—formerly horses mostly, for we were a family of horsemen; but more recently goats since the government had taken over the horse industry. Though father and I still broke horses occasionally for the Twenty-Four, we did not own or raise them any more.

Vonbulen had had a little pen in a far corner, where trade was not so brisk as it usually was in our section, and I could not understand what he was doing in ours, where he had three or four scrub pigs and a few sacks of grain. Approaching, I asked him why he was there.

"This is my pen now," he said. "Tax collector Soor told me to use it."

"You will get out of it," I replied. "You know that it is ours—every one in the teivos knows that it is and has been for many years. My grandfather built it and my family has kept it in repair. You will get out!"

"I will not get out," he replied truculently. He was a very large man and when he was angry he looked quite fierce, as he had large mustaches which he brushed upward on either side of his nose—like the tusks of one of his boars.

"You will get out or be thrown out," I told him; but he put his hand on the gate and attempted to bar my entrance.

Knowing him to be heavy minded and stupid, I thought to take him by surprise, nor did I fail as, with a hand upon the topmost rail, I vaulted the gate full in his face, and letting my knees strike his chest, I sent him tumbling backward into the filth of his swine. So hard I struck him that he turned a complete back somersault and as he scrambled to his feet, his lips fouled with oaths, I saw murder in his eye. And how he charged me! It was for all the world like the charge of the great bull I had just vanquished, except that I think that Vonbulen was angrier than the bull and not so good looking.

His great fists were flailing about in a most terrifying manner and his mouth was open just as though he intended eating me alive; but for some reason I felt no fear. In fact, I had to smile to see his face and his fierce mustache smeared with dirt.

I parried his first wild blows and then stepping in close I struck him lightly in the face—I am sure I did not strike him hard, for I did not mean to—I wanted to play with him; but the result was so astonishing to me as it must have been to him, though not so painful. He rebounded from my fist fully three feet and then went over on his back again, spitting blood and teeth from his mouth.

And then I picked him up by the scruff of his neck and the seat of his breeches, and lifting him high above my head, I hurled him out of the pen into the market place where, for the first time, I saw a large crowd of interested spectators.

Vonbulen was not a popular character in the teivos, and many were the broad smiles I saw on the faces of those of my class; but there were others who did not smile. They were Kalkars and half-breeds.

I saw all this in a single glance and then I returned to my work, for I was not through. Vonbulen lay where he had alighted and after him and onto him, one by one, I threw his sacks of grain and his scrub pigs and then I opened the gate and started to bring in my own produce and live stock. As I did so I almost ran into Soor, standing there eying me with a most malignant expression upon his face.

"What does this mean?" he fairly screamed at me.

"It means," I replied, "that no one can steal the place of a Julian as easily as Vonbulen thought."

"He did not steal it," yelled Soor. "I gave it to him. Get out! It is his."

"It is not yours to give," I replied. "I know my rights and no man shall take them from me without a fight. Do you understand me?"

And then I brushed by him without another glance and drove my wethers into the pen. As I did so I saw that no one was smiling any more—my friends looked very glum and very frightened; but a man came up from my right and stood by my side, facing Soor, and when I turned my eyes in his direction I saw that it was Jim.

Then I realized how serious my act must have seemed, and I was sorry that Jim had come and thus silently announced that he stood with me in what I had done. No others came, although there were many who hated the Kalkars fully as much as we.

Soor was furious; but he could not stop me. Only the Twenty-Four could take the pen away from me. He called me names and threatened me; but I noticed that he waited until he had walked a short distance away before he did so. It was as food to a starving man to know that even one of our oppressors feared me. So far this had been the happiest day of my life.

I hurriedly got the goats into the pen and then, with one of the cheeses in my hand, I called to Soor. He turned to see what I wanted, showing his teeth like a rat at bay.

"You told my father to bring you a present," I yelled at the top of my lungs, so that all about in every direction heard and turned toward us. "Here it is!" I cried. "Here is your bribe!" and I hurled the cheese with all my strength full in his face.

He went down like a felled ox and the people scattered like frightened rabbits. Then I went back into the pen and started to open and arrange my hides across the fence so that they might be inspected by prospective purchasers.

Jim, whose pen was next to ours, stood looking across the fence at me for several minutes. At last he spoke:

"You have done a very rash thing, Julian," he said, and then: "I envy you."

It was not quite plain what he meant and yet I guessed that

he, too, would have been willing to die for the satisfaction of having defied them. I had not done this thing merely in the heat of anger or the pride of strength; but from the memory of my father's bowed head and my mother's tears—in the realization that we were better dead than alive unless we could hold our heads aloft as men should. Yes, I still saw my father's chin upon his breast and his unsteady gait and I was ashamed for him and for myself; but I had partially washed away the stain and there had finally crystalized in my brain something that must have been forming long in solution there—the determination to walk through the balance of my life with my head up and my fists ready—a man—however short my walk might be.

6

The Court Martial

THAT AFTERNOON I saw a small detachment of the Kash Guard crossing the market place. They came directly toward my pen and stopped before it. The sergeant in charge addressed me: "You are Brother Julian 9th?" he asked.

"I am Julian 9th," I replied.

"You had better be Brother Julian 9th when you are addressed by Brother General Or-tis," he snapped back. "You are under arrest—come with me!"

"What for?" I asked.

"Brother Or-tis will tell you if you do not know—you are to be taken to him."

So! It had come and it had come quickly. I felt sorry for mother; but, in a way, I was glad. If only there had been no such person in the world as Juana St. John I should have been almost happy, for I knew mother and father would come soon and, as she always taught me, we would be reunited in a happy world on the other side—a world in which there were no Kalkars or taxes—but then there was a Juana St. John and I was very sure of this world, while not quite so sure of the other, which I had never seen, nor any one who had.

There seemed no particular reason for refusing to accompany the Kash Guard. They would simply have killed me with their bullets and if I went I might have an opportunity to wipe out some more important swine than they before I was killed—if they intended killing me. One never knows what they will do—other than that it will be the wrong thing.

61

Well, they took me to the headquarters of the teivos, way down on the shore of the lake; but as they took me in a large wagon drawn by horses it was not a tiresome trip and, as I was not worrying, I enjoyed it. We passed through many market places, for numerous districts lie between ours and headquarters, and always the people stared at me, just as I had stared at other prisoners being carted away to no one knew what fate. Sometimes they came back—sometimes they did not. I wondered which I would do.

At last we arrived at headquarters after passing through miles of lofty ruins where I had played and explored as a child. I was taken immediately into Or-tis's presence. He sat in a large room at the head of a long table, and I saw that there were other men sitting along the sides of the table, the local representatives of that hated authority known as the Twenty-Four, the form of government that the Kalkars had brought with them from the moon a century before. The Twenty-Four originally consisted of a committee of that number. Now, however, it was but a name that stood for power, for government and for tyranny. Jarth the Jemadar was, in reality, what his lunar title indicated—emperor. Surrounding him was a committee of twenty-four Kalkars; but as they had been appointed by him and could be removed by him at will, they were nothing more than his tools. And this body before which I had been haled had in our teivos the same power as the Twenty-Four which gave it birth, and so we spoke of it, too, as the Twenty-Four, or as the Teivos, as I at first thought it to be.

Many of these men I recognized as members of the Teivos. Pthav and Hoffmeyer were there, representing our district, or misrepresenting it, as father always put it, yet I was presently sure that this could not be a meeting of the Teivos proper, as these were held in another building farther south— a magnificent pillared pile of olden times that the government had partially restored as they had the headquarters, which also had been a beautiful building in a past age, its great lions still standing on either side of its broad entranceway.

No, it was not the Teivos; but what could it be, and then

it dawned upon me that it must be an arm of the new law that Or-tis had announced, and such it proved to be—a special military tribunal for special offenders. This was the first session and it chanced to be my luck that I committed my indiscretion just in time to be haled before it when it needed some one to experiment on.

I was made to stand, under guard, at the foot of the table and as I looked up and down the rows of faces on either side I saw not a friendly eye—no person of my class or race— just swine, swine, swine. Low-browed, brute-faced men, slouching in their chairs, slovenly in their dress, uncouth, unwashed, unwholesome looking—this was the personnel of the court that was to try me—for what?

Or-tis asked who appeared against me and what was the charge. Then I saw Soor for the first time. He should have been in his district collecting his taxes; but he wasn't. No, he was there on more pleasant business. He eyed me malevolently and stated the charge: resisting an officer of the law in the discharge of his duty and assaulting same with a deadly weapon with intent to commit murder.

They all looked ferociously at me, expecting, no doubt, that I would tremble with terror, as most of my class did before them; but I couldn't tremble—the charge struck me as so ridiculous. As a matter of fact, I am afraid that I grinned. I know I did.

"What is it?" asked Or-tis, "that amuses you so?"

"The charge," I replied.

"What is there funny about that?" he asked again. "Men have been shot for less—men who were not suspected of treasonable acts."

"I did not resist an officer in the discharge of his duty," I said. "It is not one of a tax collector's duties to put a family out of its pen at the market place, is it?—a pen they have occupied for three generations. I ask you, Or-tis, is it?"

Or-tis half rose from his chair. "How dare you address me thus?" he cried.

The others turned scowling faces upon me and, beating the table with their dirty fists, they all shouted and bellowed at me at once; but I kept my chin up as I had sworn to do until I died.

Finally they quieted down and again I put my question to Or-tis and I'll give him credit for answering it fairly. "No," he said, "only the Teivos may do that—the Teivos or the commandant."

"Then I did not resist an officer in the discharge of his duty," I shot back at them, "for I only refused to leave the pen that is mine. And now another question: Is a cheese a deadly weapon?"

They had to admit that it was not. "He demanded a present from my father," I explained, "and I brought him a cheese. He had no right under the law to demand it, and so I threw it at him and it hit him in the face. I shall deliver thus every such illegal tithe that is demanded of us. I have my rights under the law and I intend to see that they are respected."

They had never been talked to thus before and suddenly I realized that by merest chance I had stumbled upon the only way in which to meet these creatures. They were moral as well as physical cowards. They could not face an honest, fearless man—already they were showing signs of embarrassment. They knew that I was right and while they could have condemned me had I bowed the knee to them they hadn't the courage to do it in my presence.

The natural outcome was that they sought a scapegoat, and Or-tis was not long in finding one—his baleful eye alighted upon Soor.

"Does this man speak the truth?" he cried at the tax collector. "Did you turn him out of his pen? Did he do no more than throw a cheese at you?"

Soor, a coward before those in authority over him, flushed and stammered.

"He tried to kill me," he mumbled lamely, "and he did almost kill Brother Vonbulen."

Then I told them of that—and always I spoke in a tone of authority and I held my ground. I did not fear them and they knew it. Sometimes I think they attributed it to some knowledge I had of something that might be menacing them—for they were always afraid of revolution. That is why they ground us down so.

The outcome of it was that I was let go with a warning— a warning that if I did not address my fellows as brother I would be punished, and even then I gave the parting shot, for I told them I would call no man brother unless he was.

The whole affair was a farce; but all trials were farces, only, as a rule, the joke was on the accused. They were not conducted in a dignified or proper manner as I imagine trials in ancient times to have been. There was neither order nor system.

I had to walk all the way home—another manifestation of justice—and I arrived there an hour or two after supper time. I found Jim and Mollie and Juana at the house, and I could see that mother had been crying. She started again when she saw me. Poor mother! I wonder if it has always been such a terrible thing to be a mother; but, no, it cannot have been, else the human race would long since have been extinct—as the Kalkars will rapidly make it, anyway.

Jim had told them of the happenings in the market place— the episode of the bull, the encounter with Vonbulen and the matter of Soor. For the first time in my life, and the only time, I heard my father laugh aloud. Juana laughed, too; but there was still an undercurrent of terror that I could feel and which Mollie finally voiced.

"They will get us yet, Julian," she said; "but what you have done is worth dying for."

"Yes!" cried my father. "I can go to the butcher with a smile on my lips after this. He has done what I always wanted to do; but dared not. If I am a coward I can at least thank God that there sprang from my loins a brave and fearless man."

"You are not a coward!" I cried, and mother looked at me and smiled. I was glad that I said that, then.

You may not understand what father meant by "going to the butcher," but it is simple. The manufacture of ammunition is a lost art—that is, the high-powered ammunition that the Kash Guard likes to use—and so they conserve all the vast stores of ammunition that were handed down from ancient times—millions upon millions of rounds—or they would not be able to use the rifles that were handed down with the ammunition. They use this ammunition only in cases of dire necessity, a fact which long ago placed the firing squad of old in the same class with flying machines and automobiles. Now they cut our throats when they kill us and the man who does it is known as the butcher.

I walked home with Jim and Mollie and Juana; but more especially Juana. Again I noticed that strange magnetic force which drew me to her, so that I kept bumping into her every step or two, and, intentionally, I swung my arm that was nearest to her in the hope that my hand might touch hers, nor was I doomed to disappointment and at every touch I thrilled. I could not but notice that Juana made no mention of my clumsiness, nor did she appear to attempt to prevent our contact; but yet I was afraid of her—afraid that she would notice and afraid that she would not. I am good with horses and goats and Hellhounds; but I am not much good with girls.

We had talked upon many subjects and I knew her views and beliefs and she knew mine, so when we parted and I asked her if she would go with me on the morrow, which was the first Sunday of the month, she knew what I meant. She said that she would, and I went home very happy, for I knew that she and I were going to defy the common enemy side by side—that hand in hand we would face the Grim Reaper for the sake of the greatest cause on earth.

On the way home I overtook Peter Johansen going in the direction of our home. I could see that he had no mind to meet me and he immediately fell to explaining lengthily why he was out at night, for the first thing I did was to ask him what strange business took him abroad so often lately after the sun had set.

I could see him flush even in the dark.

"Why," he exclaimed, "this is the first time in months that I have gone out after supper," and then something about the man made me lose my temper and I blurted out what was in my heart.

"You lie!" I cried. "You lie, you damned spy!"

And then Peter Johansen went white and, suddenly whipping a knife from his clothes, he leaped at me, striking wildly for any part of me that the blade might reach. At first he almost got me, so unexpected and so venomous was the attack; but though I was struck twice on the arm and cut a little I managed to ward the point from any vital part, and in a moment I had seized his knife wrist. That was the end—I just twisted it a little—I did not mean to twist hard—and something snapped inside his wrist.

Peter let out an awful scream, his knife dropped from his fingers, and I pushed him from me and gave him a good kick as he was leaving—a kick that I think he will remember for some time. Then I picked up his knife and hurled it as far as I could in the direction of the river, where I think it landed, and went on my way toward home—whistling.

When I entered the house mother came out of her room and, putting her arms about my neck, she clung closely to me.

"Dear boy," she murmured, "I am so happy, because you are happy. She is a dear girl, and I love her as much as you do."

"What is the matter?" I asked. "What are you talking about?"

"I heard you whistling," she said, "and I knew what it meant—grown men whistle but once in their lives."

I picked her up in my arms.

"Oh, mother, dear!" I cried. "I wish it were true and maybe it will be some day—if I am not too much of a coward; but not yet."

"Then why were you whistling?" she asked, surprised and a bit skeptical, too, I imagine.

"I whistled," I explained, "because I just broke the wrist of a spy and kicked him across the road."

"Peter?" she asked, trembling.

"Yes, mother, Peter. I called him a spy and he tried to knife me."

"Oh, my son!" she cried. "You did not know. It is my fault, I should have told you. Now he will fight no more in the dark; but will come out in the open and when he does that I am lost."

"What do you mean?" I asked.

"I do not mind dying," she said; "but they will take your father first, because of me."

"What do you mean? I can understand nothing of what you are driving at."

"Then listen," she said. "Peter wants me. That is the reason he is spying on your father. If he can prove something against him and father is taken to the mines or killed, Peter will claim me."

"How do you know this?" I asked.

"Peter himself has told me that he wants me. He tried to make me leave your dear father and go with him, and when I refused he bragged that he was in the favor of the Kalkars and that he would get me in the end. He has tried to buy my honor with your father's life. That is why I have been so afraid and so unhappy; but I knew that you and father would rather die than have me do that thing, and so I have withstood him."

"Did you tell father?" I asked.

"I dared not. He would have killed Peter and that would have been the end of us, for Peter stands high in the graces of the authorities."

"I will kill him!" I said.

She tried to dissuade me, and finally I had to promise her that I would wait until I had provocation that the authorities might recognize. God knows I had provocation enough, though.

After breakfast the next day we set out singly and in different directions, as was always our custom on the first Sunday in each month. I went to Jim's first to get Juana, as she did not know the way, having never been with us. I found her ready and waiting and alone, as Jim and Mollie had started a few minutes before, and seemingly very glad to see me.

I told her nothing of Peter, as there is enough trouble in the world without burdening people with any that does not directly threaten them. I led her up the river for a mile and all the while we watched to see if we were followed. Then we found a skiff, where I had hidden it, and crossed the river. After hiding it again we continued on up for half a mile. Here was a raft that I had made myself, and on this we poled again to the other shore—if any followed us they must have swum, for there were no other boats on this part of the river.

I had come this way for several years—in fact, ever since I was fifteen years old—and no one had ever suspected or followed me, yet I never relaxed my vigilance, which may account for the fact that I was not apprehended. No one ever saw me take to either the skiff or the raft and no one could even have guessed my destination, so circuitous was the way.

A mile west of the river is a thick forest of very old trees and toward this I led Juana. At its verge we sat down, ostensibly to rest; but really to see if any one was near who might have followed us or who could accidentally discover our next move. There was no one in sight, and so, with light hearts, we arose and entered the forest.

For a quarter of a mile we made our way along a winding path and then I turned to the left at a right angle and entered thick brush where there was no trail. Always we did this, never covering the last quarter of a mile over the same route, lest we make a path that might be marked and followed.

Presently we came to a pile of brush wood, beneath one edge of which was an opening into which, by stooping low, one might enter. It was screened from view by a fallen tree, over which had been heaped broken branches. Even in winter time and early spring the opening in the brush beyond was invisible to the passers-by, if there had been any passers-by. A man trailing lost stock might come this way; but no others, for it was a lonely and unfrequented spot. During the summer, the season of the year when there was the greatest danger of discovery, the entire brush pile and its tangled screen were hidden completely beneath a mass of wild vines, so that it was with difficulty that we found it ourselves.

Into this opening I led Juana—taking her by the hand as one might a blind person, although it was not so dark within that she could not see perfectly every step she took. However, I took her by the hand, a poor excuse being better than none. The winding tunnel beneath the brush was a hundred yards long, perhaps—I wished then that it had been a hundred miles. It ended abruptly before a rough stone wall in which was a heavy door. Its oaken panels were black with age and streaked with green from the massive hinges that ran across its entire width in three places, while from the great lag screws that fastened them to the door brownish streaks of rust ran down to mingle with the green and the black. In patches moss grew upon it, so that all in all it had the appearance of great antiquity, though even the oldest among those who knew of it at all could only guess at its age. Above the door, carved in the stone, was a shepherd's crook and the words, *Dieu et mon droit.*

Halting before this massive portal I struck the panels once with my knuckles, counted five and struck again, once; then I counted three and, in the same cadence, struck three times. It was the signal for the day—never twice was it the same. Should one come with the wrong signal and later force the door he would find only an empty room beyond.

Now the door opened a crack and an eye peered forth, then it swung outward and we entered a long, low room lighted by burning wicks floating in oil. Across the width of the room were rough wooden benches and at the far end a raised platform upon which stood Orrin Colby, the blacksmith, behind an altar which was the sawn off trunk of a tree, the roots of which, legend has it, still run down into the ground beneath the church, which is supposed to have been built around it.

7

Betrayed

THERE WERE TWELVE people sitting on the benches when we entered, so that with Orrin Colby, ourselves and the man at the door we were sixteen in all. Colby is the head of our church; his great grandfather was a Methodist minister. Father and mother were there, sitting next to Jim and Mollie, and there were Samuels the Jew, Betty Worth, who was Dennis Corrigan's woman, and all the other familiar faces.

They had been waiting for us and as soon as we were seated the services commenced with a prayer, every one standing with bowed head. Orrin Colby always delivered this same short prayer at the opening of services each first Sunday of every month. It ran something like this:

> "God of our fathers, through generations of persecution and cruelty in a world of hate that has turned against You, we stand at Your right hand, loyal to You and to our Flag. To us Your name stands for justice, humanity, love, happiness and right and the Flag is Your emblem. Once each month we risk our lives that Your name may not perish from the earth. Amen!"

From behind the altar he took a shepherd's crook to which was attached a flag like that in my father's possession and held it aloft, whereat we all knelt in silence for a few seconds. Then he replaced it and we arose. Then we sang a song—it was an old, old song that started like this: "Onward, Christian

Soldiers.'' It was my favorite song. Mollie Sheehan played a violin while we sang.

Following the song Orrin Colby talked to us—he always talked about the practical things that affected our lives and our future. It was a homely talk, but it was full of hope for better times. I think that at these meetings, once each month, we heard the only suggestions of hope that ever came into our lives. There was something about Orrin Colby that inspired confidence and hope. These days were the bright spots in our drab existence.

After the talk we sang again and then Samuels the Jew prayed and the regular service was over, after which we had short talks by various members of our church. These talks were mostly on the subject which dominated the minds of all—a revolution; but we never got any further than talking. How could we? We were probably the most thoroughly subjugated people the world ever had known—we feared our masters and we feared our neighbors. We did not know whom we might trust, outside that little coterie of ours, and so we dared not seek recruits for our cause, although we knew that there must be thousands who would sympathize with us. Spies and informers were everywhere—they, the Kash Guard and the butcher, were the agencies by which they controlled us; but of all we feared most the spies and informers. For a woman, for a neighbor's house, and in one instance of which I know, for a setting of eggs, men have been known to inform on their friends—sending them to the mines or the butcher.

Following the talks we just visited together and gossiped for an hour or two, enjoying the rare treat of being able to speak our minds freely and fearlessly. I had to re-tell several times my experiences before Or-tis's new court-martial and I know that it was with difficulty that they believed that I had said the things I had to our masters and come away free and alive. They simply could not understand it.

All were warned of Peter Johansen and the names of others under suspicion of being informers were passed around that we might all be on our guard against them. We did not sing again, for even on these days that our hearts were lightest they were too heavy for song. About two o'clock the pass signal for the next meeting was given out and then we started away singly or in pairs. I volunteered to go last, with Juana, and see that the door was locked. An hour later we started out, about five minutes behind Samuels the Jew.

Juana's mother had passed down to her by word of mouth an unusually complete religious training for those days and she, in turn, had transmitted it to Juana. It seemed that they, too, had had a church in their district; but that a short time before it had been discovered by the authorities and destroyed, though none of the members of the organization had been apprehended. So close a watch was kept thereafter that they had never dared seek another meeting place.

She told me that their congregation was much like ours in personnel and with the knowledge she had of ancient religious customs it always seemed odd to her to see so different creeds worshipping under one roof in even greater harmony than many denominations of the same church knew in ancient times. Among us were descendants of Methodist, Presbyterian, Baptist, Roman Catholic and Jew that I knew of and how many more I did not know, nor did any of us care.

We worshipped an ideal and a great hope, both of which were all goodness, and we called these God. We did not care what our great-grandfathers thought about it or what some one a thousand years before had thought or done or what name they had given the Supreme Being, for we knew that there could be but one and whether we called Him one thing or another would not alter Him in any way. This much good, at least, the Kalkars had accomplished in the world; but it had come too late. Those who worshipped any god were becoming fewer and fewer. Our own congregation had fallen from twenty-two a year or so before to fifteen—until Juana made us sixteen.

Some had died natural deaths and some had gone to the mines or the butcher; but the principal reason of our decadence was the fact that there were too few children to take the place of the adults who died—that and our fear to seek converts. We were dying out, there was no doubt of it, and with us was dying all religion. That was what the lunar theory was doing for the world; but it was only what any one might have expected. Intelligent men and women realized it from almost the instant that this lunar theory stuck its ugly head above our horizon—a political faith that would make all women the common property of all men could not by any remote possibility have respect, or even aught but fear, for any religion of ancient times, and the Kalkars did, just what any one might have known they would do—they deliberately and openly crushed all churches.

Juana and I had emerged from the wood when we noticed a man walking cautiously in the shade of the trees ahead of us. He seemed to be following some one and immediately there sprang to my thoughts the ever near suspicion—spy.

The moment that he turned a bend in the pathway and was out of our sight Juana and I ran forward as rapidly as we could go that we might get a closer view of him, nor were we disappointed. We saw him and recognized him and we also saw whom he shadowed. It was Peter Johansen, carrying one arm in a sling, sneaking along behind Samuels.

I knew that if Peter was permitted to shadow Samuels home he would discover the devious way the old man followed and immediately, even though he had suspicioned nothing in particular before, he would know that Moses had been upon some errand that he didn't wish the authorities to learn of. That would mean suspicion for old Samuels and suspicion usually ended in conviction upon one charge or another. How far he had followed him we could not guess, but already we knew that it was much too near the church for safety. I was much perturbed.

Casting about in my mind for some plan to throw Peter off the track I finally hit upon a scheme which I immediately put into execution. I knew the way that the old man followed to and from church and that presently he would make a wide detour that would bring him back to the river about a quarter of a mile below. Juana and I could walk straight to the spot and arrive long before Samuels did. And this we proceeded to do.

About half an hour before we reached the point at which we knew he would strike the river, we heard him coming and withdrew into some bushes. On he came all oblivious of the creature on his trail and a moment later we saw Peter come into view and halt at the edge of the trees. Then Juana and I stepped out and hailed Samuels.

"Did you see nothing of them?" I asked in a tone of voice loud enough to be distinctly heard by Peter, and then before Samuels could reply I added: "We have searched far up the river and never a sign of a goat about—I do not believe that they came this way after all; but if they did the Hellhounds will get them after dark. Come, now, we might as well start for home and give the search up as a bad job."

I had talked so much and so rapidly that Samuels had guessed that I must have some reason for it, and so he held his peace, other than to say that he had seen nothing of any goats. Not once had Juana or I let our glances betray that we knew of Peter's presence, though I could not help but seeing him dodge behind a tree the moment that he saw us.

The three of us then continued on toward home in the shortest direction and on the way I whispered to Samuels what we had seen. The old man chuckled, for he thought as I did that my ruse must have effectually baffled Johansen—unless he had followed Moses farther than we guessed. We each turned a little white as the consequences of such a possibility were borne home upon us. We did not want Peter to know that we even guessed that we were followed, and so we never once looked behind us, not even Juana, which was remarkable for a woman, nor did we see him again, though we felt that he was following us. I for one was sure, though, that he was following at a safer distance since I had joined Samuels.

Very cautiously during the ensuing week the word was passed around by means with which we were familiar that Johansen had followed Samuels from church; but as the authorities paid no more attention to Moses than before we finally concluded that we had thrown Peter off the trail.

The Sunday following church we were all seated in Jim's

yard under one of his trees that had already put forth its young leaves and afforded shade from the sun. We had been talking of homely things—the coming crops, the newborn kids, Mollie's little pigs. The world seemed unusually kindly. The authorities had not persecuted us of late. A respite of two weeks seemed like heaven to us. We were quite sure by this time that Peter Johansen had discovered nothing and our hearts were freer than for a long time past.

We were sitting thus in quiet and contentment, enjoying a brief rest from our lives of drudgery, when we heard the pounding of horses' hoofs upon the hard earth of the path that leads down the river in the direction of the market place. Suddenly the entire atmosphere changed—relaxed nerves became suddenly taut; peaceful eyes resumed their hunted expression. Why? The Kash Guard rides.

And so they came—fifty of them—and at their head rode Brother General Or-tis. At the gateway of Jim's house they drew rein and Or-tis dismounted and entered the yard. He looked at us as a man might look at carrion; and he gave us no greeting, which suited us perfectly. He walked straight to Juana, who was seated on a little bench beside which I stood leaning against the bole of the tree. None of us moved. He halted before the girl.

"I have come to tell you," he said to her, "that I have done you the honor to choose you as my woman, to bear my children and keep my house in order."

He stood then looking at her and I could feel the hair upon my head rise and the corners of my upper lip twitched—I know not why. I only know that I wanted to fly at his throat and kill him, to tear his flesh with my teeth—to see him die! And then he looked at me and stepped back, after which he beckoned to some of his men to enter. When they had come he again addressed Juana, who had risen and stood swaying to and fro, as might one who has been dealt a heavy blow upon the head and is half stunned.

"You may come with me now," he said to her, and then I stepped between them and faced him and again he stepped back a pace.

. "She will not come with you now, or ever," I said, and my voice was very low—not above a whisper. "She is my woman—I have taken her!"

It was a lie—the last part, but what is a lie to a man who would commit murder in the same cause. He was among his men now—they were close around him and I suppose they gave him courage, for he addressed me threateningly.

"I do not care whose she is," he cried, "I want her and I shall have her. I speak for her now and I speak for her when she is a widow. After you are dead I have first choice of her and traitors do not live long."

"I am not dead yet," I reminded him. He turned to Juana.

"You shall have thirty days as the law requires; but you can save your friends trouble if you come now—they will not be molested then and I will see that their taxes are lowered."

Juana gave a little gasp and looked around at us and then she straightened her shoulders and came close to me.

"No!" she said to Or-tis. "I will never go. This is my man—he has taken me. Ask him if he will give me up to you. You will never have me—alive."

"Don't be too sure of that," he growled. "I believe that you are both lying to me, for I have had you watched and I know that you do not live under the same roof. And you!" he glared at me. "Tread carefully, for the eyes of the law find traitors where others do not see them." Then he turned and strode from the yard. A minute later they were gone in a cloud of dust.

Now our happiness and peace had fled—it was always thus—and there was no hope. I dared not look at Juana after what I had said; but then, had she not said the same thing? We all talked lamely for a few minutes and then father and mother rose to go and a moment later Jim and Mollie went indoors.

I turned to Juana. She stood with her eyes upon the ground and a pretty flush upon her cheek. Something surged up in me—a mighty force, that I had never known, possessed me, and before I realized what it impelled me to do I had seized

Juana in my arms and was covering her face and lips with kisses.

She fought to free herself, but I would not let her go.

"You are mine!" I cried. "You are my woman. I have said it—you have said it. You are my woman. God, how I love you!"

She lay quiet then and let me kiss her, and presently her arms stole about my neck and her lips sought mine in an interval that I had drawn them away and they moved upon my lips in a gentle caress that was yet palpitant with passion. This was a new Juana—a new and very wonderful Juana.

"You really love me?" she asked at last. "I heard you say it!"

"I have loved you from the moment I saw you looking up at me from beneath the Hellhound," I replied.

"You have kept it very much of a secret to yourself then," she teased me. "If you loved me so, why did you not tell me? Were you going to keep it from me all my life, or—were you afraid? Brother Or-tis was not afraid to say that he wanted me. Is my man less brave than he?"

I knew that she was only teasing me, and so I stopped her mouth with kisses and then: "Had you been a Hellhound, or Soor, or even Or-tis," I said, "I could have told you what I thought of you, but being Juana and a little girl the words would not come. I am a great coward."

We talked until it was time to go home to supper and I took her hand to lead her to my house. "But first," I said, "you must tell Mollie and Jim what has happened and that you will not be back. For a while we can live under my father's roof, but as soon as may be I will get permission from the Teivos to take the adjoining land and work it and then I shall build a house."

She drew back and flushed. "I cannot go with you yet," she said.

"What do you mean?" I asked. "You are mine!"

"We have not been married," she whispered.

"But no one is married," I reminded her. "Marriage is against the law."

"My mother was married," she told me. "You and I can be married. We have a church and a preacher. Why cannot he marry us? He is not ordained because there is none to ordain him; but being the head of the only church that he knows of or that we know of, it is evident that he can be ordained only by God and who knows but that He already has done so."

I tried to argue her out of it as now that Heaven was so near I had no mind to wait three weeks to attain it. But she would not argue—she just shook her head and at last I saw that she was right and gave in—as I would have had to do in any event.

The next day I sought Orrin Colby and broached the subject to him. He was quite enthusiastic about it and wondered that they had never thought of it before. Of course, they had not because marriage had been obsolete for so many years that no one considered the ceremony necessary, nor, in fact, was it. Men and women were more often faithful to one another through life than otherwise—no amount of ceremony or ritual could make them more so. But if a woman wants it she should have it. And so it was arranged that at the next meeting Juana and I should be married.

The next three weeks were about the longest of my life and yet they were very, very happy weeks, for Juana and I were much together, as it had finally been decided that in order to carry out our statements to Or-tis she must come and live under our roof. She slept in the living room and I upon a pile of goat skins in the kitchen. If there were any spies watching us, and I know that there were, they saw that we slept every night under the same roof.

Mother worked hard upon a new tunic and breeches for me, while Mollie helped Juana with her outfit. The poor child had come to us with only the clothes she wore upon her back; but even so, most of us had few changes—just enough to keep ourselves decently clean.

I went to Pthav, who was one of our representatives in the Teivos, and asked him to procure for me permission to work the vacant land adjoining my father's. The land all belonged to the community, but each man was allowed what he could work as long as there was plenty, and there was more than plenty for us all.

Pthav was very ugly—he seemed to have forgotten that I had saved his child's life—and said that he did not know what he could do for me, that I had acted very badly to General Or-tis and was in disfavor, beside being under suspicion in another matter.

"What has General Or-tis to do with the distribution of land by the Teivos?" I asked. "Because he wants my woman will the Teivos deny me my rights?"

I was no longer afraid of any of them and I spoke my mind as freely as I wished—almost. Of course, I did not care to give them the chance to bring me to trial as they most assuredly would have done had I really said to them all that was in my heart, but I stood up for my rights and demanded all that their rotten laws allowed me.

Pthav's woman came in while I was talking and recognized me, but she said nothing to me other than to mention that the child had asked for me. Pthav scowled at this and ordered her from the room, just as a man might order a beast around. It was nothing to me, though, as the woman was a renegade anyway.

Finally I demanded of Pthav that he obtain the concession for me unless he could give me some valid reason for refusing.

"I will ask it," he said finally, "but you will not get it—be sure of that."

I saw that it was useless and so I turned and left the room, wondering what I should do. Of course, we could remain under father's roof, but that did not seem right, as each man should make a home for himself. After father and mother died we would return to the old place, as father had after the death of my grandfather, but a young couple should start their life together alone and in their own way.

As I was leaving the house Pthav's woman stopped me. "I will do what I can for you," she whispered. She must have seen me draw away instinctively as from an unclean thing, for she flushed, and then said: "Please don't! I have suffered enough. I have paid the price of my treachery; but know, Yank," and she put her lips close to my ear, "that at heart I am more Yank than I was when I did this thing. And," she continued, "I have never spoken a word that could harm one of you. Tell them that—please tell them! I do not want them to hate me so, and, God of our Fathers! How I have suffered—the degradation, the humiliation. It has been worse than what you are made to suffer. These creatures are lower than the beasts of the forest. I could kill him if I were not such a coward. I have seen, and I know how they can make one suffer before death."

I could not but feel sorry for her, and I told her so. The poor creature appeared very grateful, and assured me that she would aid me.

"I know a few things about Pthav that he would not want Or-tis to know," she said, "and even though he beats me for it I will make him get the land for you."

Again I thanked her, and departed, realizing that there were others worse off than we—that the closer one came to the Kalkars the more hideous life became.

At last the day came, and we set out for the church. As before I took Juana, though she tried to order it differently; but I would not trust her to the protection of another. We arrived without mishap—sixteen of us—and after the religious services were over, Juana and I stood before the altar, and were married—much after the fashion of the ancients, I imagine.

Juana was the only one of us who was at all sure about the ceremony, and it had been she who trained Orrin Colby— making him memorize so much that he said his head ached for a week. All I can recall of it is that he asked me if I would take her to be my lawfully wedded wife—I lost my voice, and only squeaked a weak yes—and that he pronounced us man and wife, and then something about not letting any one put asunder what God had joined together. I felt very much married, and very happy, and then just as it was all nicely over, and everybody was shaking hands with us, there came a loud knocking at the door, and the command: "Open, in the name of the law!"

We looked at one another and gasped. Orrin Colby put a finger to his lips for silence, and led the way toward the back of the church where a rough niche was built containing a few shelves upon which stood several rude candlesticks. We knew our parts, and followed him in silence, except one who went quickly about putting out the lights. All the time the pounding on the door became more insistent; and then we could hear the strokes of what must have been an ax beating at the panels. Finally a shot was fired through the heavy wood, and we knew it was the Kash Guard.

Taking hold of the lower shelf Orrin pulled upward with all his strength with the result that all the shelving and woodwork to which it was attached slid upward revealing an opening beyond. Through this we filed, one by one, down a flight of stone steps into a dark tunnel. When the last man had passed I lowered the shelving to its former place.

Then I turned, and followed the others, Juana's hand in mine. We groped our way for some little distance in the darkness of the tunnel until Orrin halted, and whispered to me to come to him. I went and stood at his side while he told me what I was to do. He had called me because I was the tallest, and the strongest of the men. Above us was a wooden trap. I was to lift this.

It had not been moved for generations, and was very heavy with earth, and growing things above; but I put my shoulders to it, and it had to give—either it or the ground beneath my feet, and that could not give. At last I had it off, and in a few minutes I had helped them all out into the midst of a dense wood. Again we knew our parts, for many times had we been coached for just such an emergency, and one by one the men scattered in different directions.

Suiting our movements to a prearranged plan, we reached our homes from different directions, and at different times, some arriving after sundown, to the end that were we watched none might be sure that we had been upon the same errand or to the same place.

8

The Arrest of Julian 8th

MOTHER HAD SUPPER ready by the time Juana and I arrived. Father said they had seen nothing of the Kash Guard, nor had we; but we could guess at what had happened at the church. The door must finally have given to their blows. We could imagine their rage when they found that their prey had flown, leaving no trace. Even if they had found the hidden tunnel, and we doubted that they had, the discovery would profit them but little. We were very sad, though, for we had lost our church. Never again in this generation could it be used. We added another mark to the growing score against Johansen.

The next morning as I was peddling milk to those who live about the market place, Old Samuels came out of his little cottage, and hailed me.

"A little milk this morning, Julian!" he cried, and when I carried my vessel over to him he asked me inside. His cottage was very small, and simply furnished as were all those that made any pretense to furniture of any sort, some having only a pile of rags or skins in one corner for a bed, and perhaps a bench or two which answered the combined purposes of seats and table. In the yard behind his cottage he did his tanning, and there also was a little shed he called his shop where he fashioned various articles from the hides he tanned—belts, head bands, pouches, and the like.

He led me through the cottage, and out to his shed, and

when we were there he looked through the windows to see
that no one was near.

"I have something here," he said, "that I meant to bring
to Juana for a wedding gift yesterday; but I am an old man,
and forgetful, and so I left it behind. You can take it to her,
though, with the best wishes of Old Samuels the Jew. It has
been in my family since the Great War in which my people
fought by the side of your people. One of my ancestors was
wounded on a battlefield in France, and later nursed back to
health by a Roman Catholic nurse, who gave him this token
to carry away with him that he might not forget her. The
story is that she loved him; but being a nun she could not
marry. It has been handed down from father to son—it is my
most prized possession, Julian; but being an old man, and
the last of my line I wish it to go to those I love most dearly,
for I doubt that I have long to live. Again yesterday, I was
followed from the church."

He turned to a little cupboard on the wall, and removing
a false bottom took from the drawer beneath a small leather
bag which he handed to me.

"Look at it," he said, "and then slip it inside your shirt
so that none may know that you have it."

Opening the bag I brought forth a tiny image carved from
what appeared to be very hard bone—the figure of a man
nailed to a cross—a man with a wreath of thorns about his
head. It was a very wonderful piece of work—I had never
seen anything like it in my life.

"It is very beautiful," I said. "Juana will be thankful,
indeed."

"Do you know what it is?" he asked, and I had to admit
that I did not.

"It is the figure of the Son of God upon the cross," he
explained, "and it is carved from the tusk of an elephant.
Juana will—" but he got no farther. "Quick!" he whispered,
"hide it. Some one comes!"

I slipped the little figure inside my shirt just as several men
crossed from Samuels's cottage to his shop. They came directly to the door, and then we saw that they were Kash

Guards. A captain commanded them. He was one of the officers who had come with Or-tis, and I did not know him.

He looked first at me and then at Samuels, finally addressing the latter.

"From the description," he said, "you are the man I want—you are Samuels the Jew?"

Moses nodded affirmatively.

"I have been sent to question you," said the officer, "and if you know when you are well off you will tell me nothing but the truth, and all of that."

Moses made no reply—he just stood there, a little, dried-up old man who seemed to have shrunk to even smaller proportions in the brief moments since the officer had entered. Then the latter turned to me, and looked me over from head to foot.

"Who are you, and what do you here?" he asked.

"I am Julian 9th," I replied. "I was peddling milk when I stopped in to speak with my friend."

"You should be more careful of your friends, young man," he snapped. "I had intended letting you go about your business; but now that you say you are a friend of his we will just keep you, too. Possibly you can help us."

I didn't know what he wanted; but I knew that whatever it was he would get precious little help from Julian 9th. He turned to Moses.

"Do not lie to me! You went to a forbidden meeting yesterday to worship some god, and plot against the Teivos. Four weeks ago you went to the same place. Who else was there yesterday?"

Samuels looked the captain straight in the eye, and remained silent.

"Answer me, you dirty Jew!" yelled the officer, "or I will find a way to make you. Who was there with you?"

"I will not answer," said Samuels.

The captain turned to a sergeant standing behind him. "Give him the first reason why he should answer," he directed.

The sergeant, who carried his bayonet fixed to his rifle,

lowered the point until it rested against Samuels's leg, and with a sudden jab ran it into the flesh. The old man cried out in pain, and staggered back against his little bench. I sprang forward, white with rage, and seizing the sergeant by the collar of his loose tunic hurled him across the shop. It was all done in less than a second, and then I found myself facing as many loaded rifles as could crowd into the little doorway. The captain had drawn his pistol, and levelled it at my head.

They bound me, and sat me in a corner of the shop, and they were none too gentle in the way they did it, either. The captain was furious, and would have had me shot on the spot had not the sergeant whispered something to him. As it was he ordered the latter to search us both for weapons, and when they did so they discovered the little image on my person. At sight of it a sneer of triumph curled the lip of the officer.

"So-ho!" he exclaimed. "Here is evidence enough. Now we know one at least who worships forbidden gods, and plots against the laws of his land!"

"It is not his," said Samuels. "It is mine. He does not even know what it is. I was showing it to him when we heard you coming, and I told him to hide it in his shirt. It is just a curious relic that I was showing him."

"Then you are the worshiper after all," said the captain.

Old Samuels smiled a crooked smile. "Who ever heard of a Jew worshiping Christ?" he asked.

The officer looked at him sharply. "That is right," he admitted, "you would not worship Christ; but you have been worshiping something—it is all the same—they are all alike. This for all of them," and he hurled the image to the earthen floor, and ground it, in broken fragments, into the dirt with his heel.

Old Samuels went very white then, and his eyes stared wide and round; but he held his tongue. Then they started in on him again, asking him to name those who were with him the day before, and each time they asked him they prodded him with a bayonet until his poor old body streamed blood from a dozen cruel wounds. But he would not give them a single name, and then the officer ordered that a fire be built and a bayonet heated.

"Sometimes hot steel is better than cold," he said. "You had better tell me the truth."

"I will tell you nothing," moaned Samuels in a weak voice. "You may kill me; but you will learn nothing from me."

"But you have never felt red-hot steel before," the captain taunted him. "It has wrung the secrets from stouter hearts than that in the filthy carcass of a dirty old Jew. Come now, save yourself the agony, and tell me who was there, for in the end you will tell."

But the old man would not tell, and then they did the hideous thing that they had threatened—with red-hot steel they burned him after tying him to his bench.

His cries and moans were piteous—it seemed to me that they must have softened stone to compassion; but the hearts of those beasts were harder than stone.

He suffered! God of our Fathers! how he suffered; but they could not force him to tell. At last he lost consciousness and then the brute in the uniform of captain, rageful that he failed, crossed the room, and struck the poor, unconscious old man a heavy blow in the face.

After that it was my turn. He came to me.

"Tell me what you know, pig of a Yank!" he cried.

"As he died, so can I die," I said, for I thought that Samuels was dead.

"You will tell," he shrieked, almost insane with rage. "You will tell or your eyes will be burned from their sockets." He called the fiend with the bayonet—now white hot it seemed, so terrifically it glowed.

As the fellow approached me the horror of the thing they would do to me seared my brain with an anguish almost as poignant as that which the hot iron could inflict on flesh. I had struggled to free myself of my bonds while they tortured Samuels, that I might go to his aid; but I had failed. Yet, now, scarcely without realizing that I exerted myself, I rose, and the cords snapped. I saw them step back in amazement as I stood there confronting them.

"Go," I said to them. "Go before I kill you all. Even the Teivos, rotten as it is, will not stand for this usurpation of its authority. You have no right to inflict punishment. You have gone too far."

The sergeant whispered for a moment to his superior, who finally appeared to assent grudgingly to some proposition of the others and then turned, and left the little shop.

"We have no proof against you," said the sergeant to me. "We had no intention of harming you. All that we wanted was to frighten the truth out of you; but as to that," and he jerked a thumb toward Samuels, "we have the proof on him, and what we did we did under orders. Keep a still tongue in your head or it will be the worse for you, and thank the star under which you were born that you did not get worse than he."

Then he left, too, and took the soldiers with him. I saw them pass into the rear doorway of Samuels's cottage, and a moment later I heard their horses' hoofs pounding on the surface of the market place. I could scarcely believe that I had escaped. Then I did not know the reason for it; but that I was to learn later, and that it was not so much of a miracle after all.

I went right to poor old Samuels. He was still breathing, but unconscious—mercifully so. The withered old body was hideously burned, and mutilated, and one eye—but why describe their ghoulish work! I carried him into his cottage, and laid him on his cot, and then I found some flour, and covered his burns with it—that was all I knew to do for him. There were no doctors such as the ancients had, for there were no longer places of learning in which they could be trained. There were those who claimed to be able to heal. They gave herbs and strange concoctions; but as their patients usually died immediately we had little confidence in them.

After I had put the flour on his wounds, I drew up a bench, and sat down beside him so that when he regained conscious-

ness he would find a friend there to wait upon him. As I sat
there looking at him he died. Tears came to my eyes in spite
of all that I could do, for friends are few, and I had loved
this old Jew, as we all did who knew him. He had been a
gentle character, loyal to his friends, and inclined to be a
little too forgiving to his enemies—even the Kalkars. That
he was courageous his death proved.

I put another mark against the score of Peter Johansen.

The following day, father, Jim, and I buried old Samuels,
the authorities came and took all his poor little possessions,
and his cottage was turned over to another. But I had one
thing, his most prized possession, that they did not get, for
before I left him after he died, I went back into his shop, and
gathered up the fragments of the man upon the cross, and
put them into the little leather bag in which he had kept them.

When I gave them to Juana, and told her the story of them
she wept and kissed them, and with some glue such as we
make from the hides and tendons of goats we mended it so
it was difficult to tell where it had broken. After it was dry
Juana wore it in its little bag about her neck, beneath her
clothing.

A week after the death of Samuels, Pthav sent for me, and
very gruffly told me that the Teivos had issued a permit for
me to use the land adjoining that allotted to my father. As
before, his woman stopped me as I was leaving.

"It was easier than I thought," she told me, "for Or-tis
has angered the Teivos by attempting to usurp all its powers,
and knowing that he hates you they were glad to grant your
petition over his objections."

I had heard rumors lately of the growing differences between Or-tis and the Teivos, and had learned that it was these
that had saved me from the Kash Guard that day—the sergeant having warned his superior that should they maltreat
me without good and sufficient reason the Teivos could take
advantage of the fact to discipline the Guard and they were
not yet ready for the test—that was to come later.

During the next two or three months I was busy building
our home and getting my place in order. I had decided to

raise horses and obtained permission from the Teivos to do so—again over Or-tis's objections. Of course, the government controlled the entire horse traffic; but there were a few skilled horsemen permitted to raise them, though at any time their herds could be commandeered by the authorities. I knew that it might not be a very profitable business, but I loved horses and wanted to have just a few—a stallion and two or three mares. These I could use in tilling my fields and in the heavier work of hauling and at the same time I would keep a few goats, pigs and chickens to insure us a living.

Father gave me half his goats and a few chickens and from Jim I bought two young sows and a boar. Later I traded a few goats to the Teivos for two old mares that they thought were no longer worth keeping, and that same day I was told of a stallion—a young outlaw—that Hoffmeyer had. The beast was five years old and so vicious that none dared approach him and they were on the point of destroying him.

I went to Hoffmeyer and asked if I could buy the animal— I offered him a goat for it, which he was glad to accept, and then I took a strong rope and went to get my property. I found a beautiful bay with the temper of a Hellhound. When I attempted to enter the pen he rushed at me with ears back and jaws distended, but I knew that I must conquer him now or never, and so I met him with only a rope in my hand, nor did I wait for him. Instead, I ran to meet him and when he was in reach I struck him once across the face with the rope, at which he wheeled and let both hind feet fly out at me. Then I cast the noose that was at one end of the rope and caught him about the neck and for half an hour we had a battle of it.

I never struck him unless he tried to bite or strike me and finally I must have convinced him that I was master, for he let me come close enough to stroke his glossy neck, though he snorted loudly all the while I did so. When I had quieted him a bit I managed to get a half hitch around his lower jaw, and after that I had no difficulty in leading him from the pen. Once in the open I took the coils of my rope in my left hand

and before the creature knew what I was about had vaulted to his back.

He fought fair, I'll say that for him, for he stood on his feet, but for fifteen minutes he brought into play every artifice known to horsekind for unseating a rider. Only my skill and my great strength kept me on his back and at that even the Kalkars who were looking on had to applaud.

After that it was easy. I treated him with kindness, something he had never known before, and as he was an unusually intelligent animal, he soon learned that I was not only his master, but his friend. From being an outlaw he became one of the kindest and most tractable animals I have ever seen, so much so, in fact, that Juana used to ride him bareback.

I love all horses and always have, but I think I never loved any animal as I did Red Lightning, as we named him.

The authorities left us pretty well alone for some time because they were quarreling among themselves. Jim said there was an ancient saying about honest men getting a little peace when thieves fell out and it certainly fitted our case perfectly. But the peace didn't last forever, and when it broke the bolt that fell was the worst calamity that had ever come to us.

One evening father was arrested for trading at night and taken away by the Kash Guard. They got him as he was returning to the house from the goat pens and would not even permit him to bid good-by to mother. Juana and I were eating supper in our own house about three hundred yards away and never knew anything about it until mother came running over to tell us. She said that it was all done so quickly that they had father and were gone before she could run from the house to where they arrested him. They had a spare horse and hustled him onto it—then they galloped away toward the lake front. It seems strange that neither Juana nor I heard the hoof beats of the horses, but we did not.

I went immediately to Pthav and demanded to know why father had been arrested, but he professed ignorance of the whole affair. I had ridden to his place on Red Lightning and from there I started to the Kash Guard barracks where the military prison is. It was contrary to law to approach the barracks after sunset without permission, so I left Red Lightning in the shadow of some ruins a hundred yards away and started on foot toward that part of the post, where I knew the prison to be located. It consisted of a high stockade around the inside of which were rude shelters. Upon the roofs of these armed guards patroled. The center of the rectangle was an open court where the prisoners exercised, cooked their food and washed their clothing—if they cared to. There were seldom more than fifty confined there at a time, as it was only a detention camp to hold those awaiting trial and those sentenced to the mines. The latter were usually taken away when there were from twenty-five to forty of them.

They marched them in front of mounted guards a distance of about fifty miles to the nearest mines, which lie southwest of our Teivos, driving them, like cattle, with heavy whips of bullhide. To such great cruelty were they subjected, so escaped convicts told us, that always at least one out of every ten died upon the march.

Though men were sometimes sentenced for as short terms as five years in the mines, none ever returned, other than the few who escaped, so harshly were they treated and so poorly fed. They labored twelve hours a day.

I managed to reach the shadow of the wall of the stockade without being seen, for the Kash Guard was a lazy, inefficient, insubordinate soldier. He did as he pleased, though I understand that under Jarth's régime an effort was made to force discipline as he was attempting to institute a military oligarchy. Since Or-tis came they had been trying to revive the ancient military salute and the use of titles instead of the usual "Brother."

After I reached the stockade I was at a loss to communicate with my father, since any noise I might make would doubtless attract the attention of the guard. Finally through a crack between two boards, I attracted the attention of a prisoner. The man came close to the stockade and I whispered to him that I wished to speak to Julian 8th. By luck I had happened upon a decent fellow, and it was not long before he had brought father and I was talking with him in low whispers.

He told me that he had been arrested for trading by night and that he was to be tried on the morrow. I asked him if he would like to escape—that I would find the means if he wished me to, but he said that he was innocent of the charge as he had not been off our farm at night for months and that doubtless it was a case of mistaken identity and that he would be freed in the morning.

I had my doubts, but he would not listen to escape as he argued that it would prove his guilt and they would have him for sure.

"Where is there that I may go," he asked, "if I escape? I might hide in the woods, but what a life! I could never return to your mother and so sure am I that they can prove nothing against me that I would rather stand trial than face the future as an outlaw."

I think now that he refused my offer of assistance not because he expected to be released, but because he feared that evil might befall me were I to connive at his escape. At any rate, I did nothing, since he would not let me, and went home again with a heavy heart and dismal forebodings.

Trials before the Teivos were public, or at least were supposed to be, though they made it so uncomfortable for spectators that few, if any, had the temerity to attend. But under Jarth's new rule the proceedings of the military courts were secret and father was tried before such a court.

9

I Horsewhip an Officer

WE PASSED DAYS of mental anguish—hearing nothing, knowing nothing—and then one evening a single Kash Guard rode up to father's house. Juana and I were there with mother. The fellow dismounted and knocked at the door—a most unusual courtesy from one of these. He entered at my bidding and stood there a moment looking at mother. He was only a lad—a big, overgrown boy, and there was neither cruelty in his eyes nor the mark of the beast in any of his features. His mother's blood evidently predominated, and he was unquestionably not all Kalkar. Presently he spoke.

"Which is Julian 8th's woman?" he asked; but he looked at mother as though he already guessed.

"I am," said mother.

The lad shuffled his feet and caught his breath—it was like a stifled sob.

"I am sorry," he said, "that I bring you such sad news." Then we guessed that the worst had happened.

"The mines?" mother asked him, and he nodded affirmatively.

"Ten years!" he exclaimed, as one might announce a sentence of death, for such it was. "He never had a chance," he volunteered. "It was a terrible thing. They are beasts!"

I could not but show my surprise that a Kash Guard should speak so of his own kind, and he must have seen it in my face.

"We are not all beasts," he hastened to exclaim.

I commenced to question him then and I found that he had been a sentry at the door during the trial and had heard it all. There had been but one witness—the man who had informed on father, and father had been given no chance to make any defense.

I asked him who the informer was.

"I am not sure of the man," he replied; "he was a tall, stoop-shouldered man. I think I heard him called Peter."

But I had known even before I asked. I looked at mother and saw that she was dry-eyed and that her mouth had suddenly hardened into a firmness of expression such as I had never dreamed it could assume.

"Is that all?" she asked.

"No," replied the youth, "it is not. I am instructed to notify you that you have thirty days to take another man, or vacate these premises," and then he took a step toward mother.

"I am sorry, madam," he said. "It is very cruel; but what are we to do? It becomes worse each day. Now they are grinding down even the Kash Guard, so that there are many of us who—" but he stopped suddenly as though realizing that he was on the point of speaking treason to strangers, and turning on his heel, he quit the house and a moment later was galloping away.

I expected mother to break down then; but she did not. She was very brave; but there was a new and terrible expression in her eyes—those eyes that had shone forth always with love. Now they were bitter, hate-filled eyes. She did not weep—I wish to God she had—instead, she did that which I had never known her to do before—she laughed aloud. Upon the slightest pretext, or upon no pretext at all, she laughed. We were afraid for her.

The suggestion dropped by the Kash Guard started in my mind a train of thought of which I spoke to mother and Juana, and after that mother seemed more normal for a while, as though I had aroused hope, however feeble, where there had been no hope before. I pointed out that if the Kash Guard was dissatisfied the time was ripe for revolution, for if we could get only a part of them to join us, there would surely be enough of us to overthrow those who remained loyal. Then we would liberate all prisoners and set up a republic of our own such as the ancients had had.

God of our fathers! How many times—how many thousand times had I heard that plan discussed and rediscussed! We would slay all the Kalkars in the world, and we would sell the land again that men might have pride of ownership and an incentive to labor hard and develop it for their children, for well we knew by long experience that no man will develop land that reverts to the government at death, or that government may take away from him at any moment. We would encourage manufactures; we would build schools and churches; we would have music and dancing; once again we would live as our fathers had lived.

We looked for no perfect form of government, for we realized that perfection is beyond the reach of mortal men— merely would we go back to the happy days of our ancestors.

It took time to develop my plan. I talked with every one I could trust and found them all willing to join me when we had enough. In the meantime, I cared for my own place and father's as well—I was very busy and time flew rapidly.

About a month after father was taken away I came home one day with Juana who had accompanied me up river in search of a goat that had strayed. We had found its carcass, or rather its bones, where the Hellhounds had left them. Mother was not at our house, where she now spent most of her time, so I went over to father's to get her. As I approached the door I heard sounds of an altercation and scuffling that made me cover the few remaining yards at a rapid run.

Without waiting to knock, as mother had taught me always to do, I burst into the living room to discover mother in the clutches of Peter Johansen. She was trying to fight him off; but he was a large and powerful man. He heard me just as I leaped for him and, turning, grappled with me. He tried to hold me off with one hand then while he drew his knife; but I struck him in the face with one fist and knocked him from me, away across the room. He was up again in an instant, bleeding from nose and mouth, and came back at me with his knife in his hand, slashing furiously. Again I struck him and knocked him down and when he arose and came again, I seized his knife and tore the weapon from him. He had no slightest chance against me, and he saw it soon, for he commenced to back away and beg for mercy.

"Kill him, Julian," said mother. "Kill the murderer of your father."

I did not need her appeal to influence me, for the moment that I had seen Peter there I knew my long awaited time had come to kill him. He commenced to cry then—great tears ran down his cheeks and he bolted for the door and tried to escape. It was my pleasure to play with him as a cat plays with a mouse.

I kept him from the door, seizing him and hurling him bodily across the room. Then I let him reach the window, through which he tried to crawl. I permitted him to get so far that he thought he was about to escape and then I seized him again and dragged him back to the floor, and lifting him to his feet I made him fight.

I struck him lightly in the face many times and then I laid him on his back across the table, and kneeling on his chest, I spoke to him softly.

"You had my friend, old Samuels, murdered, and my father, too, and now you come to attack my mother. What did you expect, swine; but this? Have you no intelligence? You must have known that I would kill you—speak!"

"They said that they would get you today," he whimpered. "They lied to me. They went back on me. They told me that you would be in the pen at the barracks before noon. Damn them, they lied to me!"

So! That was how it was, eh? And the lucky circumstance of the strayed goat had saved me to avenge my father and succor my mother; but they would come yet. I must hurry or they might come before I was through. So I took his head between my hands and bent his neck far back over the edge of the table until I heard his spine part, and that was the end of the vilest traitor who ever lived—one who professed friendship openly and secretly conspired to ruin us. In broad daylight I carried his body to the river and threw it in. I was past caring what they knew. They were coming for me, and they would have their way with me whether they had any pretext or not. But they would have to pay a price for me, that I determined, and I got my knife and strapped it in its scabbard about my waist beneath my shirt. But they did not come—they had lied to Peter just as they lie to everyone.

The next day was market day and tax day, so I went to market with the necessary goats and produce to make my trades and pay my taxes. As Soor passed around the market place making his collections, or rather his levies, for we had to deliver the stuff to his place ourselves, I saw from the excited conversation of those in his wake that he was spreading consternation among the people of the commune.

I wondered what it might all be about, nor had I long to wait to discover, for he soon reached me. He could neither read nor write; but he had a form furnished by the government upon which were numbers that the agents were taught how to read and which stood for various classes of produce, live-stock, and manufactures. In columns beneath these numbers he made marks during the month for the amounts of my trades in each item—it was all crude, of course, and inaccurate; but as they always overcharged us and then added something to make up for any errors they might have made to our credit, the government was satisfied, even if we were not.

Being able to read and write, as well as to figure, I always knew to a dot just what was due from me in tax, and I always had an argument with Soor, from which the government emerged victorious every time.

This month I should have owed him one goat; but he demanded three.

"How is that?" I asked.

"Under the old rate you owed me the equivalent of a goat and a half; but since the tax has been doubled under the new law, you owe me three goats." Then it was I knew the cause of the excitement in other parts of the market place.

"How do you expect us to live if you take everything from us?" I asked.

"The government does not care whether you live or not," he replied, "as long as you pay taxes while you do live."

"I will pay the three goats," I said, "because I have to; but next market day I will bring you a present of the hardest cheese I can find."

He did not say anything, for he was afraid of me unless he was surrounded by Kash Guards, but he looked mighty ugly. After he had passed along to the next victim I walked over to where a number of men were evidently discussing the new tax. There were some fifteen or twenty of them, mostly Yanks, and they were angry—I could see that before I came close enough to hear what they were saying. When I joined them one asked me what I thought of this new outrage.

"Think of it!" I exclaimed. "I think what I have always thought—that as long as we submit without a murmur they will continue to increase our burden, that is already more than we can stagger under."

"They have taken even my seed beans," said one, who raised beans almost exclusively. "As you all know, last year's crop was small and beans brought a high price, so they taxed me on my trades at the high price and then collected the tax in beans at the low price of the previous year. They have been doing that all this year; but I hoped to save enough for seed until now they have doubled the tax I know that I shall have no beans to plant next year."

"What can we do about it?" asked another hopelessly. "What can we do about it?"

"We can refuse to pay the tax," I replied.

They looked at me much as men would look at one who said: "If you do not like it, you may commit suicide."

"The Kash Guard would collect the tax and it would be heavier still, for they would kill us and take our women and all that we possess," said one.

"We outnumber them," said I.

"But we cannot face rifles with our bare hands."

"It has been done," I insisted, "and it is better to die like men, facing the bullets, than by starvation, like spineless worms. We are a hundred, yes, a thousand to their one, and we have our knives, and there are pitchforks and axes, besides the clubs that we can gather. God of our Fathers! I would rather die thus, red with the blood of these swine, than live as they compel us to live!''

I saw some of them looking about to see who might have heard me, for I had raised my voice in excitement; but there were a few who looked steadily at me and nodded their heads in approval.

''If we can get enough to join us, let us do it!'' cried one.

''We have only to start,'' I said, ''and they will flock to us.''

''How should we start?'' asked another.

''I should start on Soor,'' I replied. ''I should kill him and Pthav and Hoffmeyer first, and then make a round of the Kalkar houses where we can find rifles, possibly, and kill them as we go. By the time the Kash Guard learns of it and can come in force, we shall have a large following. If we can overcome them and take their barracks we shall be too strong for any but a larger force, and it will take a month to get many soldiers here from the East. Many of the Kash Guard will join us—they are dissatisfied—one of their number told me so. It will be easy if we are but brave.''

They commenced to take a great interest and there was even a cry of ''Down with the Kalkars!'' but I stopped that in a hurry, as our greatest hope of success lay in a surprise attack.

''When shall we start?'' they asked.

''Now,'' I replied, ''if we take them unaware, we shall be successful at first, and with success others will join us. Only by numbers, overwhelming numbers, may we succeed.''

''Good!'' they cried. ''Come! Where first?''

''Soor,'' I said. ''He is at the far end of the market place. We will kill him first and hang his head on a pole. We will carry it with us and as we kill we will place each head upon a pole and take it with us. Thus we will inspire others to follow us and put fear in the hearts of our enemies.''

"Lead on, Julian 9th!" they cried. "We will follow!"

I turned and started in the direction of Soor and we had covered about half the distance when a company of Kash Guard rode into the market place at the very point where Soor was working.

You should have seen my army. Like mist before a hot sun it disappeared from view, leaving me standing all alone in the center of the market place.

The commander of the Kash Guard company must have noticed the crowd and its sudden dispersion, for he rode straight toward me, alone. I would not give him the satisfaction of thinking that I feared him and so I stood there waiting. My thoughts were of the saddest—not for myself, but for the sorry pass to which the Kalkar system had brought Americanism. These men who had deserted me would have been in happier days the flower of American manhood; but generations of oppression and servitude had turned their blood to water. To-day they turned tail and fled before a handful of half armed, poorly disciplined soldiers. The terror of the lunar fallacy had entered their hearts and rotted them.

The officer reined in before me and then it was that I recognized him—the beast who had tortured and murdered old Samuels.

"What are you doing here?" he barked.

"Minding my own business, as you had better do," I replied.

"You swine are becoming insufferable," he cried. "Get to your pen, where you belong—I will stand for no mobs and no insolence."

I just stood there looking at him; but there was murder in my heart. He loosened the bull-hide whip that hung at the pommel of his saddle.

"You have to be driven, do you?" He was livid with sudden anger and his voice almost a scream. Then he struck at me—a vicious blow with the heavy whip—struck at my face. I dodged the lash and seized it, wrenching it from his puny grasp. Then I caught his bridle and though his horse plunged and fought I lashed the rider with all my strength a dozen times before he tumbled from the saddle to the trampled earth of the market place.

Then his men were upon me and I went down from a blow on the head. They bound my hands while I was unconscious and then hustled me roughly into a saddle. I was half dazed during the awful ride that ensued—we rode to the military prison at the barracks and all the way that fiend of a captain rode beside me and lashed me with his bull-hide whip.

10

Revolution

THEN THEY THREW me into the pen where the prisoners were kept and after they had left I was surrounded by the other unfortunates incarcerated there. When they learned what I had done they shook their heads and sighed. It would be all over with me in the morning, they said—nothing less than the butcher for such an offense as mine.

I lay upon the hard ground, bruised and sore, thinking not of my future but of what was to befall Juana and mother if I, too, were taken from them. The thought gave me new strength and made me forget my hurts, for my mind was busy with plans, mostly impossible plans, for escape—and vengeance. Vengeance was often uppermost in my mind.

Above my head, at intervals, I heard the pacing of the sentry upon the roof. I could tell, of course, each time that he passed and the direction in which he was going. It required about five minutes for him to pass above me, reach the end of his post and return—that was when he went west. Going east he took but a trifle over two minutes. Therefore, when he passed me going west his back was toward me for about two and a half minutes; but when he went east it was only for about a minute that his face was turned from the spot where I lay.

Of course, he could not see me while I lay beneath the shed; but my plan—the one I finally decided upon—did not include remaining in the shed. I had evolved several subtle schemes for escape; but finally cast them all aside and chose, instead, the boldest that occurred to me. I knew that at best the chances were small that I could succeed in my plan and therefore the boldest seemed as likely as any other and it at least had the advantage of speedy results. I would be free or I would be dead in a few brief moments after I essayed it.

I waited, therefore, until the other prisoners had quieted down and comparative silence in the direction of the barracks and the parade assured me that there were few abroad. The sentry came and went and came again upon his monotonous round. Now he was coming toward me from the east and I was ready, standing just outside the shed beneath the low eaves which I could reach by jumping. I heard him pass and gave him a full minute to gain the distance I thought necessary to drown the sounds of my attempt from his ears. Then I leaped for the eaves, caught with my fingers, and drew myself quickly to the roof.

I thought that I did it very quietly, but the fellow must have had the ears of a Hellhound, for no more had I drawn my feet beneath me for the quick run across the roof than a challenge rang out from the direction of the sentry and almost simultaneously the report of a rifle.

Instantly all was pandemonium. Guards ran, shouting, from all directions, lights flashed in the barracks, rifles spoke from either side of me and from behind me, while from below rose the dismal howlings of the prisoners. It seemed then that a hundred men had known of my plan and been lying in wait for me; but I was launched upon it and even though I had regretted it, there was nothing to do but carry it through to whatever was its allotted end.

It seemed a miracle that none of the bullets struck me; but, of course, it was dark and I was moving rapidly. It takes seconds to tell about it; but it required less than a second for me to dash across the roof and leap to the open ground beyond the prison pen. I saw lights moving west of me and so I ran east toward the lake and presently the firing ceased as they lost sight of me, though I could hear sounds of pursuit. Nevertheless, I felt that I had succeeded and was congratulating myself upon the ease with which I had accomplished the seemingly impossible when there suddenly rose before me out of the black night the figure of a huge soldier pointing a rifle point blank at me. He issued no challenge nor asked any question—just pulled the trigger. I could hear the hammer strike the firing pin; but there was no explosion. I did not know what the reason was, nor did I ever know. All that was apparent was that the rifle misfired and then he brought his bayonet into play while I was springing toward him.

Foolish man! But then he did not know that it was Julian 9th he faced. Pitifully, futilely he thrust at me and with one hand I seized the rifle and tore it from his grasp. In the same movement I swung it behind me and above my head, bringing it down with all the strength of one arm upon his thick skull. Like a felled ox he tumbled to his knees and then sprawled forward upon his face. He never knew how he died.

Behind me I heard them coming closer and they must have seen me, for they opened fire again and I heard the beat of horses' hoofs upon my right and left. They were surrounding me upon three sides and upon the fourth was the great lake. A moment later I was standing upon the edge of the ancient breakwater while behind me rose the triumphant cries of my pursuers. They had seen me and they knew that I was theirs.

At least, they thought they knew so. I did not wait for them to come closer; but raising my hands above me I dove head foremost into the cool waters of the lake. Swimming rapidly beneath the surface I kept close in the shadows and headed north.

I had spent much of my summer life in the water of the river so that I was much at home in that liquid element as in air, but this, of course, the Kash Guard did not know, for even had they known that Julian 9th could swim they could not at that time have known which prisoner it was who had escaped and so I think they must have thought what I wanted them to think—that I had chosen self-drowning to recapture.

However, I was sure they would search the shore in both directions and so I kept to the water after I came to the surface. I swam farther out until I felt there was little danger of being seen from shore, for it was a dark night. And thus I swam on until I thought I was opposite the mouth of the river when I turned toward the west, searching for it.

Luck was with me. I swam directly into it and a short distance up the sluggish stream before I knew that I was out of the lake; but even then I did not take to the shore, preferring to pass the heart of the ancient city before trusting myself to land.

At last I came out upon the north bank of the river, which is farthest from the Kash Guard barracks, and made my way as swiftly as possible up stream in the direction of my home. Here, hours later, I found an anxious Juana awaiting me, for already she had heard what had transpired in the market place. I had made my plans and had soon explained them to Juana and mother. There was nothing for them but to acquiesce, as only death could be our lot if we remained in our homes another day. I was astonished, even, that they had not already fallen upon Juana and mother. As it was they might come any minute. There was no time to lose.

Hastily wrapping up a few belongings I took the Flag from its hiding place above the mantel and tucked it in my shirt—then we were ready. Going to the pens we caught Red Lightning and the two mares and three of my best milk goats. These latter we tied and after Juana and mother had mounted the mares I laid one goat in front of each across a mare's withers and the third before myself upon Red Lightning, who did not relish the strange burden and gave me considerable trouble at first.

We rode out up river, leaving the pens open that the goats might scatter and possibly cover our trail until we could turn off the dusty path beyond Jim's house. We dared not stop to bid Jim and Mollie good-by lest we be apprehended there by our enemies and bring trouble to our good friends. It was a sad occasion for poor mother, leaving thus her home and those dear neighbors who had been as close to her as her own; but she was as brave as Juana.

Not once did either of them attempt to dissuade me from the wild scheme I had outlined to them. Instead, they encouraged me and Juana laid her hand upon my arm as I rode beside her, saying: "I would rather that you died thus than that we lived on as downtrodden serfs, without happiness and without hope."

"I shall not die," I said, "until my work is done, at least. Then if die I must I shall be content to know that I leave a happier country for my fellow men to live in."

"Amen!" whispered Juana.

That night I hid them in the ruins of the old church, which we found had been partially burned by the Kalkars. For a moment I held them in my arms—my mother, and my wife—and then I left them to ride toward the southwest and the coal mines. The mines lie about fifty miles away and west of south according to what I had heard. I had never been to them; but I knew that I must find the bed of an ancient canal and follow it through the district of Joliet and between fifteen and twenty miles beyond, where I must turn south and, after passing a large lake, I would presently come to the mines. I rode the balance of the night and into the morning until I commenced to see people astir in the thinly populated country through which I passed.

Then I hid in a wood through which a stream wound and here, found pasture for Red Lightning and rest for myself. I had brought no food, leaving what little bread and cheese we had brought from the house for mother and Juana. I did not expect to be gone over a week and I knew that with goat's milk and what they had on hand in addition to what they could find growing wild, there would be no danger of starvation before I returned—after which we expected to live in peace and plenty for the rest of our days.

My journey was less eventful than I had anticipated. I passed through a few ruined villages and towns of greater or less antiquity, the largest of which was ancient Joliet, which was abandoned during the plague fifty years ago, the Teivos headquarters and station being removed directly west a few miles to the banks of a little river. Much of the territory I traversed was covered with thick woods, though here and there were the remnants of clearings which were not yet entirely reclaimed by nature. Now and again I passed those gaunt and lonely towers in which the ancients stored the winter feed for their stock. Those that have endured were of concrete and some showed but little the ravages of time, other than the dense vines that often covered them from base to capital, while several were in the midst of thick forests with old trees almost entwining them, so quickly does Nature reclaim her own when man has been displaced.

After I passed Joliet I had to make inquires. This I did boldly of the few men I saw laboring in the tiny fields scattered along my way. They were poor clods, these descendants of ancient America's rich and powerful farming class.

Early in the second morning I came within sight of the stockade about the mines. Even at a distance I could see that it was a weak, dilapidated thing and that the sentries pacing along its top were all that held the prisoners within. As a matter of fact, many escaped; but they were soon hunted down and killed as the farmers in the neighborhood always informed on them. The commandant at the prison had conceived the fiendish plan of slaying one farmer for every prisoner who escaped and was not recaught.

I hid until night and then, cautiously, I approached the stockade, leaving Red Lightning securely tied in the woods. It was no trick to reach the stockade, so thoroughly was I hidden by the rank vegetation growing upon the outside. From a place of concealment I watched the sentry, a big fellow; but apparently a dull clod who walked with his chin upon his breast and with the appearance of being half asleep.

The stockade was not high and the whole construction was similar to that of the prison pen at Chicago, evidently having been designed by the same commandant in years gone by. I could hear the prisoners conversing in the shed beyond the wall and presently when one came near to where I listened I tried to attract his attention by making a hissing sound.

After what seemed a long time to me, he heard me; but even then it was some time before he appeared to grasp the idea that some one was trying to attract his attention. When he did he moved closer and tried to peer through one of the cracks; but as it was dark out he could see nothing.

"Are you a Yank?" I asked. "If you are I am a friend."

"I am a Yank," he replied. "Did you expect to find a Kalkar working in the mines?"

"Do you know a prisoner called Julian 8th?" I inquired.

He seemed to be thinking for a moment and then he said: "I seem to have heard the name. What do you want of him?"

"I want to speak to him—I am his son."

"Wait!" he whispered. "I think that I heard a man speak that name to-day. I will find out—he is near by."

I waited for perhaps ten minutes when I heard some one approaching from the inside and presently a voice asked if I was still there.

"Yes," I said. "Is that you, father?" for I thought that the tones were his.

"Julian, my son!" came to me almost as a sob. "What are you doing here?"

Briefly I told him and then of my plan. "Have the convicts the courage to attempt it?" I asked, in conclusion.

"I do not know," he said, and I could not but note the tone of utter hopelessness in his voice. "They would wish to; but here our spirits and our bodies both are broken. I do not know how many would have the courage to attempt it. Wait and I will talk with some of them—all are loyal; but just weak from overwork, starvation, and abuse."

I waited for the better part of an hour before he returned. "Some will help," he said, "from the first, and others if we are successful. Do you think it worth the risk—they will kill you if you fail—they will kill us all."

"And what is death to that which you are suffering?" I asked.

"I know," he said, "but the worm impaled upon the hook still struggles and hopes for life. Turn back, my son; we can do nothing against them."

"I will not turn back," I whispered. "I will not turn back."

"I will help you; but I cannot speak for the others. They may and they may not."

We had spoken only when the sentry had been at a distance, falling into silence each time he approached the point where we stood. In the intervals of silence I could hear the growing restlessness of the prisoners and I guessed that what I had said to the first man was being passed around from mouth to mouth within until already the whole adjacent shed was seething with something akin to excitement. I wondered if it would arouse their spirit sufficiently to carry them through the next ten minutes. If it did success was assured.

Father had told me all that I wanted to know—the location of the guard house and the barracks and the number of Kash Guard posted here—only fifty men to guard five thousand! How much more eloquently than words did this fact bespeak the humiliation of the American people and the utter contempt in which our scurvy masters hold us—fifty men to guard five thousand!

And then I started putting my plan into execution—a mad plan which had only its madness to recommend it. The sentry approached and came opposite where I stood and I leaped for the eaves as I had leaped for the eaves of the prison pen at Chicago, only this time I leaped from the outside where the eaves are closer to the ground and so the task was easier. I leaped and caught hold. Then I scrambled up behind the sentry and before his dull wits told him that there was someone behind him I was upon his back and the same fingers that threw a mad bull closed upon his windpipe. The struggle was brief—he died quickly and I lowered him to the roof. Then I took his uniform from him and donned it, with his ammunition belt, and I took his rifle and started out upon his post, walking with slow tread and with my chin upon my breast as he had walked.

At the end of my post I waited for the sentry I saw coming up and when he was close to me I turned back and he turned back away from me. Then I wheeled and struck him an awful blow upon the head with my rifle. He died more quickly than the other—instantly, I should say.

I took his rifle and ammunition from him and lowered them inside the pen to waiting hands. Then I went on to the next sentry, and the next, until I had slain five more and passed their rifles to the prisoners below. While I was doing this five prisoners who had volunteered to father climbed to the roof of the shed and stripped the dead men of their uniforms and donned them.

It was all done quietly and in the black night none might see what was going on a few feet away. I had to stop when I came near to the guard house. Then I turned back and presently slid into the pen with my accomplices who had been going among the other prisoners with father arousing them to mutiny. Now were most of them ready to follow me, for so far my plan had proven successful. With equal quietness we overcame the men at the guard house and then moved on in a silent body toward the barracks.

So sudden and so unexpected was our attack that we met with little resistance. We were almost five thousand to forty now. We swarmed in upon them like wild beasts upon a foe and we shot them and bayonetted them until none remained alive. Not one escaped. And now we were flushed with success so that the most spiritless became a veritable lion for courage.

We who had taken the uniform of the Kash Guard discarded them for our own garb, as we had no mind to go abroad in the hated livery of our oppressors. That very night we saddled their horses with the fifty saddles that were there and fifty men rode the balance of the horses bareback. That made one hundred mounted men and the others were to follow on foot—to Chicago. "On to Chicago!" was our slogan.

We traveled cautiously, though I had difficulty in making them do so, so intoxicated were they with their first success. I wanted to save the horses and also I wanted to get as many men into Chicago as possible, so we let the weakest ride, while those of us who were strong walked, though I had a time of it getting Red Lightning to permit another on his sleek back.

Some fell out upon the way from exhaustion or from fear, for the nearer Chicago we approached the more their courage ebbed. The very thought of the feared Kalkars and their Kash Guard took the marrow from the bones of many. I do not know that one may blame them, for the spirit of man can endure only so much and when it is broken only a miracle can mend it in the same generation.

We reached the ruined church a week from the day I left mother and Juana there and we reached it with less than two thousand men, so rapid had been the desertion in the last few miles before we entered the district.

Father and I could scarcely wait to see our loved ones and so we rode on ahead to greet them, and inside the church we found three dead goats and a dying woman—my mother with a knife protruding from her breast. She was still conscious when we entered and I saw a great light of happiness in her eyes as they fell upon father and upon me. I looked around for Juana and my heart stood still, fearing that I would not find her—and fearing that I would.

Mother could still speak, and as we leaned over her as father held her in his arms, she breathed a faint story of what had befallen them. They had lived in peace until that very day when the Kash Guard had stumbled upon them—a large detachment under Or-tis himself. They had seized them to take them away; but mother had had a knife hidden in her clothing and had utilized it as we saw rather than suffer the fate she knew awaited them. That was all, except that Juana had had no knife and Or-tis had carried her off.

I saw mother die, then, in father's arms and I helped him bury her after our men came and we had shown them what the beasts had done, though they knew well enough and had suffered themselves enough to know what was to be expected of the swine.

11

The Butcher

WE WENT ON then, father and I filled with grief and bitterness and hatred even greater than we had known before. We marched toward the market place of our district, and on the way we stopped at Jim's and he joined us. Mollie wept when she heard what had befallen mother and Juana, but presently she controlled herself and urged us on and Jim with us, though Jim needed no urging. She kissed him good-by with tears and pride mingled in her eyes, and all he said was: "Good-by, girl. Keep your knife with you always."

And so we rode away with Mollie's "May the Saints be with you!" in our ears. Once again we stopped, at our abandoned goat pens, and there we dug up the rifle, belt and ammunition of the soldier father had slain years before. These we gave to Jim.

Before we reached the market place our force commenced to dwindle again—most of them could not brave the terrors of the Kash Guard upon which they had been fed in whispered story and in actual experience since infancy. I do not say that these men were cowards—I do not believe that they were cowards and yet they acted like cowards. It may be that a lifetime of training had taught them so thoroughly to flee the Kash Guard that now no amount of urging could make them face it. The terror had become instinctive as is man's natural revulsion for snakes. They could not face the Kash Guard any more than some men can touch a rattler, even though it may be dead.

It was market day and the place was crowded. I had divided my force so that we marched in from two directions in wide fronts, about five hundred men in each party, and surrounded the market place. As there were only a few men from our district among us, I had given orders that there was to be no killing other than that of the Kash Guards until we who knew the population could pick out the right men.

When the nearest people first saw us they did not know what to make of it, so complete was the surprise. Never in their lives had they seen men of their own class armed and there were a hundred of us mounted. Across the plaza a handful of Kash Guard were lolling in front of Hoffmeyer's office. They saw my party first, as the other was coming up from behind them, and they mounted and came toward us. At the same moment I drew the Flag from my breast and, waving it above my head, urged Red Lightning forward, shouting, as I rode: "Death to the Kash Guard! Death to the Kalkars!"

And then, of a sudden, the Kash Guard seemed to realize that they were confronted by an actual force of armed men and their true color became apparent—all yellow. They turned to flee, only to see another force behind them. The people had now caught the idea and the spirit of our purpose and they flocked around us shouting, screaming, laughing, crying.

"Death to the Kash Guard!" "Death to the Kalkars!" "The Flag!" I heard more than once, and "Old Glory!" from some who, like myself, had not been permitted to forget. A dozen men rushed to my side and grasping the streaming banner pressed it to their lips, while tears coursed down their cheeks. "The Flag! The Flag!" they cried. "The Flag of our fathers!"

It was then, before a shot had been fired, that one of the Kash Guard rode toward me with a white cloth above his head. I recognized him immediately as the youth who had brought the cruel order to mother and who had shown sorrow for the acts of his superiors.

"Do not kill us," he said, "and we will join with you. Many of the Kash Guard at the barracks will join, too."

And so the dozen soldiers in the market place joined us, and a woman ran from her house carrying the head of a man stuck upon a short pole and she screamed forth her hatred against the Kalkars—the hatred that was the common bond between us all. As she came closer I saw that it was Pthav's woman and the head upon the short pole was the head of Pthav. That was the beginning—that was the little spark that was needed. Like maniacs, laughing horribly, the people charged the houses of the Kalkars and dragged them forth to death.

Above the shrieking and the groans and the din could be heard shouts for the Flag and the names of loved ones who were being avenged. More than once I heard the name of Samuels the Jew. Never was a man more thoroughly avenged than he that day.

Dennis Corrigan was with us, freed from the mines, and Betty Worth, his woman, found him there, his arms red to the elbows with the blood of our oppressors. She had never thought to see him alive, and when she heard his story, and of how they had escaped, she ran to me and nearly pulled me from Red Lightning's back trying to hug and kiss me.

It was she who started the people shouting for me until a mad, swirling mob of joy-crazed people surrounded me. I tried to quiet them, for I knew that this was no way in which to forward our cause, and finally I succeeded in winning a partial silence. Then I told them that this madness must cease, that we had not yet succeeded, that we had won only a single small district and that we must go forward quietly and in accordance with a sensible plan if we were to be victorious.

"Remember," I admonished them, "that there are still thousands of armed men in the city and that we must overthrow them all, and then there are other thousands that the Twenty-Four will throw in upon us, for they will not surrender this territory until they are hopelessly defeated from here to Washington—and that will require months and maybe years."

They quieted down a little then and we formed plans for
marching immediately upon the barracks that we might take
the Kash Guard by surprise. It was about this time that father
found Soor and killed him.

"I told you," said father, just before he ran a bayonet
through the tax collector, "that some day I would have my
little joke, and this is the day."

Then a man dragged Hoffmeyer from some hiding place
and the people literally tore him to pieces, and that started
the pandemonium all over again. There were cries of "On
to the barracks!" and "Kill the Kash Guard!" followed by
a concerted movement toward the lake front. On the way our
numbers were increased by volunteers from every house—
either fighting men and women from the houses of our class,
or bloody heads from the houses of the Kalkars, for we carried them all with us, waving above us upon the ends of poles
and at the head of all I rode with Old Glory, now waving
from a tall staff.

I tried to maintain some semblance of order, but it was
impossible, and so we streamed along, screaming and killing, laughing and crying, each as the mood claimed him.
The women seemed the maddest, possibly because they had
suffered most, and Pthav's woman led them. I saw others
there with one hand clutching a suckling baby to a bare breast
while the other held aloft the dripping head of a Kalkar, an
informer, or a spy. One could not blame them who knew the
lives of terror and hopelessness they had led.

We had just crossed the new bridge over the river into the
heart of the great, ruined city, when the Kash Guard fell upon
us from ambush with their full strength. They were poorly
disciplined; but they were armed, while we were not disciplined at all nor scarcely armed. We were nothing but an
angry mob into which they poured volley after volley at close
range.

Men, women and babies went down and many turned and
fled; but there were others who rushed forward and grappled
hand to hand with the Kash Guard, tearing their rifles from
them. We who were mounted rode among them. I could not

carry the Flag and fight, so I took it from the staff and re-placed it inside my shirt and then I clubbed my rifle and guiding Red Lightning with my knees I drove into them.

God of our fathers! But it was a pretty fight. If I had known that I was to die the next minute I would have died gladly for the joy I had in those few minutes. Down they went before me, to right and to left, reeling from their saddles with crushed skulls and broken bodies, for wherever I hit them made no difference in the result—they died if they came within reach of my rifle, which was soon only a bent and twisted tube of bloody metal.

And so I rode completely through them with a handful of men behind me. We turned then to ride back over the crum-bling ruins that were in this spot only mounds of debris and from the elevation of one of these hillocks of the dead past I saw the battle down by the river and a great lump came into my throat. It was all over—all but the bloody massacre. My poor mob had turned at last to flee. They were jammed and stuck upon the narrow bridge and the Kash Guard were firing volleys into that wedged mass of human flesh. Hundreds were leaping into the river only to be shot from the banks by the soldiers.

Twenty-five mounted men surrounded me—all that was left of my fighting force—and at least two thousand Kash Guard lay between us and the river. Even could we have fought our way back we could have done nothing to save the day or our own people. We were doomed to die, but we decided to inflict more punishment before we died.

I had in mind Juana in the clutches of Or-tis—not once had the frightful thought left my consciousness—and so I told them that I would ride to headquarters and search for her and they said that they would ride with me and that we would slay whom we could before the soldiers returned.

Our dream had vanished, our hopes were dead. In silence we rode through the streets toward the barracks. The Kash Guard had not come over to our side as we had hoped—possibly they would have come had we some measure of success in the city; but there could be no success against armed troops for a mob of men, women and children.

I realized too late that we had not planned sufficiently, yet we might have won had not someone escaped and ridden ahead to notify the Kash Guard. Could we have taken them by surprise in the barracks the outcome might have been what it had been in the market places through which we had passed. I had realized our weakness and the fact that if we took time to plan and arrange some spy or informer would have divulged all to the authorities long before we could have put our plans into execution. Really, there had been no other way than to trust to a surprise attack and the impetuosity of our first blow.

I looked about among my followers as we rode along. Jim was there, but not father—I never saw him again. He probably fell in the battle at the new bridge. Orrin Colby, blacksmith and preacher, rode at my side, covered with blood—his own and Kash Guard. Dennis Corrigan was there, too.

We rode right into the barrack yard, for with their lack of discipline and military efficiency they had sent their whole force against us with the exception of a few men who remained to guard the prisoners and a handful at the headquarters building. The latter was overcome with scarcely a struggle and from one whom I took prisoner I learned where the sleeping quarters of Or-tis were located.

Telling my men that our work was done I ordered them to scatter and escape as best they might, but they said that they would remain with me. I told them that the business I was on was such that I must handle it alone and asked them to go and free the prisoners while I searched for Juana. They said that they would wait for me outside and we parted.

Or-tis's quarters were on the second floor of the building in the east wing and I had no difficulty in finding them. As I approached the door I heard the sound of voices raised in anger within and of rapid movement as though some one was running hither and thither across the floor. I recognized Or-tis's voice—he was swearing foully, and then I heard a woman's scream and I knew it was Juana.

I tried the door and found it locked. It was a massive door, such as the ancients built in their great public buildings, such as this had originally been, and I doubted my ability to force it. I was mad with apprehension and lust for revenge and if maniacs gain tenfold in strength when the madness is upon them I must have been a maniac that moment, for when, after stepping back a few feet, I hurled myself against the door, the shot bolt tore through the splintering frame and the barrier swung in upon its hinges with a loud bang.

Before me, in the center of the room, stood Or-tis with Juana in his clutches. He had her partially upon a table and with one hairy hand he was choking her. He looked up at the noise of my sudden entry, and when he saw me he went white and dropped Juana, at the same time whipping a pistol from its holder at his side. Juana saw me, too, and springing for his arm dragged it down as he pulled the trigger so that the bullet went harmlessly into the floor.

Before he could shake her off I was upon him and had wrenched the weapon from his grasp. I held him in one hand as one might a little child—he was utterly helpless in my grip—and I asked Juana if he had wronged her.

"Not yet," she said, "He just came in after sending the Kash Guard away. Something has happened. There is going to be a battle; but he sneaked back to the safety of his quarters."

Then she seemed to notice for the first time that I was covered with blood. "There has been a battle!" she cried, "and you have been in it."

I told her that I had and that I would tell her about it after I had finished Or-tis. He commenced to plead and then to whimper. He promised me freedom and immunity from punishment and persecution if I would let him live. He promised never to bother Juana again and to give us his protection and assistance. He would have promised me the sun and the moon and all the little stars, had he thought I wished them, but I wished only one thing just then and I told him so—to see him die.

"Had you wronged her," I said, "you would have died a

slow and terrible death; but I came in time to save her, and so you are saved that suffering."

When he realized that nothing could save him he began to weep, and his knees shook so that he could not stand, and I had to hold him from the floor with one hand and with my other clenched I dealt him a single terrific blow between the eyes—a blow that broke his neck and crushed his skull. Then I dropped him to the floor and took Juana in my arms.

Quickly, as we walked toward the entrance of the building, I told her of all that had transpired since we parted, and that now she would be left alone in the world for a while, until I could join her. I told her where to go and await me in a forgotten spot I had discovered upon the banks of the old canal on my journey to the mines. She cried and clung to me, begging to remain with me, but I knew it could not be, for already I could hear fighting in the yard below. We would be fortunate indeed if one of us escaped. At last she promised on condition that I would join her immediately, which, of course, I had intended doing as soon as I had the chance.

Red Lightning stood where I had left him before the door. A company of Kash Guard, evidently returning from the battle, were engaged with my little band that was slowly falling back toward the headquarters building. There was no time to be lost if Juana was to escape. I lifted her to Red Lightning's back from where she stooped, and threw her dear arms about my neck, covering my lips with kisses.

"Come back to me soon," she begged, "I need you so— and it will not be long before there will be another to need you, too."

I pressed her close to my breast. "And if I do not come back," I said, "take this and give it to my son to guard as his fathers before him have." I placed the Flag in her hands.

The bullets were singing around us and I made her go, watching her as the noble horse raced swiftly across the parade and disappeared among the ruins to the west. Then I turned to the fighting to find but ten men left to me. Orrin Colby was dead and Dennis Corrigan. Jim was left and nine others. We fought as best we could, but we were cornered now, for other guards were streaming onto the parade from other directions and our ammunition was expended.

They rushed us then—twenty to one—and though we did the best we could they overwhelmed us. Lucky Jim was killed instantly, but I was only stunned by a blow upon the head.

That night they tried me before a court-martial and tortured me in an effort to make me divulge the names of my accomplices. But there were none left alive that I knew of, even had I wished to betray them. As it was, I just refused to speak. I never spoke again after bidding Juana good-by, other than the few words of encouragement that passed between those of us who remained fighting to the last.

Early the next morning I was led forth to the butcher.

I recall every detail up to the moment the knife touched my throat—there was a slightly stinging sensation followed instantly by—oblivion.

It was broad daylight when he finished—so quickly had the night sped—and I could see by the light from the port hole of the room where we sat that his face looked drawn and pinched and that even then he was suffering the sorrows and disappointments of the bitter, hopeless life he had just described.

I rose to retire. "That is all?" I asked.

"Yes," he replied, "that is all of that re-incarnation."

"But you recall another?" I persisted. He only smiled as I was closing the door.

THE END

THE RED HAWK

1

The Flag

THE JANUARY SUN beat hotly upon me as I reined Red Lightning in at the summit of a barren hill and looked down toward the rich land of plenty that stretched away below me as far as the eye could see. In that direction was the mighty sea, a day's ride, perhaps, to the westward—the sea that none of us had ever looked upon; the sea that had become as fabulous as a legend of the ancients during the nearly four hundred years since the Moon men swept down upon us and overwhelmed the earth in their mad and bloody carnival of revolution.

In the near distance the green of the orange groves mocked us from below, and great patches that were groves of leafless nut trees, and there were sandy patches toward the south that were vineyards waiting for the hot suns of April and May before they, too, broke into riotous, tantalizing green. And from this garden spot of plenty a curling trail wound up the mountainside to the very level where we sat gazing down upon this last stronghold of our foes.

When the ancients built that trail it must have been wide and beautiful indeed, but in the centuries that elapsed man and the elements have sadly defaced it. The rains have washed it away in places, and the Kalkars have made great gashes in it to deter us, their enemies, from invading their sole remaining lands and driving them into the sea; and upon their side of the gashes they had built forts where they keep warriors always. It is so upon every pass that leads down into their country. And well for them that they do so guard themselves!

Since fell my great ancestor, Julian 9th, in the year 2122, at the end of the first uprising against the Kalkars, we have been driving them slowly back across the world. That was more than three hundred years ago. For a hundred years they have held us here, a day's ride from the ocean. Just how far it is we do not know; but in 2408 my grandfather, Julian 18th, rode alone almost to the sea.

He had won back nearly to safety when he was discovered and pursued almost to the tents of his people. There was a battle, and the Kalkars who had dared invade our country were destroyed, but Julian 18th died of his wounds without being able to tell more than that a wondrously rich country lay between us and the sea, which was not more than a day's ride distant. A day's ride, for us, might be anything under a hundred miles.

We are desert people. Our herds range a vast territory where feed is scarce, that we may be always near the goal that our ancestors set for us three centuries ago—the shore of the western sea into which it is our destiny to drive the remnants of our former oppressors.

In the forests and mountains of Arizona there is rich pasture, but it is far from the land of the Kalkars where the last of the tribe of Or-tis make their last stand, and so we prefer to live in the desert near our foes, driving our herds great distances to pasture when the need arises, rather than to settle down in a comparative land of plenty, resigning the age old struggle, the ancient feud between the house of Julian and the house of Or-tis.

A light breeze moves the black mane of the bright bay stallion beneath me. It moves my own black mane where it falls loose below the buckskin thong that encircles my head and keeps it from my eyes. It moves the dangling ends of the Great Chief's blanket strapped behind my saddle.

On the twelfth day of the eighth month of the year just gone this Great Chief's blanket covered the shoulders of my father, Julian 19th, from the burning rays of the summer's desert sun. I was twenty on that day, and on that day my father fell before the lance of an Or-tis in the Great Feud, and I became the Chief of Chiefs.

Surrounding me to-day as I sit looking down upon the land of my enemies are fifty of the fierce chieftains of the hundred clans that swear allegiance to the house of Julian. They are bronzed and, for the most part, beardless men.

The insignias of their clans are painted in various colors upon their foreheads, their cheeks, their breasts. Ocher they use, and blue and white and scarlet. Feathers rise from the headbands that confine their hair—the feathers of the vulture, the hawk, and the eagle. I, Julian 20th, wear a single feather. It is from a red-tailed hawk—the clan sign of my family.

We are all garbed similarly. Let me describe the Wolf, and in his portrait you will see a composite of us all. He is a sinewy, well built man of fifty, with piercing gray-blue eyes beneath straight brows. His head is well shaped, denoting great intelligence. His features are strong and powerful and of a certain fierce cast that might well strike terror to a foeman's heart—and does, if the Kalkar scalps that fringe his ceremonial blanket stand for aught. His breeches, wide about the hips and skin tight from above the knees down, are of the skin of the buck deer. His soft boots, tied tight about the calf of each leg, are also of buck. Above the waist he wears a sleeveless vest of calfskin tanned with the hair on. The Wolf's is of fawn and white.

Sometimes these vests are ornamented with bits of colored stone or metal sewn to the hide in various designs. From the Wolf's headband, just above the right ear, depends the tail of a timber wolf—the clan sign of his family.

An oval shield upon which is painted the head of a wolf hangs about this chief's neck, covering his back from nape to kidneys. It is a stout, light shield—a hardwood frame covered with bullhide. Around its periphery have been fastened the tails of wolves. In such matters each man, with the assistance of his women folk, gives rein to his fancy in the matter of ornamentation.

Clan signs and chief signs, however, are sacred. The use of one to which he is not entitled might spell death for any man. I say "might" because we have no inflexible laws. We have few laws.

The Kalkars were forever making laws, so we hate them. We judge each case upon its own merits, and we pay more attention to what a man intended doing than what he did.

The Wolf is armed, as are the rest of us, with a light lance about eight feet in length, a knife, and a straight two-edged sword. A short, stout bow is slung beneath his right stirrup leather, and a quiver of arrows is at his saddlebow.

The blades of his sword and his knife and the metal of his lance tip come from a far place called Kolrado, and are made by a tribe that is famous because of the hardness and the temper of the metal of their blades. The Utaws brings us metal also, but theirs is inferior, and we use it only for the shoes that protect our horses' feet from the cutting sands and the rocks of our hard and barren country.

The Kolrados travel many days to reach us, coming once in two years. They pass, unmolested, through the lands of many tribes because they bring what none might otherwise have, and what we need in our never ending crusade against the Kalkars. That is the only thread that holds together the scattered clans and tribes that spread east and north and south beyond the ken of man. All are animated by the same purpose—to drive the last of the Kalkars into the sea.

From the Kolrados we get meager news of clans beyond them toward the rising sun. Far, far to the east, they say,—so far that in a lifetime no man might reach it—lies another great sea, and that there, as here upon the world's western edge, the Kalkars are making their last stand. All the rest of the world has been won back by the people of our own blood—by Americans.

We are always glad to see the Kolrados come, for they bring us news of other peoples; and we welcome the Utaws, too, although we are not a friendly people, killing all others who come among us, for fear, chiefly, that they may be spies sent by the Kalkars.

It is handed down from father to son that this was not always so, and that once the people of the world went to and fro safely from place to place, and that then all spoke the same language; but now it is different. The Kalkars brought hatred and suspicion among us until now we trust only the members of our own clans and tribe.

The Kolrados, from coming often among us, we can understand, and they can understand us, by means of a few words and many signs, although when they speak their own language among themselves we cannot understand them, except for an occasional word that is like one of ours. They say that when the last of the Kalkars is driven from the world we must live at peace with one another; but I am afraid that that will never come to pass, for who would go through life without breaking a lance or dipping his sword point now and again into the blood of a stranger? Not the Wolf, I swear; nor no more the Red Hawk.

By the Flag! I take more pleasure in meeting a stranger upon a lonely trail than in meeting a friend, for I cannot set my lance against a friend and feel the swish of the wind as Red Lightning bears me swiftly down upon the prey and I crouch in the saddle, nor thrill to the shock as we strike.

I am the Red Hawk. I am but twenty, yet the fierce chiefs of a hundred fierce clans bow to my will. I am a Julian—the twentieth Julian—and from this year 2430 I can trace my line back five hundred and thirty-four years to Julian 1st, who was born in 1896. From father to son, by word of mouth, has been handed down to me the story of every Julian, and there is no blot upon the shield of one in all that long line, nor shall there be any blot upon the shield of Julian 20th.

From my fifth year to my tenth I learned, word for word, as had my father before me, the deeds of my forbears, and to hate the Kalkars and the tribe of Or-tis. This, with riding, was my schooling. From ten to fifteen I learned to use lance and sword and knife, and on my sixteenth birthday I rode forth with the other men—a warrior.

As I sat there this day looking down upon the land of the accused Kalkars, my mind went back to the deeds of the fifteenth Julian, who had driven the Kalkars across the desert and over the edge of these mountains into the valley below just one hundred years before I was born, and I turned to the Wolf and pointed down toward the green groves and the distant hills and off beyond to where the mysterious ocean lay.

"For a hundred years they have held us here," I said. "It is too long."

"It is too long," the Wolf agreed.

"When the rains are over the Red Hawk leads his people into the land of plenty."

The Rock raised his spear and shook it savagely toward the valley far below. The scalp-lock fastened just below its metal-shod tip trembled in the wind. "When the rains are over!" cried the Rock. His fierce eyes glowed with the fire of fanaticism.

"The green of the groves we will dye red with their blood!" cried the Rattlesnake.

"With our swords, not our mouths," I said, and wheeled Red Lightning toward the east.

The Coyote laughed, and the others joined with him as we wound downward out of the hills toward the desert.

On the afternoon of the following day we came within sight of our tents, where they were pitched beside the yellow flood of the river. Five miles before that we had seen a few puffs of smoke rise from the summit of a hill to the north of us. It told the camp that a body of horsemen was approaching from the west. It told us that our sentry was on duty and that doubtless all was well.

At my signal my warriors formed themselves in two straight lines, crossing each other at their centers. A moment later another smoke signal arose, informing the camp that we were friends and us that our signal had been rightly read.

Presently, in a wild charge, whooping and brandishing our spears, we charged down among the tents. Dogs, children, and slaves scampered for safety, the dogs barking, the children and the slaves yelling and laughing. As we swung ourselves from our mounts before our tents, slaves rushed out to seize our bridle reins, the dogs leaped, growling, upon us in exuberant welcome, while the children fell upon their sires, their uncles, or their brothers, demanding the news of the ride or a share in the spoils of conflict or chase. Then we greeted our women.

I had no wife, but there were my mother and my two sisters, and I found them awaiting me in the inner tent, seated upon a low couch that was covered, as was the floor, with the bright blankets that our slaves weave from the wool of sheep. I knelt and took my mother's hand and kissed it, and then I kissed her upon the lips, and in the same fashion I saluted my sisters, the elder first.

It is custom among us; but it is also our pleasure, for we both respect and love our women. Even if we did not, we should appear to, if only for the reason that the Kalkars do otherwise. They are brutes and swine.

We do not permit our women a voice in the councils of the men, but none the less they do influence our councils from the seclusion of their inner tents. It is indeed an unusual mother among us who does not make her voice heard in the council through her husband or her sons, and she does it through the love and respect in which they hold her, and not by scolding and nagging.

They are wonderful, our women. It is for them and the Flag that we have fought the foe across a world for three hundred years. It is for them that we shall go forth and drive him into the sea.

As the slaves prepared the evening meal I chatted with my mother and my sisters. My two brothers, the Vulture and Rain Cloud, lay also at my mother's feet. The Vulture was eighteen, a splendid warrior, a true Julian.

Rain Cloud was sixteen then, and I think the most beautiful creature I had ever seen. He had just become a warrior, but so sweet and lovable was his disposition that the taking of human life appeared a most incongruous calling for him; yet he was a Julian, and there was no alternative.

Every one loved him, and respected him, too, even though he had never excelled in feats of arms, for which he seemed to have no relish; but they respected him because they knew that he was brave and that he would fight as courageously as any of them, even though he might have no stomach for it. Personally, I considered Rain Cloud braver than I, for I knew that he would do well the thing he hated, while I would be only doing well the thing I loved.

The Vulture resembled me in looks and the love of blood, so we left Rain Cloud at home to help guard the women and the children, which was no disgrace, since it is a most honorable and sacred trust, and we went forth to the fighting when there was likely to be any, and when there wasn't we went forth and searched for it. How often have I ridden the trails leading in across our vast frontiers longing for a sight of a strange horseman against whom I might bend my lance!

We asked no questions then when we had come close enough to see the clan sign of the stranger and to know that he was of another tribe and likely he was as keen for the fray as we, otherwise he would have tried to avoid us. We each drew rein at a little distance and set his lance, and each called aloud his name, and then with a mighty oath each bore down upon the other, and then one rode away with a fresh scalplock and a new horse to add to his herd, while the other remained to sustain the vulture and the coyote.

Two or three of our great, shaggy hounds came in and sprawled among us as we lay talking with mother and the two girls, Nallah and Neeta. Behind my mother and sisters squatted three slave girls, ready to do their bidding, for our women do not labor. They ride and walk and swim and keep their bodies strong and fit that they may bear mighty warriors, but labor is beneath them, as it is beneath us.

We hunt and fight and tend our own herds, for that is not menial, but all other labor the slaves perform. We found them here when we came. They have been here always—a stolid, dark-skinned people, weavers of blankets and baskets, makers of pottery, tillers of the soil. We are kind to them, and they are happy.

The Kalkars, who preceded us, were not kind to them. It has been handed down to them from father to son, for more than a hundred years, that the Kalkars were cruel to them, and they hate their memory; yet, were we to be driven away by the Kalkars, these simple people would remain and serve anew their cruel masters, for they will never leave their soil.

They have strange legends of a far time when great horses of iron raced across the desert, dragging iron tents filled with people behind them, and they point to holes in the mountainsides through which these iron monsters made their way to the green valleys by the sea, and they tell of men who flew like birds and as swiftly; but of course we know that such things were never true and are but the stories that the old men and the women among them told to the children for their amusement. However, we like to listen to them.

I told my mother of my plans to move down into the valley of the Kalkars after the rains.

She was silent some time before making a reply.

"Yes, of course," she said: "you would be no Julian were you not to attempt it. At least twenty times before in a hundred years have our warriors gone down in force into the valley of the Kalkars and been driven back. I wish that you might have taken a wife and left a son to be Julian 21st before you set out upon this expedition from which you may not return. Think well of it, my son, before you set forth. A year or two will make no great difference. But you are the Great Chief, and if you decide to go, we can but wait here for your return and pray that all is well with you."

"But you do not understand, mother," I replied. "I said that we are going to move down in the valley of the Kalkars after the rains. I did not say that we are coming back again. I did not say that you would remain here and wait for our return. You will accompany us.

"The tribe of Julian moves down into the valley of the Kalkars when the rains are over, and they take with them their women and their children and their tents and all their flocks and herds and every other possession that is movable, and—they do not return to live in the desert ever more."

She did not reply, but only sat in thought.

Presently a man slave came to bid us warriors to the evening meal. The women and the children eat this meal within their tents, but the warriors gather around a great circular table, called the Council Ring.

There were a hundred of us there that night. Flares in the hands of slaves gave us light and there was light from the cooking fire that burned within the circle formed by the table. The others remained standing until I had taken my seat, which was the signal that the eating might begin.

Slaves brought meat and vegetables—beef and mutton, both boiled and broiled, potatoes, beans and corn, and there were bowls of figs and dried grapes and dried plums. There were also venison and bear meat and fish.

There was a great deal of talk and a great deal of laughter, loud and boisterous, for the evening meal in the home camp is always a gala event. We ride hard and we ride often and we ride long, often we are fighting, and much of the time away from home. Then we have little to eat and nothing to drink but water, which is often warm and unclean and always scarce in our country.

We sit upon a long bench that encircles the outer periphery of the table, and as I took my seat the slaves, bearing platters of meat, passed along the inner rim of the table. As they came opposite each warrior he arose and leaning far across the board, seized a portion of meat with a thumb and finger and cut it deftly away with his sharp knife. The slaves moved in slow procession without pause, and there was a constant gleam and flash of blades and movement and change of color as the painted warriors arose and leaned across the table, the firelight playing upon their beads and metal ornaments and the gay feathers of their headdresses. And the noise!

Pacing to and fro behind the warriors were twoscore shaggy hounds waiting for the scraps that would presently be tossed them—large, savage beasts bred to protect our flocks from coyote and wolf, Hellhound and lion; and quite capable of doing it, too.

As the warriors fell to eating, the din subsided, and at a word from me a youth at my elbow struck a deep note from a drum. Instantly there was silence. Then I spoke:

"For a hundred years we have dwelt beneath the heat of this barren wasteland, while our foes occupied a flowering garden, their cheeks fanned by the cooling breezes of the sea. They live in plenty; their women eat of luscious fruits, fresh from the trees, while ours must be satisfied with the dried and wrinkled semblance of the real.

"Ten slaves they have to do their labor for every one that we possess; their flocks and herds find lush pasture and sparkling water beside their masters' tents, while ours pick a scant existence across forty thousand square miles of sandy, rockbound desert. But these things gall the soul of Red Hawk least of all. The wine turns bitter in my mouth when in my mind's eye I look out across the rich valleys of the Kalkars and I recall that here alone in all the world that we know there flies not the Flag."

A great growl rose from the fierce throats.

"Since my youth I have held one thought sacred in my breast against the day that the blanket of the Great Chief should fall upon my shoulders. That day has come, and I but await the time that the rains shall be safely over before making of that thought a deed. Twenty times in a hundred years have the Julian warriors ridden down into the Kalkar country in force, but their women and their children and their flocks remained behind in the desert—an unescapable argument for their return.

"It shall not be so again. In April the tribe of Julian leaves the desert forever. With our tents and our women and all our flocks and herds we shall descend and live among the orange groves. This time there shall be no turning back. I, the Red Hawk, have spoken."

The Wolf leaped to his feet, his naked blade flashing in the torchlight.

"The Flag!" he cried.

A hundred warriors sprang erect, a hundred swords arose, shimmering, above our heads.

"The Flag! The Flag!"

I stepped to the table top and raised a tankard of wine aloft.

"The Flag!" I cried again; and we all drank deep.

And then the women came, my mother carrying the Flag, furled upon a long staff. She halted there, at the foot of the table, the other women massed behind her, and she undid the cords that held it and let the Flag break out in the desert breeze, and we all kneeled and bent our heads to the faded bit of fabric that has been handed down from father to son through all the vicissitudes and hardships and bloodshed of more than five hundred years since the day that it was carried to victory by Julian 1st in a long forgotten war.

This, the Flag, is known from all other flags as the Flag of Argon, although its origin and the meaning of the word that describes it are lost in the mists of time. It is of alternate red and white stripes, with a blue square in one corner upon which are sewn many white stars. The white is yellow with age, and the blue and the red are faded, and it is torn in places, and there are brown spots upon it—the blood of Julians who have died protecting it, and the blood of their enemies. It fills us with awe, for it has the power of life and death, and it brings the rains and the winds and the thunder. That is why we bow down before it.

2

Exodus

APRIL ARRIVED, AND with it the clans, coming at my bidding. Soon there would be little danger of heavy rains in the coast valleys. To have been caught there in a week of rain with an army would have been fatal, for the mud is deep and sticky and our horses would have mired and the Kalkars fallen upon us and destroyed us.

They greatly outnumber us, and so our only hope must lie in our mobility. We realize that we are reducing this by taking along our women and our flocks; but we believe that so desperate will be our straits that we must conquer, since the only alternative to victory must be death—death for us and worse for our women and children.

The clans have been gathering for two days, and all are there—some fifty thousand souls; and of horses, cattle, and sheep there must be a thousand thousand, for we are rich in live stock. In the last two months, at my orders, all our swine have been slaughtered and smoked, for we could not be hampered by them on the long desert march, even if they could have survived it.

There is water in the desert this time of year and some feed, but it will be a hard, a terrible march. We shall lose a great deal of our stock, one in ten, perhaps; the Wolf thinks it may be as high as five in ten.

We shall start to-morrow an hour before sunset, making a short march of about ten miles to a place where there is a spring along the trail the ancients used. It is strange to see all across the desert evidence of the great work they accomplished. After five hundred years the location of their well graded trail, with its wide, sweeping curves, is plainly discernible. It is a narrow trail, but there are signs of another, much wider, that we discover occasionally. It follows the general line of the other, crossing it and recrossing it, without any apparent reason, time and time again. It is almost obliterated by drifting sand, or washed away by the rain of ages. Only where it is of material like stone has it endured.

The pains those ancients took with things! The time and men and effort they expended! And for what? They have disappeared, and their works with them.

As we rode that first night Rain Cloud was often at my side, and as usual he was gazing at the stars.

"Soon you will know all about them," I said, laughing, "for you are always spying upon them. Tell me some of their secrets."

"I am learning them," he replied seriously.

"Only the Flag, who put them there to light our way at night, knows them all," I reminded him.

He shook his head. "They were there, I think, long before the Flag existed."

"Hush!" I admonished him. "Speak no ill of the Flag."

"I speak no ill of it," he replied. "It stands for all to me. I worship it, even as you; yet still I think the stars are older than the Flag, as the earth must be older than the Flag."

"The Flag made the earth," I reminded him.

"Then where did it abide before it made the earth?" he asked.

I scratched my head. "It is not for us to ask," I replied. "It is enough that our fathers told us these things. Why would you question them?"

"I would know the truth."

"What good will it do you?" I asked.

This time it was Rain Cloud who scratched.

"It is not well to be ignorant," he replied at last. "Beyond the desert, wherever I have ridden, I have seen hills. I know not what lies beyond those hills. I should like to see. To the west is the ocean. In my day, perhaps, we shall reach it. I shall build a canoe and go forth upon the ocean and see what lies beyond.''

''You will come to the edge of the world and tumble over it, and that will be the end of your canoe and you.''

''I do not know about that,'' he replied. ''You think the earth is flat.''

''And who is there that does not think so? Can we not see that it is flat? Look about you—it is like a large, round, flat cake.''

''With land in the center and water all round the land?'' he asked.

''Of course.''

''What keeps the water from running off the edge?'' he wanted to know.

I had never thought about that, and so I returned the only answer that I could think of at the time.

''The Flag, of course,'' I said.

''Do not be a fool, my brother,'' said Rain Cloud. ''You are a great warrior and a mighty chief; you should be wise, and the wise man knows that nothing, not even the Flag, can keep water from running down hill if it is not confined.''

''Then it must be confined,'' I argued. ''There must be land to hold the water from running over the edge of the world.''

''And what is beyond that land?''

''Nothing,'' I replied confidently.

''What do the hills stand on? What does the earth stand on?''

''It floats on a great ocean,'' I explained.

''With hills around it to keep its water from running over its edge?''

''I suppose so.''

''And what upholds that ocean and those hills?'' he went on.

''Do not be foolish,'' I told him. ''I suppose there must be another ocean below that one.''

"And what holds it up?"

I thought he would never stop. I do not enjoy thinking about such useless things. It is a waste of time, yet now that he had started me thinking, I saw that I should have to go on until I had satisifed him. Somehow I had an idea that dear little Rain Cloud was poking fun at me, and so I bent my mind to the thing and really thought, and when I did think I saw how foolish is the belief that we all hold.

"We know only about the land that we can see and the oceans that we know exist, because others have seen them," I said at last. "These things, then, of which we know, constitute the earth. What upholds the earth we do not know, but doubtless it floats about in the air as float the clouds. Are you satisfied?"

"Now I will tell you what I think," he said. "I have been watching the sun, the moon, and the stars every night since I was old enough to have a thought beyond my mother's breast. I have seen, as you can see, as every one with eyes can see, that the sun, the moon, and the stars are round like oranges. They move always in the same paths through the air, though all do not move upon the same path. Why should the earth be different? It probably is not. It, too, is round, and it moves upon its path. What keeps them all from falling, I do not know."

I laughed at that, and called to Nallah, our sister, who rode near by. "Rain Cloud thinks that the earth is round like an orange."

"We should slip off if that were true," she said.

"Yes, and all the water would run off it," I added.

"There is something about it that I do not understand," admitted Rain Cloud, "yet still I think that I am right. There is so much that none of us knows. Nallah spoke of the water running off the earth if it were round. Did you ever think of the fact that all the water of which we know runs down forever from the higher places? How does it get back again?"

"The rains and snows," I replied quickly.

"Where do they come from?"

"I do not know."

"There is so much that we do not know," sighed Rain Cloud; "yet all that we can spare the time for is thoughts of fighting. I shall be glad when we have chased the last of the Kalkars into the sea, so that some of us may sit down in peace and think."

"It is handed down to us that the ancients prided themselves upon their knowledge, but what did it profit them? I think we are happier. They must have had to work all their lives to do the things they did and to know all the things they knew, yet they could eat no more or sleep no more or drink no more in a lifetime than can we. And now they are gone forever from the earth and all their works with them, and all their knowledge is lost."

"And presently we will be gone," said Rain Cloud.

"And we will have left as much as they to benefit those who follow," I replied.

"Perhaps you are right, Red Hawk," said Rain Cloud; "yet I cannot help wanting to know more than I do know."

The second march was also made at night, and was a little longer than the first. We had a good moon, and the desert night was bright. The third march was about twenty-five miles; and the fourth a short one, only ten miles. And there we left the trail of the ancients and continued in a south-westerly direction to a trail that followed a series of springs that gave us short marches the balance of the way to a lake called Bear by our slaves.

The way, of course, was all well known to us, and so we knew just what was ahead and dreaded the fifth march, which was a terrible one, by far the worst of them all. It lay across a rough and broken area of desert and crossed a range of barren mountains. For forty-five miles it wound its parched way from water hole to water hole.

For horsemen alone it would have been a hard march, but with cattle and sheep to herd across that waterless waste it became a terrific undertaking. Every beast that was strong enough carried hay, oats or barley, in sacks, for we could not depend entirely upon the sparse feed of the desert for so huge a caravan; but water we could not carry in sufficient quantities for the stock. We transported enough, however, on the longer marches to insure a supply for the women and all children under sixteen, and on the short marches enough for nursing mothers and children under ten.

We rested all day before the fifth march began, setting forth about three hours before sundown. From fifty camps in fifty parallel lines we started. Every man, woman and child was mounted. The women carried all children under five, usually seated astride a blanket on the horse's rump behind the mother. The rest rode alone. The bulk of the warriors and all the women and children set out ahead of the herds, which followed slowly behind, each bunch securely hemmed in by outriders and followed by a rear guard of warriors.

A hundred men on swift horses rode at the head of the column, and as the night wore on gradually increased their lead until they were out of sight of the remainder of the caravan. Their duty was to reach the camp site ahead of the others and fill the water tanks that slaves had been preparing for the last two months.

We took but a few slaves with us, only personal attendants for the women and such others as did not wish to be separated from their masters and had chosen to accompany us. For the most part the slaves preferred to remain in their own country, and we were willing to let them, since it made fewer mouths to feed upon the long journey, and we knew that in the Kalkar country we should find plenty to take their places, as we would take those from the Kalkars we defeated.

At the end of five hours we were strung out in a column fully ten miles long, and our outriders on either flank were often half a mile apart; but we had nothing to fear from the attacks of human enemies, the desert being our best defense against such. Only we of the desert knew the desert trails and the water holes, only we are inured to the pitiless hardships of its barrenness, its heat, and its cruelties.

But we have other enemies, and on this long march they

clung tenaciously to our flanks, almost surrounding the great herds with a cordon of gleaming eyes and flashing fangs—the coyotes, the wolves, and the Hellhounds. Woe betide the straggling sheep or cow that they might cut off from the protection of the rear guard or the flankers. A savage chorus, a rush, and the poor creature was literally torn to pieces upon its feet. A woman or child with his mount would have suffered a similar fate, and even a lone warrior might be in great danger. If the brutes knew their own strength, they could, I believe, exterminate us, for their numbers are appalling; there must have been as high as a thousand following us upon that long march at a single time.

But they hold us in great fear because we have waged relentless warfare against them for hundreds of years, and the fear of us must be bred in them. Only when in great numbers and goaded by starvation will they attack a full grown warrior. They kept us busy all during the long nights of this wearisome march, and they kept our shaggy hounds busy, too. The coyotes and the wolves are easy prey for the hounds, but the Hellhounds are a match for them, and it is these that we fear most. Our hounds, and with the fifty clans there must have been gathered a full two thousand of them, work with tireless efficiency and a minimum of wasted effort when on the march.

In camp they are constantly fighting among themselves, but on the march, never. From the home camp they indulge in futile chases after rabbits, but on the march they consume no energy uselessly. The dogs of each clan have their pack leader, usually an experienced dog owned by the hound-chief of the clan. The Vulture is our hound-chief, and his hound, old Lonay, is pack leader. He does his work and leads his pack with scarce a word from the Vulture. He has about fifty hounds in his pack, twenty-five of which he posts at intervals about the herd, and with the other twenty-five old Lonay brings up the rear.

A high-pitched yelp from one of his sentries is a signal of attack, and brings Lonay and his fighting dogs to the rescue. Sometimes there will be a sudden rush of coyotes, wolves and Hellhounds simultaneously from two or three points, and then the discipline and intelligence of old Lonay and his pack merit the affection and regard in which we hold these great, shaggy beasts.

Whirling rapidly two or three times, Lonay emits a series of deep-throated growls and barks, and instantly the pack splits into two or three or more units, each of which races to a different point of trouble. If at any point they are outnumbered and the safety of the herd imperiled, they set up a great wailing which is the signal that they need the help of warriors, a signal that never goes unheeded. In similar cases, or in the hunt, the hounds of other packs will come to the rescue, and all will work together harmoniously, yet if one of these same hounds should wander into the others' camp a half hour later he would be torn to pieces.

But enough of this, and of the long, tiresome march. It was over at last. The years of thought that I had given it, the two months of preparation that had immediately preceded it, the splendid condition of all our stock, the training and the temper of my people bore profitable fruit, and we came through without the loss of a man, woman or child, and with the loss of less than two in a hundred of our herds and flocks. The mountain crossing on that memorable fifth march took the heaviest toll, mostly lambs and calves falling by the trail side.

With two days out for rest we came, at the end of the tenth march and the twelfth day, to the lake called Bear and into a rich mountain country, lush with feed and game. Here deer and wild goats and wild sheep abounded, with rabbit and quail and wild chicken, and the beautiful wild cattle that the legends of our slaves tell us are descended from the domestic stock of the ancients.

It was not my plan to rest here longer than was necessary to restore in full the strength and spirits of the stock. Our horses were not jaded, as we had had sufficient to change often. In fact, we warriors had not ridden our war horses once upon the journey. Red Lightning had trotted into the last camp fat and sleek.

To have remained here long would have been to have apprised the enemy of our plans, for the Kalkars and their slaves hunt in these mountains which adjoin their land, and should a single hunter see this vast concourse of Julians our coming would have been known throughout the valleys in a single day, and our purpose guessed by all.

So, after a day of rest, I sent the Wolf and a thousand warriors westward to the main pass of the ancients with orders to make it appear that we were attempting to enter the valley there in force. For three days he would persist in this false advance, and in that time I felt that I should have drawn all the Kalkar fighting men from the valley lying southwest of the lake of the Bear. My lookouts were posted upon every eminence that gave view of the valleys and the trails between the main pass of the ancients and that through which we should pour down from the Bear out into the fields and groves of the Kalkars.

The third day was spent in preparation. The last of the arrows were finished and distributed. We looked to our saddle leathers and our bridles. We sharpened our swords and knives once more and put keener points upon our lances. Our women mixed the war paint and packed our belongings again for another march. The herds were gathered and held in close, compact bunches.

Riders reported to me at intervals from the various lookouts and from down the trail to the edge of the Kalkar farms. No enemy had seen us, but that they had seen the Wolf and his warriors we had the most reassuring evidence in the reports from our outposts that every trail from south and west was streaming with Kalkar warriors and that they were converging upon the pass of the ancients.*

During the third day we moved leisurely down the mountain trails and as night fell our vanguard of a thousand warriors debouched into the groves of the Kalkars. Leaving four thousand warriors, mostly youths, to guard the women, the children, the flocks and the herds, I set out rapidly in a north-

*Probably Cajon Pass.

westerly direction toward the pass of the ancients at the head of full twenty thousand warriors.

Our war horses we had led all day as we came slowly out of the mountains riding other animals, and not until we were ready to start upon the twenty-five-mile march to the pass of the ancients did we saddle and mount the fleet beasts upon which the fate of the Julians might rest this night. In consequence our horses were fresh from a two weeks' rest. Three hours of comparatively easy riding should see us upon the flanks of the enemy.

The Rock, a brave and seasoned warrior, I had left behind to guard the women, the children, and the stock. The Rattlesnake, with five thousand warriors, bore along a more westerly trail, after fifteen miles had been covered, that he might fall upon the rear of the enemy from one point while I fell upon them from another, and at the same time place himself between their main body, lying at the foot of the pass, and the source of their supplies and reënforcements.

With the Wolf, the mountains, and the desert upon one side, and the Rattlesnake and I blocking them upon the south and the southeast, the position of the Kalkars appeared to me to be hopeless.

Toward midnight I called a halt to await the report of scouts who had preceded us, and it was not long before they commenced to come in. From them I learned that the camp fires of the Kalkars were visible from an eminence less than a mile ahead. I gave the signal to advance.

Slowly the great mass of warriors moved forward. The trail dipped down into a little valley and then wound upward to the crest of a low ridge, where, a few minutes later, I reined in Red Lightning.

Before me spread a broad valley bathed in the soft light of moon and stars. Dark masses in the nearer foreground I recognized as orange groves even without the added evidence of the sweet aroma of their blossoms that was heavy on the still night air. Beyond, to the northwest, a great area was dotted with dying camp fires.

I filled my lungs with the cool, sweet air; I felt my nerves tingle; a wave of exultation surged through me; Red Lightning trembled beneath me. After nearly four hundred years a Julian stood at last upon the threshold of complete revenge!

3

Armageddon

VERY QUIETLY WE crept down among the orange groves, nearer, ever nearer, to the sleeping foe. Somewhere to the west of us, beneath the silvery moon, the Rattlesnake was creeping stealthily forward to strike. Presently the stillness of the night would be broken by the booming of his war drums and the hoarse cries of his savage horde. It would be the signal that would send the Wolf down from the mountain heights above them and the Red Hawk from the orange groves below them to sink fang and talon into the flesh of the hated Kalkars, and ever the Rattlesnake would be striking at their heels.

Silently we awaited the signal from the Rattlesnake. A thousand bowmen unslung their bows and loosened arrows in their quivers; swords were readjusted, their hilts ready to the hand; men spat upon their right palm that their lance grip might be the surer. The night dragged on toward dawn.

The success of my plan depended upon a surprise attack while the foe slept. I knew that the Rattlesnake would not fail me, but something must have delayed him. I gave the signal to advance silently. Like shadows we moved through the orange groves and deployed along a front two miles in length, a thousand bowmen in the lead and behind these line after line of lancers and swordsmen.

Slowly we moved forward toward the sleeping camp. How like the lazy, stupid Kalkars that no sentries were posted at their rear! Doubtless there were plenty of them on the front exposed to the Wolf. Where they could see an enemy they could prepare for him, but they have not imagination enough to foresee aught.

Only the desert and their great numbers have saved them from extermination during the last hundred years.

Scarce a mile away now we could catch occasional glimpses of the dying embers of the nearest fires, and then from the east there rolled across the valley the muffled booming of distant war drums. A momentary silence followed, and then, faintly, there broke upon our ears the war cries of our people. At my signal our own drums shattered the silence that had surrounded us.

It was the signal for the charge. From twenty thousand savage throats arose the awful cries of battle, twenty thousand pairs of reins were loosed, and eighty thousand iron shod hoofs set the earth atremble as they thundered down upon the startled enemy, and from the heights above came the growl of the drums of the Wolf and the eerie howls of his painted horde.

It was dawn as we smote the camp. Our bowmen, guiding their mounts with their knees and the swing of their bodies, raced among the bewildered Kalkars, loosing their barbed shafts into the cursing, shrieking mob that fled before them only to be ridden down and trampled by our horses' feet.

Behind the bowmen came the lancers and the swordsmen, thrusting and cutting at those who survived. From our left came the tumult of the Rattlesnake's assault, and from far ahead and above us the sounds of battle proclaimed that the Wolf had fallen on the foe.

Ahead I could see the tents of the Kalkar leaders, and toward these I spurred Red Lightning. Here would be the representatives of the house of Or-tis, and here would be the battle center.

Ahead the Kalkars were forming in some semblance of order to check and repel us. They are huge men and ferocious fighters, but I could see that our surprise attack had unnerved them. They gave before us before their chiefs could organize them for resistance, yet again and again they reformed and faced us.

We were going more slowly now, the battle had become largely a matter of hand-to-hand combats; they were checking us, but they were not stopping us. So great were their numbers that even had they been unarmed it would have been difficult to force our horses through their massed ranks.

Back of their front line they were saddling and mounting their horses, which those who had borne the brunt of our first onslaught had been unable to do. We had cut the lines to which their animals had been tethered, and driven them, terrified, ahead of us to add to the confusion of the enemy. Riderless horses were running wildly everywhere, those of the Kalkars and many of our own, whose riders had fallen in battle.

The tumult was appalling, for to the shrieks of the wounded and the groans of the dying were added the screams of stricken horses and the wild, raucous war cries of battle-maddened men, and underlying all, the dull booming of the war drums. Above us waved the Flag, not the Flag of Argon, but a duplicate of it, and here were the drums and a massed guard of picked men.

The Flag and the drums moved forward as we moved. And near me was the clan flag of my family with the Red Hawk upon it, and with it were its drums. In all there were a hundred clan flags upon that field this day, and the drums of each rolled out, incessantly, defiance of the enemy.

Their horsemen now were rallied, and the dismounted men were falling back behind them, and presently a Kalkar chief upon a large horse confronted me. Already was my blade red with their blood. I had thrown away my lance long since, for we were fighting in too close quarters for its effective use, but the Kalkar had his spear and there was a little open space between us, and in the instant he crouched and put spurs to his horse and bore down upon me.

He was a large man, as most Kalkars are, for they have bred with that alone in mind for five hundred years, so that many of them are seven feet in height and over. He looked very fierce, did this fellow, with his black whiskers and his little bloodshot eyes.

He wore a war bonnet of iron to protect his head from sword cuts and a vest of iron covered his chest against the thrusts of sword or lance or the barbed tips of arrows. We Julians, or Americans, disdain such protection, choosing to depend upon our skill and agility, not hampering ourselves and our horses with the weight of all this metal.

My light shield was on my left forearm, and in my right hand I grasped my two-edged sword. A pressure of my knees, an inclination of my body, a word in his pointed ear, were all that was needed to make Red Lightning respond to my every wish, even though the reins hung loose.

The fellow bore down upon me with a loud yell, and Red Lightning leaped to meet him. The Kalkar's point was set straight at my chest, and I had only a sword on that side to deflect it, and at that I think I might have done so had I cared to try, even though the Kalkar carries a heavy lance and this one was backed by a heavy man and a heavy horse.

These things make a difference, I can tell you out of wide experience. The weight behind a lance has much to do with the success or failure of many a combat. A heavy lance can be deflected by a light sword, but not as quickly as a light lance, and the point of a lance is usually within three feet of you before your blade parries its thrust—within three feet of you and traveling as fast as a running horse can propel it.

You can see that the blow must be a quick and heavy one if it is to turn the lance point even a few inches in the fraction of a second before it enters your flesh.

I usually accomplish it with a heavy downward and outward cut, but in that cut there is always the danger of striking your horse's head unless you rise in your stirrups and lean well forward before delivering it, so that, in reality, you strike well ahead of your horse's muzzle.

This is best for parrying a lance thrust for the groin or belly, but this chap was all set for my chest, and I would have had to have deflected his point too great a distance in the time at my disposal to have insured the success of my defense. And so I changed my tactics.

With my left hand I grasped Red Lightning's mane and at the instant that the Kalkar thought to see his point tear through my chest I swung from my saddle and lay flat against Red Lightning's near side, while the Kalkar and his spear brushed harmlessly past an empty saddle. Empty for but an instant, though.

Swinging back to my seat in the instant that I wheeled Red Lightning, I was upon the Kalkar from the rear even as the fighting mass before him brought him to a halt. He was swinging to have at me again, but even as he faced me my sword swung down upon his iron bonnet, driving pieces of it through his skull and into his brain. A fellow on foot cut viciously at me at the instant I was recovering from the blow I had dealt the mounted Kalkar, so that I was able only partly to parry with my shield, with the result that his point opened up my right arm at the shoulder—a flesh wound, but one that bled profusely, although it did not stay the force of my return, which drove through his collar bone and opened up his chest to his heart.

Once again I spurred in the direction of the tents of the Or-tis, above which floated the red banners of the Kalkars, and around which were massed the flower of the Kalkar forces; too thickly massed, perhaps, for most effective defense, since we were driving them in from three sides and packing them there as tightly as eggs in the belly of a she-salmon.

But now they surged forward and drove us back by weight of numbers, and now we threw ourselves upon them again until they, in their turn, were forced to give the ground that they had won. Sometimes the force of our attack drove them to one side, while at another point their warriors were pushing out into the very body of the massed clans, so that here and there our turning movements would cut off a detachment of the enemy, or again a score or more of our own men would be swallowed by the milling Kalkar horde, until, as the day wore on, the great field became a jumbled mass of broken detachments of Julian and Kalkar warriors, surging back and forth over a bloody shambles, the iron shoes of their reeking mounts trampling the corpse of friends and foe alike into the gory mire.

There were lulls in the fighting, when, as though by mutual assent, both sides desisted for brief intervals of rest, for we had fought to the limit of endurance. Then we sat, often stirrup to stirrup with a foeman, our chests heaving from our exertions, our mounts, their heads low, blowing and trembling.

Never before had I realized the extreme of endurance to which a man may go before breaking, and I saw many break that day, mostly Kalkars, though, for we are fit and strong at all times. It was only the very young and the very old among us who succumbed to fatigue, and but a negligible fraction of these, but the Kalkars dropped by hundreds in the heat of the day. Many a time that day as I faced an enemy I would see his sword drop from nerveless fingers and his body crumble in the saddle and slip beneath the trampling feet of the horses before ever I had struck him a blow.

Once, late in the afternoon, during a lull in the battle, I sat looking about the chaos of the field. Red with our own blood from a score of wounds and with the blood of friend and foe, Red Lightning and I stood panting in the midst of the welter. The tents of the Or-tis lay south of us—we had fought halfway around them—but they were scarce a hundred yards nearer for all those bitter hours of battle. Some of the warriors of the Wolf were near me, showing how far that old, gray chieftain had fought his way since dawn, and presently behind a mask of blood I saw the flashing eyes of the Wolf himself, scarce twenty feet away. "The Wolf!" I cried; and he looked up and smiled in recognition.

"The Red Hawk is red indeed," he bantered; "but his pinions are yet unclipped."

"And the fangs of the Wolf are yet undrawn," I replied.

A great Kalkar, blowing like a spent hound, was sitting his tired horse between us. At our words he raised his head.

"You are the Red Hawk?" he asked.

"I am the Red Hawk," I replied.

"I have been searching for you these two hours," he said.

"I have not been far, Kalkar," I told him. "What would you of the Red Hawk?"

"I bear word from Or-tis, the Jemadar."

"What word has an Or-tis for a Julian?" I demanded.

"The Jemadar would grant you peace," he explained.

I laughed. "There is only one peace which we may share together," I said, "and that is the peace of death—that peace I will grant him and he will come hither and meet me. There is nothing that an Or-tis has the power to *grant* a Julian."

"He would stop the fighting while you and he discuss the terms of peace," insisted the Kalkar. "He would stop this bloody strife that must eventually annihilate both Kalkar and Yank." He used an ancient term which the Kalkars have applied to us for ages in a manner of contempt, but which we have been taught to consider as an appellation of honor, although its very meaning is unknown to us and its derivation lost in antiquity.

"Go back to your Jemadar," I said, "and tell him that the world is not wide enough to support both Kalkar and Yank, Or-tis and Julian; that the Kalkars must slay us to the last man, or be slain."

He wheeled his horse toward the tent of the Or-tis, and the Wolf bade his warriors to let him pass. Soon he was swallowed by the close packed ranks of his own people, and then a Kalkar struck at one of us from behind and the battle raged again.

How many men had fallen one might not even guess, but the corpses of warriors and horses lay so thick that the living mounts could but climb and stumble over them, and sometimes barriers of them nearly man high lay between me and the nearest foeman, so that I was forced to jump Red Lightning over the gory obstacles to find new flesh for my blade. And then, slowly, night descended until man could not tell foe from friend, but I called to my tribesmen about me to pass along the word that we would not move from our ground that night, staying on for the first streak of dawn that would permit us to tell a Kalkar from a Yank.

Once again the tents of the Or-tis were north of me. I had fought completely around them during the long day, gaining two hundred yards in all, perhaps; but I knew that they had weakened more than we, and that they could not stand even another few hours of what they had passed through this day. We were tired, but not exhausted, and our war horses, after a night's rest, would be good for another day, even without food.

As darkness forced a truce upon us all I began to reform my broken clans, drawing them into a solid ring about the position of the Kalkars. Sometimes we would find a lone Kalkar among us, cut off from his fellows; but these we soon put out of danger, letting them lie where they fell. We had drawn off a short distance, scarce more than twenty yards from the Kalkars, and there in small detachments we were dismounting and removing saddles for a few minutes to rest and cool our horses' backs, and to dispatch the wounded, giving merciful peace to those who must otherwise have soon died in agony. This favor we did to foe as well as friend.

All through the night we heard a considerable movement of men and horses among the Kalkars, and we judged that they were reforming for the dawn's attack, and then, quite suddenly and without warning of any sort, we saw a black mass moving down upon us. It was the Kalkars—the entire body of them—and they rode straight for us, not swiftly, for the corpse-strewn, slippery ground prevented that, but steadily, overwhelmingly, like a great, slow moving river of men and horses.

They swept into us and over us, or they carried us along with them. Their first line broke upon us in a bloody wave and went down, and those behind passed over the corpses of those that had fallen. We hacked until our tired arms could scarce raise a blade shoulder high. Kalkars went down screaming in agony; but they could not halt, they could not retreat, for the great, ever moving mass behind them pushed them onward; nor could they turn to right or left, because we hemmed them in on both flanks; nor could they flee ahead, for there, too, were we.

Borne on by this resistless tide, I was carried with it. It surrounded me. It pinioned my arms at my sides. It crushed at my legs. It even tore my sword from my hand. At times, when the force ahead stemmed it on for a moment and the force behind continued to push on, it rose in the center until horses were lifted from the ground, and then those behind sought to climb over the backs of those in front, until the latter were borne to earth and the others passed over their struggling forms, or the obstacle before gave way and the flood smoothed out and passed along again between the flashing banks of Julian blades, hewing, ever hewing, at the surging Kalkar stream.

Never have I looked upon such a sight as the moon revealed that night—never in the memory or the tradition of man has there been such a holocaust. Thousands upon thousands of Kalkars must have fallen upon the edge of that torrent as it swept its slow way between the blades of my painted warriors, who hacked at the living mass until their arms fell numb at their sides from utter exhaustion, and then gave way to the eager thousands pressing from behind.

And ever onward I was borne, helpless to extricate myself from the sullen, irresistible flood that carried me southward down the broadening valley. The Kalkars about me did not seem to realize that I was an enemy, or notice me in any way, so intent were they upon escape. Presently we had passed the field of yesterday's thickest fighting, the ground was no longer strewn with corpses and the speed of the rout increased, and as it did so the massed warriors spread to right and left sufficiently to permit more freedom of individual action, still not enough to permit me to worm my way from the current.

That I was attempting to do so, however, was what attracted attention to me at first, and then the single red hawk feather and my other trappings, so different from those of the Kalkars.

"A Yank!" cried one near me, and another drew his sword

and struck at me; but I warded the blow with my shield as I drew my knife, a pitiful weapon wherewith to face a swordsman.

"Hold!" cried a voice of authority near by. "It is he whom they call the Red Hawk, their chief. Take him alive, to the Jemadar."

I tried to break through their lines, but they closed in upon me, and although I used my knife to good effect upon several of them, they overbore me with their numbers, and then one of them must have struck me upon the head with the flat of his sword, for of a sudden everything went black, and of that moment I remember only reeling in my saddle.

4

The Capitol

WHEN I REGAINED consciousness it was night again. I was lying upon the ground, out beneath the stars. For a moment I experienced a sense of utter comfort, but as my tired nerves awoke they spoke to me of pain and stiffness from many wounds, and my head throbbed with pain. I tried to raise a hand to it and it was then that I discovered that my wrists were bound. I could feel the matted stiffness of my scalp and I knew that it was caked with dried blood, doubtless from the blow that had stunned me.

In attempting to move that I might ease my cramped muscles I found that my ankles were fastened together as well as my wrists, but I managed to roll over, and raising my head a little from the ground I looked about and saw that I was surrounded by sleeping Kalkars and that we lay in a barren hollow ringed by hills. There were no fires and from this fact and the barrenness and seclusion of the camp I guessed that we were snatching a brief rest in hiding from a pursuing foe.

I tried to sleep, but could do so only fitfully, and presently I heard men moving about and soon they approached and awakened the warriors sleeping near me. The thongs were removed from my ankles shortly thereafter and Red Lightning was brought and I was helped into the saddle. Immediately after, we resumed the march. A glance at the stars showed me that we were moving west. Our way led through hills and was often rough, evidencing that we were following no beaten trail, but rather that the Kalkars were attempting to escape by a devious route.

I could only guess at the numbers of them, but it was evident that there was not the great horde that had set forth from the battlefield below the pass of the ancients. Whether they had separated into smaller bands, or the balance had been slain I could not even conjecture; but that their losses must have been tremendous I was sure.

We traveled all that day, stopping only occasionally when there was water for the horses and the men. I was given neither food nor water, nor did I ask for either. I would die rather than ask a favor of an Or-tis. In fact, I did not speak all that day, nor did any of the Kalkars address me.

I had seen more Kalkars in the last two days than in all my life before and was now pretty familiar with the appearance of them. They range in height from six to eight feet, the majority of them being midway between these extremes. Many of them are bearded, but some shave the hair from all or portions of their faces. A great many wear beards upon their upper lips only.

There is a great variety of physiognomy among them, for they are a half-caste race, being the result of hundreds of years of inter-breeding between the original moon men and the women of the earth whom they seized for slaves when they overran and conquered the world. Among them there is occasionally an individual who might pass anywhere for a Yank, insofar as external appearances are concerned; but the low, coarse, brutal features of the Kalkar preponderate.

They wear a white blouse and breeches of cotton woven by their slaves and long, woolen cloaks fabricated by the same busy hands. Their women help in this work as well as in the work of the fields, for the Kalkar women are no better than slaves, with the possible exception of those who belong to the families of the Jemadar and his nobles. Their cloaks are of red, with collars of various colors, or with borders or other designs to denote rank.

Their weapons are similar to ours, but heavier. They are

but indifferent horsemen. That, I think, is because they ride only from necessity and not, as we, from love of it.

That night, after dark, we came to a big Kalkar camp. It was one of the camps of the ancients, the first that I ever had seen. It must have covered a great area and some of the huge stone tents were still standing. It was in these that the Kalkars lived or in dirt huts leaning against them. In some places I saw where the Kalkars had built smaller tents from the building materials salvaged from the ruins of the ancient camp, but as a rule they were satisfied with hovels of dirt, or the half fallen and never repaired structures of the ancients.

This camp lies about forty-five or fifty miles west of the battlefield, among beautiful hills and rich groves, upon the banks of what must once have been a mighty river, so deeply has it scoured its pathway into the earth in ages gone.*

I was hustled into a hut where a slave woman gave me food and water. There was a great deal of noise and excitement outside, and through the open doorway I could hear snatches of conversation as Kalkars passed to and fro. From what I heard I gathered that the defeat of the Kalkars had been complete and that they were flying toward the coast and their principal camp, called The Capitol, which the slave woman told me lay a few miles southwest. This, she said, was a wonderful camp, with tents reaching so high into the heavens that often the moon brushed against their tops as she made her way through the sky.

They had released my hands, but my feet were still bound and two Kalkars squatted just outside the door of the hut to see that I did not escape. I asked the slave woman for some warm water to wash my wounds and she prepared it for me. Not only that, the kindly soul saw to my wounds herself, and after they had been cleansed she applied a healing lotion which greatly soothed them, and then she bound them as best she could.

I felt much refreshed by this and with the food and drink in me was quite happy, for had I not accomplished what my

*The camp described probably occupies the site of present day Pasadena.

people had been striving after for a hundred years, a foothold on the western coast. This first victory had been greater than I had dared to hope and if I could but escape and rejoin my people I felt that I could lead them to the waters of the ocean with scarce a halt while the Kalkars still were suffering the demoralization of defeat.

It was while I was thinking these thoughts that a Kalkar chief entered the hut. Beyond the doorway the score of warriors that had accompanied him, waited.

"Come!" commanded the Kalkar, motioning me to arise.

I pointed to my tethered ankles.

"Cut his bonds," he directed the slave woman.

When I was free I arose and followed the Kalkar without. Here the guards surrounded me and we marched away between avenues of splendid trees such as I never had seen before, to a tent of the ancients, a partly ruined structure of imposing height that spread over a great area of ground. It was lighted upon the inside by many flares and there were guards at the entrance and slaves holding other flares.

They led me into a great chamber that must be much as the ancients left it, although I had seen from the outside that in other places the roof of the tent had fallen in and its walls were crumbling. There were many high Kalkars in this place and at the far end of the room, upon a platform, one sat alone on a huge, carved bench—a bench with a high back and arms. It was just large enough for a single man. It is what we call a small bench.

The Kalkars call it *chair*; but this one, I was to learn, they call *throne*, because it is the small bench upon which their ruler sits. I did not know this at the time.

I was led before this man. He had a thin face and a long, thin nose, and cruel lips and crafty eyes. His features, however, were good. He might have passed in any company as a full-blood Yank. My guard halted me in front of him.

"This is he, Jemadar," said the chief who fetched me.

"Who are you?" demanded the Jemadar, addressing me.

His tone did not please me. It was unpleasant and dictatorial. I am not accustomed to that, even from equals, and a

Julian has no superiors. I looked upon him as scum. There-fore, I did not reply.

He repeated his question angrily. I turned to the Kalkar chief who stood at my elbow. "Tell this man that he is ad-dressing a Julian," I said, "and that I do not like his manner. Let him ask for it in a more civil tone if he wishes informa-tion."

The eyes of the Jemadar narrowed angrily. He half arose from his small bench. "A Julian!" he exclaimed. "You are all Julians—but you are *the* Julian. You are the Great Chief of the Julians. Tell me," his tone became suddenly civil, almost ingratiating, "is it not true that you are *the* Julian, The Red Hawk who led the desert hordes upon us?"

"I am Julian 20th, The Red Hawk," I replied; "and you?"

"I am Or-tis, the Jemadar," he replied.

"It has been long since an Or-tis and a Julian met," I said.

"Heretofore they always have met as enemies," he re-plied. "I have sent for you to offer peace and friendship. For five hundred years we have fought uselessly and senselessly because two of our forebears hated each other. You are the twentieth Julian I am the sixteenth Or-tis. Never before have we seen each other, yet we must be enemies. How silly!"

"There can be no friendship between a Julian and an Or-tis," I replied coldly.

"There can be peace," he said, "and friendship will come later, maybe long after you and I are dead. There is room in this great, rich country for us all. Go back to your people. I will send an escort with you and rich presents. Tell them that the Kalkars would share their country with the Yanks. You will rule half of it and I will rule the other half. If the power of either is threatened the other will come to his aid with men and horses. We can live in peace and our people will prosper. What say you?"

"I sent you my answer yesterday," I told him. "It is the same to-day—the only peace that you and I can share is the peace of death. There can be but one ruler for this whole country and he will be a Julian—if not I, the next in line. There is not room in all the world for both Kalkar and Yank.

For three hundred years we have been driving you toward the sea. Yesterday we started upon the final drive that will not stop until the last of you has been driven from the world you ruined. That is my answer, Kalkar.''

He flushed and then paled. ''You do not guess our strength,'' he said after a moment's silence. ''Yesterday you surprised us, but even so you did not defeat us. You do not know how the battle came out. You do not know that after you were captured our forces turned upon your weakened warriors and drove them back into the recesses of the mountains. You do not know that even now they are suing for peace. If you would save their lives and yours as well, you will accept my offer.''

''No, I do not know these things, nor do you,'' I replied with a sneer; ''but I do know that you lie. That has always been the clan sign of the Or-tis.''

''Take him away!'' cried the Jemadar. ''Send this message to his people: I offer them peace on these terms—they may have all the country east of a straight line drawn from the pass of the ancients south to the sea; we will occupy the country to the west of that line. If they accept I will send back their great chief. If they refuse, he will go to the butcher, and remind them that he will not be the first Julian that an Or-tis has sent to the butcher. If they accept there are to be no more wars between our people.''

They took me back then to the hut of the old slave and there I slept until early morning, when I was awakened by a great commotion without. Men were shouting orders and cursing as they ran hurriedly to and fro. There was the trampling of horses' feet, the clank and clatter of trappings of war. Faintly, as from a great distance, I heard, presently, a familiar sound and my blood leaped in answer. It was the war cry of my people and beneath it ran the dull booming of their drums.

''They come!'' I must have spoken aloud, for the old slave woman, busy with some household duty, turned toward me.

''Let them come,'' she said. ''They cannot be worse than these others, and it is time that we changed masters. It has been long now since the rule of the ancients, who, it is said, were not unkind to us. Before them were other ancients, and before those still others. Always they came from far places, ruled us and went their way, displaced by others. Only we remain, never changing.

"Like the coyote, the deer and the mountains we have been here always. We belong to the land, we are the land— when the last of our rulers has passed away we shall still be here, as we were in the beginning—unchanged. They come and mix their blood with ours, but in a few generations the last traces of it have disappeared, swallowed up by the slow, unchanging flood of ours. You will come and go, leaving no trace; but after you are forgotten we shall still be here."

I listened to her in surprise for I never had heard a slave speak as this one, and I should have been glad to have questioned her further. Her strange prophesy interested me. But now the Kalkars entered the hovel. They came hurriedly and as hurriedly departed, taking me with them. My wrists were tied again and I was almost thrown upon Red Lightning's back. A moment later we were swallowed up by the torrent of horsemen surging toward the southwest.

Less than two hours later we were entering the greatest camp that man has ever looked upon. For miles we rode through it, our party now reduced to the score of warriors who guarded me. The others had halted at the outskirts of the camp to make a stand against my people and as we rode through the strange trails of the camp we passed thousands upon thousands of Kalkars rushing past us to defend the Capitol.

We passed vast areas laid out in squares, as was the custom of the ancients, a trail upon each side of the square, and within the grass-grown mounds that covered the fallen ruins of their tents. Now and again a crumbling wall raised its ruin above the desolation, or some more sturdily constructed structure remained almost intact except for fallen roof and floors. As we advanced we encountered more and more of the latter, built of that strange, rocklike substance the secret of which has vanished with the ancients.

Now these mighty tents of a mighty people became larger. Whole squares of them remained and there were those that reared their weatherworn heads far into the sky. It was easy to believe that at night the moon might scrape against them. Many were very beautiful, with great carvings upon them and more and more of them, as we advanced, had their roofs and floors intact. These were the habitations of the Kalkars. They arose upon each side of the trails like the sides of sheer mountain cañons, their fronts pierced by a thousand openings.

The trail between the tents was deep with dust and filth. In places the last rains had washed clean the solid stone pavement of the ancients, but elsewhere the debris of ages lay thick, rising above the bottom of the lower opening in the tents in many places and spreading itself inward over the floors of the structures.

Bushes and vines and wild oats grew against the walls and in every niche that was protected from the trampling feet of the inhabitants. Offal of every description polluted the trails until my desert bred nose was distressed at the stench. Coarse Kalkar women, with their dirty brats, leaned from the openings above the level of the trail and when they caught sight of me they screamed vile insults.

As I looked upon these stupendous tents, the miles upon miles of them stretching away in every direction, and sought to conceive of the extent of the incalculable effort, time and resources expended by the ancients in the building of them, and then looked upon the filthy horde to whose vile uses they had unwittingly been dedicated my mind was depressed by contemplation of the utter futility of human effort. How long and at what cost had the ancients striven to the final achievement of their mighty civilization! And for what?

How long and at what cost had we striven to wrest its wreckage from the hands of their despoilers! And for what? There was no answer—only that I knew we should go on and on, and generations after us would go on and on, striving, always striving, for that which was just beyond our grasp—

victims of some ancient curse laid upon our earliest progenitor, perhaps.

And I thought of the slave woman and her prophesy. Her people would remain, steadfast, like the hills, aspiring to nothing, achieving nothing, except perhaps that one thing we all crave in common—contentment. And when the end comes, whatever that end shall be, the world will doubtless be as well off because of them as because of us, for in the end there will be nothing.

My guard turned in beneath the high arched entrance of a mighty structure. From the filth of its spacious floor rose mighty columns of polished stone, richly variegated. The tops of the columns were carved and decorated in colors and in gold. The place was filled with horses, tied to long lines that stretched almost the length of the room, from column to column. At one end a broad flight of stone steps led upward.

After we dismounted I was led up these steps. There were many Kalkars coming and going. We passed them as I was conducted along a narrow avenue of polished white stone upon either side of which were openings in the walls leading to other chambers.

Through one of these openings we turned into a large chamber and there I saw again the Or-tis whom I had seen the night before. He was standing before one of the openings overlooking the trail below, talking with several of his nobles. One of the latter glanced up and saw me as I entered, calling the Jemadar's attention to me.

Or-tis faced me. He spoke to one near him who stepped to another opening in the chamber and motioned to someone without. Immediately a Kalkar guard entered bringing a youth of one of my desert clans. At sight of me the young warrior raised his hand to his forehead in salute.

"I give you another opportunity to consider my offering of last night," said the Or-tis, addressing me. "Here is one of your own men who can bear your message to your people if you still choose to condemn them to a futile and bloody struggle, and with it he will bear a message from me—that you go to the butcher in the morning if your warriors do not retire and your chiefs engage to maintain peace hereafter. In that event you will be restored to your people. If you give me this promise yourself you may carry your own message to the tribes of Julian.''

"My answer," I replied, "is the same as it was last night, as it will be to-morrow." Then I turned to the Yank warrior. "If you are permitted to depart, go at once to the Vulture and tell him that my last command is that he carry the Flag onward to the sea. That is all.''

The Or-tis was trembling with disappointment and rage. He laid a hand upon the hilt of his sword and took a step toward me; but whatever he intended he thought better of it and stopped. "Take him above," he snapped to my guard; "and to the butcher in the morning.

"I will be present," he said to me, "to see your head roll into the dust and your carcass fed to the pigs.''

They took me from the chamber then and led me up and up along an endless stairway, or at least it seemed endless before we finally reached the highest floor of the great tent. There they pushed me into a chamber the doorway to which was guarded by two giant warriors.

Squatting upon the floor of the chamber, his back leaning against the wall, was a Kalkar. He glanced up at me as I entered, but said nothing. I looked about the bare chamber, its floor littered with the dust and debris of ages, its walls stained by the dirt and grease from the bodies that had leaned against it, to the height of a man.

I approached one of the apertures in the front wall. Far below me, like a narrow buckskin thong, lay the trail filled with tiny people and horses no bigger than rabbits. I could see the pigs rooting in the filth—they and the dogs are the scavengers of the camp.

For a long time I stood looking out over what was to me a strange landscape. The tent in which I was confined was among the highest of the nearer structures of the ancients and from its upper floor I could see a vast expanse of tent roofs, some of the structures apparently in an excellent state

of preservation, while here and there a grass-grown mound
marked the site of others that had fallen.

Evidences of fire and smoke were numerous, and it was
apparent that whatever the ancients had built of other materials than their enduring stone had long since disappeared,
while many of the remaining buildings had been eaten by
flame and left mere shells, as was attested by hundreds of
smoke blackened apertures within the range of my vision.

As I stood gazing out over the distant hills beyond the
limits of the camp I became aware of a presence at my elbow.
Turning I saw that it was the Kalkar whom I had seen sitting
against the wall as I entered the chamber.

"Look well, Yank," he said, in a not unpleasant voice,
"for you have not long to look." He was smiling grimly.
"We have a wonderful view from here," he continued; "on
a clear day you can see the ocean and the island."

"I should like to see the ocean," I said.

He shook his head. "You are very near," he said, "but
you will never see it. I should like to see it again myself, but
I shall not."

"Why?" I asked.

"I go with you to the butcher in the morning," he replied
simply.

"You?"

"Yes, I."

"And why?"

"Because I am a true Or-tis," he replied.

"Why should they send an Or-tis to the butcher?" I demanded. "It is not strange that an Or-tis should send me,
the Julian, to him; but why should an Or-tis send an Or-tis?"

"He is not a true Or-tis who sends me," replied the man,
and then he laughed.

"Why do you laugh?"

"Is it not a strange joke of fate," he cried, "that sees *the*
Julian and *the* Or-tis going to the butcher together? By the
blood of my sires! I think our feud be over, Julian, at least
so far as you and I are concerned."

"It can never be over, Kalkar," I replied.

He shook his head. "Had my father lived and carried out his plans I think it might have ended," he insisted.

"While an Or-tis and a Julian lived? Never!"

"You are young, and the hate that has been suckled into you and yours from your mothers' breasts for ages runs hot in your veins; but my father was old and he saw things as few of my kind, I imagine, ever have seen them. He was a kindly man and very learned and he came to hate the Kalkars and the horrid wrong the first Or-tis did the world and our people when he brought them hither from the Moon, even as you and yours have hated them always. He knew the wrong and he wished to right it.

"Already he had planned means whereby he might get into communication with the Julians and join with them in undoing the crime that our ancestor committed upon the world. He was Jemadar, but he would have renounced his throne to be with his own kind again. Our blood strain is as clear as yours—we are American. There is no Kalkar or half-breed blood in our veins. There are perhaps a thousand others among us who have brought down their birthright unsullied. These he would have brought with him, for they all were tired of the Kalkar beasts.

"But some of the Kalkar nobles learned of the plan and among them was he who calls himself Or-tis and Jemadar. He is the son of a Kalkar woman by a renegade uncle of mine. There is Or-tis blood in his veins, but a drop of Kalkar makes one all Kalkar, therefore he is no Or-tis.

"He assassinated my father and then set out to exterminate every pure-blooded Or-tis and all those other uncontaminated Americans who would not swear fealty to him. Some have done so to save their hides, but many have gone to the butcher. Insofar as I know, I am the last of the Or-tis line. There were two brothers and a sister, all younger than I. We scattered and I have not heard of them since, but I am sure that they are dead. The usurper will not tell me—he only laughed in my face when I asked him.

"Yes, if my father had lived the feud might have been

ended; but to-morrow the butcher will end it. However, the other way would have been better. What think you, Julian?''

I stood meditating in silence for a long time. I wondered if, after all, the dead Jemadar's way would not have been better.

5

The Sea

IT SEEMED STRANGE indeed to me that I stood conversing thus amicably with an Or-tis. I should have been at his throat, but there was something about him that disarmed me, and after his speech I felt, I am almost ashamed to say, something of friendliness for him.

He was an American after all, and he hated the common enemy. Was he responsible for the mad act of an ancestor dead now nearly four hundred years? But the hate that was almost a part of my being would not down entirely—he was still an Or-tis. I told him as much.

"I do not know that I can blame you," he said; "but what matters it? To-morrow we shall both be dead. Let us at least call a truce until then."

He was a pleasant-faced young fellow, two or three years my senior, perhaps, with a winning way that disarmed malice. It would have been very hard to have hated this Or-tis.

"Agreed!" I said, and held out my hand. He took it and then he laughed.

"Thirty-four ancestors would turn over in their graves if they could see this!" he cried.

We talked there by the opening for a long time, while in the trail below us constant streams of Kalkars moved steadily to the battlefront. Faintly, from a great distance, came the booming of the drums.

"You beat them badly yesterday," he said. "They are filled with terror."

"We will beat them again to-day and to-morrow and the next day until we have driven them into the sea," I said.

"How many warriors have you?" he asked.

"There were full twenty-five thousand when we rode out of the desert," I replied proudly.

He shook his head dubiously. "They must have ten or twenty times twenty-five thousand," he told me.

"Even though they have forty times twenty-five thousand we shall prevail," I insisted.

"Perhaps you will, for you are better fighters; but they have so many youths growing into the warrior class every day. It will take years to wear them down. They breed like rabbits. Their women are married before they are fifteen, as a rule. If they have no child at twenty they are held up to scorn and if they are still childless at thirty they are killed, and unless they are mighty good workers they are killed at fifty anyhow—their usefulness to the State is over."

Night came on. The Kalkars brought us no food or water. It became very dark. In the trail below and in some of the surrounding tents flares gave a weird, flickering light. The sky was overcast with light clouds. The Kalkars in the avenue beyond our doorway dozed. I touched the Or-tis upon the shoulder where he lay stretched beside me on the hard floor.

"What is it?" he whispered.

"I am going," I said. "Do you wish to come?"

He sat up. "How are you going?" he demanded, still in a low whisper.

"I do not know, nor how far I shall go; but I am going, if only far enough to cheat the butcher."

He laughed. "Good! I will go with you."

It had taken me a long time to overcome the prejudice of heredity and I had thought long before I could bring myself to ask an Or-tis to share with me this attempt to escape; but now it was done. I hoped I would not regret it.

I arose and moved cautiously toward the doorway. A wick, burning from the nozzle of a clay vessel filled with oil, gave forth a sickly light. It shone upon two hulking Kalkars nodding against the wall as they sat upon the stone floor of the avenue.

My knife, of course, had been taken from me and I was unarmed; but here was a sword within my reach and another for the Or-tis. The hilt of one protruded from beneath the cloak of the nearer Kalkar. My hand, reaching forth, was almost upon it when he moved. I could not wait to learn if he was awaking or but moving in his sleep. I lunged for the hilt, grasped it and the fellow was awake. At the same instant the Or-tis sprang upon the other.

He whom I had attacked lumbered to his feet, clawing at the hand that had already half drawn his sword from its scabbard, and at the same time he set up a terrific yelling. I struck him on the jaw with my clenched fist. I struck him as hard as I could strike as he loomed above me his full eight feet.

The Or-tis was having a bad time with his man, who had seized him by the throat and was trying to draw a knife to finish him. The knife must have become stuck in its scabbard for a moment, or his long, red cloak was in the way. I do not know. I saw only a flash of it from the corner of my eye as my man stiffened and then sank to the floor.

Then I wheeled upon the other, a naked blade in my hand. He threw the Or-tis aside when he saw me and whipped out his own sword, but he was too slow. As I ran my point into his heart I heard the sound of running footsteps ascending the stairway and the shouts of men. I handed the sword I carried to the Or-tis and snatched the other from the fellow I had just finished.

Then I kicked the puny flare as far as I could kick it and called to the Or-tis to follow me. The light went out and together we ran along the dark avenue toward the stairway, up which we could hear the warriors coming in response to the cries of our late antagonists.

We reached the head of the stairs but a moment before the Kalkars appeared. There were three of them and one carried a weak, smoking flare that did little but cast large, grotesque, dancing shadows upon wall and stair and reveal our targets to us without revealing us to them.

"Take the last one," I whispered to the Or-tis.

We leaned over the railing and as he smote the head of the last of the three I finished the second. The first, carrying the flare, turned to find himself facing two swords. He gave a shriek and started down the avenue.

That would not do. If he had kept still we might have let him live, for we were in a hurry; but he did not keep still and so we pursued him. He reminded me of a comet as he fled through the dark with his tail of light, only it was such a little tail. He was a fast comet, though, and we could not catch him until the end of the avenue brought him to bay, then, in turning, he slipped and fell.

I was upon him in the same instant, but some fancy stayed my blade when I might have run it through him. Instead I seized him, before he could recover himself, and lifting him from the floor I hurled him through the aperture at the end of the avenue. He still clung to his lamp, and as I leaned out above him he appeared a comet indeed, although he was quickly extinguished when he struck the pavement in the courtyard far below.

The Or-tis chuckled at my elbow. "The stupid clod!" he ejaculated. "He clung to that flare even to death, when, had he thrown it away and dodged into one of these many chambers he could have eluded us and still live."

"Perhaps he needed it to light his way to hell," I suggested.

"They need no help in that direction," the Or-tis assured me, "for they will all get there, if there be such a place."

We retraced our steps to the stairway again, but once more we heard men ascending. The Or-tis plucked me by the sleeve. "Come," he whispered; "it is futile to attempt escape in this direction now that the guard is aroused. I am familiar with this place. I have been here many times. If we have the nerve we may yet escape. Will you follow me?"

"Certainly," I replied.

The corpses of two of our recent antagonists lay at our feet at the head of the stairs, where we stood. Or-tis stooped and snatched their cloaks and bonnets from them. "We shall need

these if we reach the ground—alive,'' he said. ''Follow me
closely.''

He turned and continued along the corridor, presently entering a chamber at the left.

Behind us we could hear the Kalkars ascending the stairs.
They were calling to their fellows above, from whom they
would never receive a reply; but they were evidently coming
slowly, for which we were both thankful.

Or-tis crossed the chamber to an aperture in the wall. ''Below is the courtyard,'' he said. ''It is a long way down. These
walls are laid in uneven courses. An agile man might make
his way to the bottom without falling. Shall we try it? We
can go down close to these apertures and thus rest often if
we wish.''

''You go on one side and I will go on the other,'' I told
him.

He rolled the two cloaks and the bonnets into a bundle
and dropped them into the dark void beneath, then we slid
over the edge of the aperture. Clinging with my hands I found
a foothold and then another below the first.

The ledges were about half the width of my hand. Some
of them were rounded by time and the weather. These did
not afford a very good hold. However, I reached the aperture
below without mishap and there, I am free to confess, I was
glad to pause for a moment, as I was panting as though I had
run a mile.

Or-tis came down in safety, too. ''The butcher appears
less terrible,'' he said.

I laughed. ''He would have it over quicker,'' I replied.

The next stage we descended two floors before we halted.
I came close to slipping and falling twice in that distance. I
was wet with sweat as I took a seat beside my companion.

I do not like to recall that adventure. It sends shivers
through me always, even now; but at last it was over—we
reached the bottom together and donned the cloaks and the
bonnets of the Kalkars. The swords, for which we had no
scabbards, we slipped through our own belts, the cloaks hiding the fact that they were scabbardless.

The smell of horses was strong in our nostrils as we crept toward a doorway. All was darkness within, as we groped forward to find that we were in a small chamber with a door at the opposite side. Nearly all the doors of the ancients have been destroyed, either by the fires that have destroyed the interiors of most of the buildings, by decay or by the Kalkars that have used them for fuel; but there are some left—they are the metal doors, and this was one.

I pushed it open enough to see if there was a light beyond. There was. It was in the great chamber on the first floor where the horses were tethered. It was not a brilliant light, but a sad, flickering light. Even the lights of the Kalkars are grimy and unclean. It cast a pallid luminescence beneath it, elsewhere were heavy shadows. The horses, when they moved, cast giant shadows upon the walls and floor and upon the great polished stone columns.

A guard loafed before the door that led to the trail in front of the tent. It was composed of five or six men. I suppose there were others in some near-by chamber. The doorway through which we peered was in shadow.

I pushed it open enough to admit our bodies and we slipped through. In an instant we were hidden from the sight of the guard among the horses. Some of them moved restlessly as we approached them. If I could but find Red Lightning!

I had searched along one line almost the full length of the chamber and had started along a second when I heard a low nicker close by. It was he! Love of the Flag! It was like finding my own brother.

In the slovenly manner of the Kalkars the saddles and bridles lay in the dirt in the aisle behind the horses. Fortunately I found my own, more easily, of course, because it is unlike those of the Kalkars, and while I slipped them quietly upon Red Lightning the Or-tis, selecting a mount haphazardly, was saddling and bridling it.

After a whispered consultation we led our horses to the rear of the room and mounted among the shadows, unobserved by the guard. Then we rode out from behind the picket lines and moved slowly toward the entrance, talking and laughing in what we hoped might appear an unconcerned manner, the Or-tis riding on the side nearest the guard and a little in advance, that Red Lightning might be hidden from them, for we thought that they might recognize him more quickly than they would us.

As they saw us coming they ceased their chatter and looked up, but we paid no attention to them, riding straight on for the aperture that led into the trail outside the structure. I think we might have passed them without question had there not suddenly burst from the doorway of what was, I judge, the guard room, an excited figure who shouted lustily to all within hearing of his voice:

"Let no one leave! The Julian and the Or-tis have escaped!" he screamed.

The guards threw themselves across the entrance and at the same instant I put spurs to Red Lightning, whipped out my sword and bore down upon them, the Or-tis following my example. I cut at one upon my left front and Red Lightning bore down another beneath his iron hoofs.

We were out upon the trail and the Or-tis was beside us. Reining to the left we bore south a few yards and then turned west upon another trail, the shouts and curses of the Kalkars ringing in our ears.

With free rein we let our mounts out to far greater speed than the darkness and the littered trail gave warrant, and it was not until we had put a mile behind us that we drew in to a slower gait. The Or-tis spurred to my side.

"I had not thought it could be done, Julian," he said; "yet here we ride, as free as any men in all the country wide."

"But still within the shadow of the butcher," I replied. "Listen! They are following hot-foot." The pounding of the hoofs of our pursuers' horses arose louder and louder behind us as we listened. Again we spurred on, but presently we came to a place where a ruined wall had fallen across the trail.

"May the butcher get me!" cried the Or-tis! "that I should have forgotten that this trail is blocked. We should have turned north or south at the last crossing. Come, we must ride back, and quickly, too, if we are to reach it before they.''

Wheeling, we put our mounts to the run back along the trail over which we had but just come. It was but a short distance to the cross trail, yet our case looked bad, for even in the darkness the pursuing Kalkars could now be seen, so close were they. It was a question as to which would reach the crossing first.

"You turn to the south," I cried to the Or-tis, "and I will turn to the north. In that way one of us may escape.''

"Good!" he agreed. "There are too many of them for us to stand and fight.''

He was right—the trail was packed with them, and we could hear others coming far behind the van. It was like a young army. I hugged the left hand side of the trail and Or-tis the right. We reached the crossing not a second in advance of the leaders of the pursuit.

Into the blackness of the new trail I plunged and behind me came the Kalkars. I urged Red Lightning on and he responded as I knew he would. It was madness to ride through the black night along a strange trail at such speed, yet it was my only hope.

Quickly, my fleet stallion drew away from the clumsy, ill-bred mounts of my pursuers. At the first crossing I turned again to the west, and although here I encountered a steep and winding hill it was fortunately but a short ride to the top and after that the way was along a rolling trail, but mostly downhill.

The structures of the ancients that remained standing became fewer and fewer as we proceeded, and in an hour they had entirely disappeared. The trail, however, was fairly well marked and after a single, short turn to the south it continued westward over rolling country in almost a straight line.

I had reduced my speed to conserve Red Lightning's strength, and as no sign of pursuit developed I jogged along at a running walk, a gait which Red Lightning could keep up for hours without fatigue. I had no idea where the trail was leading me, and at the time I did not even know that it was bearing west, for the heavens were still overcast, although I judged that this must be the fact. My first thought was to put as much distance as possible between me and the Kalkar camp and at the first streak of dawn take to the hills and then work my way north and east in an attempt to rejoin my people.

And so I moved on, through country that was now level and now rolling, for the better part of three hours. A cool breeze sprang up and blew in my face. It had a damp freshness and a strange odor with which I was entirely unfamiliar. I was tired from my long exertions, from loss of sleep and from lack of food and water, yet this strange breeze revived me and filled me with new strength and life.

It had become very dark, although I knew that dawn must be near. I wondered how Red Lightning could pick his way through the utter blackness. This very thought was in my mind when he came to a sudden halt.

I could see nothing, yet I could tell that Red Lightning had some good reason for his action. I listened, and there came to my ears a strange, sullen roar—a deep pounding, such as I never had heard before. What could it be?

I dismounted to rest my beloved mount, while I listened and sought for an explanation of this monotonously reiterated sound. At length I determined to await dawn before continuing. With the bridle reins about my wrist I lay down, knowing that, if danger threatened, Red Lightning would warn me. In another minute I was asleep.

How long I slept I do not know—an hour, perhaps—but when I awoke it was daylight and the first thing that broke upon my sensibilities was the dull, monotonous booming, the pounding, pounding that had lulled me to sleep so quickly.

Never shall I forget the scene that burst upon my astonished eyes as I rose to my feet. Before me was a sheer cliff dropping straight away at my feet, upon the very verge of which Red Lightning had halted the previous night; and beyond, as far as the eye could reach, was water—a vast expanse of water, stretching on and on and on—*the sea*! At last a Julian had looked upon it.

It rolled up on the sands below me, pounding, surging, booming. It rolled back again, resistless, restless; and, at once, terrifying and soothing—terrifying in its immensity and mystery, soothing in the majestic rhythm of its restlessness.

I had looked upon it—the goal of four hundred years of strife—and it gave to me renewed strength and determination to lead my people to it. There it lay, as it had always lain, unaltered, unalterable.

Along its shore line, sweeping away upon either hand toward distant haze dimmed headlands, was a faint scratch at the foot of its bold cliffs that may mark the man-made trail of the ancients, but of man or his works there is no other sign. In utter solitude its rolling waters break upon its sands, and there is no ear to hear.

To my right an old trail led down into a deep cañon that opened upon the beach. I mounted Red Lightning and followed its windings along the half obliterated trail of the ancients, down among giant oaks and sycamores and along the cañon's bottom to the beach. I wanted to feel the cool waters and to quench my thirst.

Red Lightning must have been thirsty, too, but the great waves rolling in frightened him so that it was with difficulty that I urged him to the water's edge; but training and heredity are stronger than fear, and at last he walked out upon the sands until the waters, surging in, broke about his pasterns. Then I threw myself from him at full length upon the beach and as the next wave rolled in I buried my face in it and quaffed one deep drink.

One was enough. Sputtering, choking and gagging, I sprang to my feet. What poisoned liquid rolled in this hellish cauldron? I became very sick. Never in my life had I experienced such ill sensations.

I thought that I was dying, and in my agony I saw Red Lightning dip his velvet muzzle into the treacherous liquid.

Red Lightning took one draught, as had I, and then, snorting, he leaped back from that vast pool of iniquity. For a moment he stood there wide-eyed, staring at the water, pained surprise in his eyes.

Then he fell to trembling as, upon wide spread feet, he swayed to and fro. He was dying—together we were dying at the foot of the goal we had achieved after four hundred years of battle and suffering.

I prayed that I might live even if it were only long enough for me to reach my people and warn them against this hideous monster lying in wait for them. Better that they flee back to their desert than trust themselves to this unknown world where even the fairest of waters held death.

But I did not die. Neither did Red Lightning die. I was very sick for an hour; but after that I rapidly recovered. It was a long time after before I learned the truth about sea water.

6

Saku the Nipon

HUNGRY AND THIRSTY, Red Lightning and I set off up the cañon away from the sea, presently entering the first side cañon* bearing in a northerly direction, for it was my desire to pass through these mountains in the hope of finding a valley running east and west which I could follow back in the direction of my people.

We had proceeded only a short distance up the side cañon when I discovered a spring of pure water and around it an abundance of fine pasture. It was, nevertheless, with some feeling of trepidation that I sampled the liquid; but the first mouthful reassured me and a moment later Red Lightning and I were drinking avidly from the same pool. Then I removed his saddle and bridle and turned him loose to browse upon the lush grasses, while I removed my clothing and bathed my body, which was, by now, sorely in need of it.

I felt much refreshed, and could I have found food should soon have been myself again; but without bow and arrows my chances seemed slight unless I were to take the time to construct a snare and wait for prey.

This, however, I had no mind to do, since I argued that sooner or later I must run across human habitation, where, unless greatly outnumbered by armed men, I would obtain food.

---

*Probably Rustic Cañon, which enters Santa Monica Cañon a short distance above the sea.

For an hour I permitted Red Lightning to line his belly with nutritious grasses and then I called him to me, resaddled, and was on my way again up the wooded, winding cañon, following a well marked trail in which constantly appeared the spoor of coyote, wolf, Hellhound, deer and lion, as well as those of domestic animals and the sandaled feet of slaves, but I saw no signs of shod horses to indicate the presence of Kalkars. The imprints of sandals might mark only the passage of native hunters, or they might lead to a hidden camp. It was this latter that I hoped.

Throughout all the desert and mountain country the camps of the slaves are to be found, for they are not all attached to the service of the whites, there being many who live roving lives, following the game and the pasture and ever eluding the white man. It was the Kalkars who first gave them the name of slave, they say, but before that they were known to the ancients by the name of In-juns.

Among themselves they use only their various tribal names, such as Hopi, Navaho, Mojave, to mention the better known tribes with which we came in contact on the desert and in the mountains and forests to the east. With the exception of the Apache and the far Yaqui, and of the latter we knew little except by repute, they are a peaceful people and hospitable to friendly strangers. It was my hope, therefore, to discover a camp of these natives, where I was sure that I would be received in peace and given food.

I had wound upward for perhaps three miles when I came suddenly upon a little, open meadow and the realization of my wish, for there stood three of the pointed tents of slaves consisting of a number of poles leaning inward and lashed together at the top, the whole covered by a crazy patchwork consisting of the skins of animals sewn together. These tents, however, were peculiar, in that they were very small.

As I came in sight of the camp I was discovered by a horde of scrawny curs that came bristling and yapping toward me, apprising their masters of the presence of a stranger. A head appeared in the opening of one of the tents and was as quickly withdrawn.

I called aloud that I would speak with their chief and then I waited through a full minute of silence. Receiving no reply I called again, more peremptorily, for I am not accustomed to waiting long for obedience.

This time I received a reply. "Go away, Kalkar," cried a man's voice. "This is our country. Go away or we will kill you."

Evidently these people dared voice their antagonism to the Kalkars, and from my knowledge of the reputation of the latter I knew this to be the most unusual in any country that they dominated. That they hated them I was not surprised— all people hate them. It was upon the assumption of this common hatred that I based my expectation of friendly assistance from any slave with whom I might come in contact in the Kalkar country.

"I am not a Kalkar," I therefore replied to the voice, whose owner still remained behind the skins of his diminutive tent, upon the floor of which he must have been sitting, since no man could stand upright in it.

"What are you?" asked the voice.

"I am a desert Yank," I replied, guessing that he would be more familiar with that word than American or Julian.

"You are a Kalkar," he insisted. "Do I not see your skin, even if your cloak and bonnet were not enough to prove you a Kalkar?"

"But I am not a Kalkar. I have but just escaped them and I have been long without food. I wish food and then I will go on, for I am in search of my own people who are fighting the Kalkars at the edge of their great camp to the east."

He stuck his head through the flap then and eyed me closely. His face was small and much wrinkled and he had a great shock of stiff, black hair that stuck out in all directions and was not confined by any band. I thought that he must still be sitting or squatting upon the ground, so low was his head, but a moment later, when, evidently having decided to investigate my claims more closely, he parted the flap and stepped out of the tent, I was startled to see a man little more than three feet tall standing before me.

He was stark naked and carried a bow in one hand and several arrows in the other. At first I thought he might be a child, but his old and wrinkled face as well as the well developed muscles moving beneath his brown skin belied that.

Behind him came two other men of about the same height and simultaneously from the other two tents appeared six or eight more of these diminutive warriors. They formed a semicircle about me, their weapons in readiness.

"From what country do you come?" demanded the little chief.

I pointed toward the east. "From the desert beyond your farthest mountains," I replied.

He shook his head. "We have never been beyond our own hills," he said.

It was most difficult to understand him, although I am familiar with the dialects of a score of tribes and the mongrel tongue that is employed by both the Kalkars and ourselves to communicate with the natives, yet we managed to make ourselves understood to each other.

I dismounted and approached them, my hand held out toward them as is the custom of my people in greeting friends, with whom we always clasp hands after an absence, or when meeting friendly strangers for the first time. They did not seem to understand my intentions and drew back, fitting arrows to their bows.

I did not know what to do. They were so small that to have attacked them would have seemed to me like putting children to the sword, and too, I craved their friendship, for I believed that they might prove of inestimable value to me in discovering the shortest route back to my people, that was at the same time most free of Kalkar camps.

I dropped my hand and smiled, at a loss as to how best to reassure them. The smile must have done it, for immediately the old man's face broke into a grin.

"You are not a Kalkar," he said; "they never smile at us." He lowered his weapon, his example being followed by the others. "Tie your horse to a tree. We will give you food."

He turned toward the tents and called to the women to come out and prepare food.

I dropped my reins to the ground, which is all the tying that Red Lightning requires, and advanced toward the little men, and when I had thrown aside my Kalkar coat and bonnet they crowded around me with questions and comment.

"No, he is not a Kalkar," said one. "His cloak and bonnet are Kalkar, but not his other garments."

"I was captured by the Kalkars," I explained, "and to escape I covered myself with this cloak which I had taken from a Kalkar that I killed."

A stream of women and children now issued from the tents, whose capacity must have been taxed beyond their limit. The children were like toys, so diminutive were they, and, like their fathers and mothers, quite naked, nor was there among them all the sign of an ornament or decoration of any nature.

They crowded around me, filled with good natured curiosity, and I could see that they were a joyous, kindly little people; but even as I stood there encircled by them I could scarcely bring myself to believe in their existence, rather thinking that I was the victim of a capricious dream, for never had I seen or heard of such a race of tiny humans.

As I had this closer and better opportunity to study them I saw that they were not of the same race as the slaves, or Injuns; but were of a lighter shade of brown, with different shaped heads and slanting eyes. They were a handsome little people and there was about the children that which was at once laughable and appealing, so that one could not help but love them and laugh with them.

The women busied themselves making fire and bringing meat—a leg of venison and flour for bread, with fresh fruits such as apricots, strawberries and oranges. They chattered and laughed all the time, casting quick glances at me and then giggling behind their hands.

The children and the dogs were always under foot, but no one appeared to mind them and no one spoke a cross word, and often I saw the men snatch up a child and caress it. They seemed a very happy people—quite unlike any other people who have lived long in a Kalkar country. I mentioned this fact to the chief and asked him how they could be so happy under the cruel domination of the Kalkars.

"We do not live under their rule," he replied. "We are a free people. When they attempted to harass us, we made war upon them."

"You made war upon the Kalkars?" I demanded incredulously.

"Upon those who came into our hills," he replied. "We never leave the hills. We know every rock and tree and trail and cave, and being a very little people and accustomed to living always in the hills we can move rapidly from place to place.

"Long ago the Kalkars used to send warriors to kill us, but they could never find us, though first from one side and then from another our arrows fell among them, killing many. We were all about them, but they could not see us. Now they leave us alone. The hills are ours from the great Kalkar camp to the sea and up the sea for many marches. The hills furnish us with all that we require and we are happy."

"What do you call yourselves?" I asked. "From where do you come?"

"We are Nipons," he replied. "I am Saku, chief of this district. We have always been here in these hills. The first Nipon, our ancestor, was a most honorable giant who lived upon an island far, far out in the middle of the sea. His name was Mik-do. He lives there now. When we die we go there to live with him. That is all."

"The Kalkars no longer bother you?" I asked.

"Since the time of my father's father they have not come to fight with us," replied Saku. "We have no enemies other than Raban, the giant, who lives on the other side of the hills. He comes sometimes to hunt us with his dogs and his slaves. Those whom he kills or captures, he eats.

"He is a very terrible creature, is Raban. He rides a great horse and covers himself with iron so that our arrows and our spears do not harm him. He is three times as tall as we."

I assumed that, after the manner of the ignorant, he was referring to an imaginary personification of some greatly feared manifestation of natural forces—storm, fire or earthquake, perhaps—probably fire, since his reference to the devouring of his people by this giant suggested fire, and, so, dismissed the subject from my mind, along with Mik-do and the fabulous island in the sea.

How filled is the mind of the ignorant native with baseless beliefs and superstitions. He reminded me of our own slaves who told of the iron horses drawing tents of iron and of men flying through the air.

As I ate I questioned Saku concerning the trails leading back in the direction of my people. He told me that the trail upon which he was camped led to the summit of the hills, joining with another that led straight down into a great valley which he thought would lead me to my destination, but of that he was not sure, having only such knowledge of the extent of the valley as one might glean from viewing it from the summit of his loftiest hills.

Against this trail, however, he warned me explicitly, saying that I might use it in comparative safety only to the summit, for upon the other side it led straight down past the great, stone tent of Raban the giant.

"The safer way," he said, "is to follow the trail that winds along the summit of the hills, back toward the camp of the Kalkars—a great trail that was built in the time of Mik-do—and from which you can ride down into the valley along any one of many trails. Always you will be in danger of Raban until you have gone a day's march beyond his tent, for he rides far in search of prey; but at least you will be in less danger than were you to ride down the cañon* in which he lives."

But Raban, the imaginary giant, did not worry me much and although I thanked Saku for his warnings, and let him

*Probably Rustic Cañon, which enters Santa Monica Cañon a short distance above the sea.

believe that I would follow his advice, I was secretly determined to take the shortest route to the valley beyond the hills.

Having finished my meal I thanked my hosts and was preparing to depart when I saw the women and children pulling down the tents to an accompaniment of much laughter and squealing while several of the men started up the cañon, voicing strange cries. I looked at Saku questioningly.

"We are moving up the cañon for deer," he explained, "and will go with you part of the way to the summit. There are many trees across the trail that would hinder you, and these we will move or show you a way around."

"Must you carry all this camp equipment?" I asked him, seeing the women struggling with the comparatively heavy hide tents, which they were rolling and tying into bundles, while others gathered the tent poles and bound them together.

"We will put them on our horses," he explained, pointing up the cañon.

I looked in the direction he indicated to see the strangest creatures I had ever looked upon—a string of tiny, woolly horses that were being driven toward camp by the men who had recently gone up the cañon after them. The little animals were scarce half the height of Red Lightning and they moved at so slow a pace that they seemed scarce to move at all. They had huge bellies and most enormous ears set upon great, uncouth heads. In appearance they seemed part sheep, part horse and a great deal of the long-eared rabbit of the desert.

They were most docile creatures and during the business of strapping the loads to them the children played about between their feet or were tossed to their backs, where they frolicked, while the sad-eyed, dejected creatures stood with drooping heads and waving ears. When we started on the march all the children were mounted upon these little horses, sometimes perched upon the top of a load, or again there would be three or four of them upon the back of a single beast.

It did not take me long to discover that Red Lightning and I had no place in this cavalcade, for if we went behind we were constantly trampling upon the heels of the slow moving little horses, and if we went ahead we lost them in a few yards, and so I explained to Saku that my haste made it necessary for me to go on, but that if I came to any obstacle I could not surmount alone I would wait there for them to overtake me.

I thanked him again for his kindness to me and we exchanged vows of friendship which I believe were as sincere upon his part as they were upon mine. They were a happy, lovable little people and I was sorry to leave them.

Pushing rapidly ahead I encountered no insuperable obstacles and after a couple of hours I came out upon a wide trail at the summit of the hills and saw spread before me a beautiful valley extending far to the east and to the west. At my feet was the trail leading down past the tent of the imaginary Raban and toward this I reined Red Lightning.

I had not yet crossed the old trail of the ancients when I heard the sound of the flying feet of horses approaching from the west. Here the trail winds upward and passes around the shoulder of a hill and as I looked I saw a running horse come into view and at its heel another in hot pursuit. The rider of the second horse was evidently a Kalkar warrior, as a red robe whipped in the wind behind him, and the figure upon the leading animal I could not identify at first, but as they drew rapidly nearer the streaming hair of its head suggested that it must be a woman.

A Kalkar up to their old tricks, I thought, as I sat watching them. So intent was the man upon his prey that he did not notice me until after he had seized the bridle rein of his quarry and brought both animals to a halt not a score of feet from me, then he looked up in surprise. His captive was looking at me, too.

She was a girl with wide, frightened eyes—appealing eyes that even while they appealed were dulled by hopelessness, for what aid might she expect from one Kalkar against another, and of course she must have believed me a Kalkar.

She was a Kalkar woman, but still she was a woman, and so I was bound to aid her. Even had I not felt thus obligated by her sex I should have killed her companion in any event, for was he not a stranger in addition to being a Kalkar?

I let my Kalkar cloak slip to the ground and I tossed my Kalkar bonnet after it.

"I am The Red Hawk!" I cried as I drew the sword from my belt and touched Red Lightning with my spurs.

"Fight, Kalkar!"

The Kalkar tried to bring his spear into play, but it was slung across his back, and he couldn't unsling it in time; so he, too, drew a sword, and, to gain time, he reined his horse behind that of the girl, But she was master of her own mount now, and with a shake of her reins she had urged her horse forward, uncovering the Kalkar, and now he and I were face to face.

He towered above me and he had the protection of his iron vest and iron bonnet, while I was without even the protection of a shield; but whatever advantage these things might have given him, they were outweighed by the lightness and agility of Red Lightning and the freedom of my own muscles, unencumbered by heavy metal protections.

His big, clumsy horse was ill-mannered, and, on top of all else, the Kalkar's swordsmanship was so poor that it seemed ill-befitting a brave warrior to take his almost defenseless life; but he was a Kalkar, and there was no alternative. Had I found him naked and unarmed in bed and unconscious with fever, it would still have been my duty to dispatch him, although there had been no glory in it.

I could not, however, bring myself to the point of butchering him without appearing at least to give him a chance, and so I played with him, parrying his cuts and thrusts and tapping him now and then upon his metal bonnet and vest. This must have given him hope, for suddenly he drew off and then rushed me, his sword swinging high above his head. What a chance he offered, blundering down upon me with chest and belly and groin exposed, for his iron shirt could never stop a Julian's point.

So wondrously awkward was his method of attack that I waited to see the nature of his weird technique before dispatching him. I was upon his left front, and when he was almost upon me he struck downward at me and to his left, but he could not think of two things at once—his horse and his opponent—and as he did not strike quite far enough to the left his blade clove his mount's skull between the ears, and the poor brute, which was rushing forward at the time, fell squarely upon its face, and, turning completely over, pinioned its rider beneath its corpse.

I dismounted to put the man out of his misery, for I was sure he must be badly injured, but I found that he was stone dead. His knife and spear I appropriated, as well as his heavy bow and arrows, although I was distrustful as to my skill with the last weapon, so much lighter and shorter are the bows to which I am accustomed.

I had not concerned myself with the girl, thinking, of course, that during the duel she would take advantage of the opportunity to escape; but when I looked up from the corpse of the Kalkar she was still there, sitting her horse a few yards away and eyeing me intently.

7

Bethelda

"WELL!" I EXCLAIMED. "Why have you not flown?"

"And where?" she demanded. "Back to your Kalkar friends," I replied.

"It is because you are not a Kalkar that I did not fly," she said.

"How do you know that I am no Kalkar," I demanded, "and why, if I am not, should you not fly from me, who must be an enemy of your people?"

"You called him 'Kalkar' as you charged him," she explained, "and one Kalkar does not call another Kalkar that. Neither am I a Kalkar."

I thought then of what the Or-tis had told me of the thousand Americans who had wished to desert the Kalkars and join themselves with us. This girl must be of them, then.

"Who are you?" I asked.

"My name is Bethelda," she replied. "And who are you?"

She looked me squarely in the eyes with a fearless frankness that was anything but Kalkarian. It was the first time that I had had a good look at her, and, by the Flag, she was not displeasing to look at! She had large, gray-green eyes and heavy lashes and a cheerful countenance that seemed even now to be upon the verge of laughter. There was something almost boyish about her, and yet she was all girl. I stood looking at her for so long a time without speaking that a frown of impatience clouded her brow.

"I asked you who you are," she reminded me.

"I am Julian 20th, the Red Hawk," I replied, and I thought for an instant that her eyes went a little wider and that she looked frightened; but I must have been mistaken, for I was to learn later that it took more than a name to frighten Bethelda.

"Tell me where you are going," I said, "and I will ride with you, lest you be again attacked."

"I do not know where to go," she replied, "for wherever I go I meet enemies."

"Where are your people?" I demanded.

"I fear that they are all slain," she told me, a quiver in her voice.

"But where were you going? You must have been going somewhere."

"I was looking for a place to hide," she said. "The Nipons would let me stay with them, if I could find them. My people were always kind to them. They would be kind to me."

"Your people were of the Kalkars, even though you say you are no Kalkar, and the Nipons hate them. They would not take you in."

"My people were Americans. They lived among the Kalkars, but they were not Kalkars. We lived at the foot of these hills for nearly a hundred years, and we often met the Nipons. They did not hate us, though they hated the Kalkars about us."

"Do you know Saku?" I asked.

"Since I was a little child I have known Saku the Chief," she replied.

"Come, then," I said; "I will take you to Saku."

"You know him? He is near?"

"Yes. Come!"

She followed me down the trail up which I had so recently come, and although I begrudged the time that it delayed me, I was glad that I might have her off my hands so easily and so quickly; for of certainty I could not leave her alone and unprotected, nor could I take her upon my long journey with me, even could I have prevailed upon my people to accept her.

In less than an hour we came upon Saku's new camp, and the little people were surprised indeed to see me, and overjoyed when they discovered Bethelda, more than assuring me by their actions that the girl had been far from stating the real measure of the esteem in which the Nipons held her. When I would have turned to ride away they insisted that I remain until morning, pointing out to me that the day was already far gone, and that being unfamiliar with the trails I might easily become lost and thus lose more time than I would gain.

The girl stood listening to our conversation, and when I at last insisted that I must go because, having no knowledge of the trails anyhow, I would be as well off by night as by day, she offered to guide me.

"I know the valley from end to end," she said. "Tell me where you would go and I will lead you there as well by night as by day."

"But how would you return?" I asked.

"If you are going to your people perhaps they would let me remain, for am I not an American, too?"

I shook my head. "I am afraid that they would not," I told her. "We feel very bitterly toward all Americans that cast their lot with the Kalkars—even more bitterly than we feel toward the Kalkars themselves."

"I did not cast my lot with the Kalkars," she said proudly. "I have hated them always—since I was old enough to hate. If four hundred years ago my people chose to do a wicked thing, is it any fault of mine? I am as much an American as you, and I hate the Kalkars more because I know them better."

"My people would not reason that way," I said. "The women would set the hounds on you, and you would be torn to pieces."

She shivered. "You are as terrible as the Kalkars," she said bitterly.

"You forget the generations of humiliation and suffering

that we have endured because of the renegade Americans who brought the Kalkar curse upon us,'' I reminded her.

"We have suffered, too,'' she said, "and we are as innocent as you,'' and then suddenly she looked me squarely in the eyes. "How do you feel about it? Do you, too, hate me worse than if I were a Kalkar? You saved my life, perhaps, to-day. You could do that for one you hate?''

"You are a girl,'' I reminded her, "and I am an American—a Julian,'' I added.

"You saved me only because I am a girl?'' she insisted.

I nodded.

"You are a strange people,'' she said, "that you could be so brave and generous to one you hate, and yet refuse the simpler kindness of forgiveness—forgiveness of a sin that we did not commit.''

I recalled the Or-tis, who had spoken similarly, and I wondered if perhaps they might not be right; but we are a proud people and for generations before my day our pride had been ground beneath the heels of the victorious Kalkar. Even yet the wound was still raw. And we are a stubborn people—stubborn in our loves and our hatreds.

Already I had regretted my friendliness with Or-tis, and now I was having amicable dealings with another Kalkar—it was difficult for me to think of them as other than Kalkars. I should be hating this one—I should have hated the Or-tis—but for some reason I found it not so easy to hate them.

Saku had been listening to our conversation, a portion of which at least he must have understood.

"Wait until morning,'' he said, "and then she can at least go with you as far as the top of the hills and point out the way for you; but you will be wise to take her with you. She knows every trail, and it will be better for her to go with you to your own people. She is not Kalkar, and if they catch her they will kill her.

"Were she Kalkar we would hate her and chase her away; but though she is welcome among us it would be hard for her to remain. We move camp often, and often our trails lead where one so large as she might have difficulty in following, nor would she have a man to hunt for her, and there are times when we have to go without food because we cannot find enough even for our own little people.''

''I will wait until morning,'' I said; ''but I cannot take her with me; my people would kill her.''

I had two motives in remaining over the night. One was to go forth early in the morning and kill game for the little Nipons in payment for their hospitality, and the other was to avail myself of the girl's knowledge of the trails, which she could point out from some lofty hilltop. I had only a general idea of the direction in which to search for my people, and as I had seen from the summit that the valley beyond was entirely surrounded by hills I realized that I might gain time by waiting until morning, when the girl should be able to point out the route to the proper pass to my destination.

After the evening meal that night I kept up a fire for the girl, as the air was chill and she was not warmly clad. The little people had only their tents and a few skins for their own protection, nor was there room in the former for the girl, so already overcrowded were they. The Nipons retired to their rude shelters almost immediately after eating, leaving the girl and me alone. She huddled close to the fire and she looked very forlorn and alone.

''Your people are all gone?'' I asked.

''My own people—my father, my mother, my three brothers—all are dead, I think,'' she replied. ''My mother and father I know are dead. She died when I was a little girl. Six months ago my father was killed by the Kalkars. My three brothers and I scattered, for we heard that they were coming to kill us also.

''I have heard that they captured my brothers; but I am not sure. They have been killing many in the valley lately, for here dwell nearly all the pure descendants of Americans, and those of us who were thought to favor the true Or-tis were marked for slaughter by the false Or-tis.

''I had been hiding in the home of a friend of my father, but I knew that if I were found there it would bring death to him and his family, and so I came away, hoping to find a place where I might be safe from them; but I guess there is no place for me—even my friends, the Nipons, though they would let me stay with them, admit that it would be a hardship to provide for me.''

''What will you do?'' I asked. Somehow I felt very sorry for her.

''I shall find some nearly inaccessible place in the hills and build myself a shelter,'' she replied.

''But you cannot live here in the hills alone,'' I remonstrated.

She shrugged her shoulders. ''Where may I live, then?''

''For a little while, perhaps,'' I suggested, ''until the Kalkars are driven into the sea.''

''Who will drive them into the sea?'' she asked.

''We,'' I replied proudly. .

''And if you do, how much better off shall I be? Your people will set their hounds upon me—you have said so yourself. But you will not drive the Kalkars into the sea. You have no conception of their numbers. All up and down the coasts, days' journeys north and south, wherever there is a fertile valley, they have bred like flies. For days they have been coming from all directions, marching toward the Capitol. I do not know why they congregate now, nor why only the warriors come. Are they threatened, do you think?'' A sudden thought seemed to burst upon her. ''It cannot be,'' she exclaimed, ''that the Yanks have attacked them! Have your people come out of the desert again?''

''Yes,'' I replied. ''Yesterday we attacked their great camp; to-day my warriors must have eaten their evening meal in the stone tents of the Kalkars.''

''You mean the Capitol?''

''Yes.''

''Your forces have reached the Capitol? It seems incredible! Never before have you come so far. You have a great army?''

''Twenty-five thousand warriors marched down out of the desert beneath the Flag,'' I told her, ''and we drove the

Kalkars from the pass of the ancients back to the Capitol, as you call their great camp.''

"You have lost many warriors?"

"Many fell," I replied; "thousands."

"Then you are not twenty-five thousand now, and the Kalkars are like ants. Kill them, and more will come. They will wear you down until your few survivors will be lucky if they can escape back to their desert.''

"You do not know us," I told her. "We have brought our women, our children, our flocks and herds down into the orange groves of the Kalkars, and there we shall remain. If we cannot drive the Kalkars into the sea to-day, we shall have to wait until to-morrow. It has taken us three hundred years to drive them this far, but in all that time we have never given back a step that we have once gained; we have never retreated from any position to which we have brought our families and our stock.''

"You have a large family?" she asked.

"I have no wife," I replied as I arose to add fuel to the fire. As I returned with a handful of sticks I saw that she hugged closer to the blaze and that she shivered with the cold. I removed my Kalkar robe and threw it across her shoulders.

"No," she cried, rising. "I cannot take it. You will be cold.''

"Keep it," I said. "The night will be cold, and you cannot go until morning without covering.''

She shook her head.

"No," she repeated. "I cannot accept favors from an enemy who hates me.''

She stood there, holding the red robe out toward me. Her chin was high and her expression haughty.

I stepped forward and took the robe and as her hand dropped to her side I threw the woolen garment about her once more and held it there upon her slim figure. She tried to pull away from it, but my arm was about her, holding the robe in place, and as I guessed her intention I pressed the garment more closely around her, which drew her to me until we stood face to face, her body pressed against mine. As I looked down into her upturned face our eyes met, and for a moment we stood there as if turned to stone.

I do not know what happened. Her eyes, wide and half frightened, looked up into mine, her lips were parted, and she caught her breath once in what was almost a sob. Just for an instant we stood thus, and then her eyes dropped and she bent her head and turned it half away and at the same time her muscles relaxed and she went almost limp in my arms.

Very gently I lowered her to her seat beside the fire and adjusted the robe about her. Something had happened to me. I did not know what it was, but of a sudden nothing seemed to matter so much in all the world as the comfort and safety of Bethelda.

In silence I sat down opposite her and looked at her as though I never before had laid eyes upon her, and well might it have been that I had never; for, by the Flag, I had not seen her before, or else, like some of the tiny lizards of the desert, she had the power to change her appearance as they change their colors, for this was not the same girl to whom I had been talking a moment since; this was a new and wonderful creature of a loveliness beyond all compare.

No, I did not know what had happened, nor did I care. I just sat there and devoured her with my eyes. And then she looked up and spoke four words that froze my heart in my bosom.

She looked up and her eyes were dull and filled with pain. Something had happened to her, too—I could see it.

"I am an Or-tis," she said, and dropped her head again.

I could not speak. I just sat there staring at the slender little figure of my blood enemy, sitting, dejected, in the fire-light. After a long time she lay down beside the fire and slept, and I suppose that I must have slept, too, for once, when I opened my eyes, the fire was out, I was almost frozen, and the light of a new day was breaking over rugged hilltops to the east. I arose and rekindled the fire. After that I would get Red Lightning and ride away before she awakened; but when

I had found him, feeding a short distance from the camp, I did not mount and ride away, but came back to the camp again. Why, I do not know. I did not want to see her again ever, yet something drew me to her.

She was awake and standing looking all about, up and down the cañon, when I first saw her, and I was sure that there was an expression of relief in her eyes when she discovered me.

She smiled wistfully, and I could not be hard, as I should have been to a blood enemy.

I was friendly with her brother, I thought—why should I not be friendly with her? Of course, I shall go away and not see her again; but at least I may be pleasant to her while I remain. Thus I argued, and thus I acted.

"Good morning," I said as I approached. "How are you?"

"Splendid," she replied. "And how are you?"

Her tones were rich and mellow and her eyes intoxicated me like old wine. Oh, why was she an enemy?

The Nipons came from their little tents. The naked children scampered around, playing with the dogs in an attempt to get warm. The women built the fires, around which the men huddled while their mates prepared the morning meal.

After we had eaten I took Red Lightning and started off down the cañon to hunt, and although I was dubious as to what results I should achieve with the heavy Kalkar bow, I did better than I had expected, for I got two bucks, although the chase carried me much farther from camp than I had intended going.

The morning must have been half spent as Red Lightning toiled up the cañon trail beneath the weight of the two carcasses and myself to the camp. I noticed that he seemed nervous as we approached, keeping his ears pricked forward and occasionally snorting, but I had no idea of the cause of his perturbation and was only the more on the alert myself, as I always am when warned by Red Lightning's actions that something may be amiss.

And when I came to the camp site I did not wonder that

he had been aroused, for his keen nostrils had scented tragedy long before my dull senses could become aware of it. The happy, peaceful camp was no more. The little tents lay flat upon the ground and near them the corpses of two of my tiny friends—two little naked warriors. That was all. Silence and desolation brooded where there had been life and happiness a few short hours before. Only the dead remained.

Bethelda! What had become of her? What had happened? Who had done this cruel thing? There was but a single answer—the Kalkars must have discovered this little camp and rushed it. The Nipons that had not been killed doubtless escaped, and the Kalkars had carried Bethelda away a captive.

Suddenly I saw red. Casting the carcasses of the bucks to the ground, I put spurs to Red Lightning and set out up the trail where the fresh imprint of horses' hoofs pointed the direction in which the murderers had gone. There was the spoor of several horses in the trail, and among them one huge imprint fully twice the size of the dainty imprint of Red Lightning's shoe. While the feet of all the Kalkar horses are large, this was the largest I had ever seen.

From the signs of the trail, I judged that not less than twenty horses were in the party, and while at first I had ridden impetuously in pursuit, presently my better judgment warned me that I could best serve Bethelda through strategy, if at all, since it was obvious that one man could not, single-handed, overthrow a score of warriors by force alone.

And now, therefore, I went more warily, though had I been of a mind to do so I doubt that I could have much abated my speed, for there was a force that drove me on, and if I let my mind dwell long on the possibility of the dangers confronting Bethelda I forgot strategy and cunning and all else save brute force and blood.

Vengeance! It is of my very marrow, bred into me through generations that have followed its emblem, the Flag, westward along its bloody trail toward the sea. Vengeance and the Flag and the Julian—they are one. And here was I, Lord of Vengeance, Great Chief of the Julians, Protector of the

Flag, riding hot-foot to save or avenge a daughter of the Ortis! I should have flushed for shame, but I did not. Never had my blood surged so hot even to the call of the Flag. Could it be, then, that there was something greater than the Flag? No, that I could not admit; but I had found something that imparted to the Flag a greater meaning to me.

8

Raban

I CAME TO the summit without overtaking them, but I could tell from the spoor that they were not far ahead of me. The cañon trail is very winding and there is a great deal of brush, so that, oftentimes, a horseman a score of yards ahead of you is out of your sight and the noise of your own mount's passage drowns that of the others. For this reason I did not know, as long as I was in the cañon, how close I might be to them, but when I reached the summit it was different. Then I could see further in all directions.

The murderers were not in sight upon the great highway of the ancients, and I rode swiftly to where the trail drops down upon the north side of the mountains to the great valley that I had seen the day before. There are fewer trees and lower brush upon this side, and below me I could see the trail at intervals as it wound downward, and as I looked I saw the first of a party of horsemen come into sight around the shoulder of a hill as they made their way down into the cañon.

To my right, a short distance, was a ridge leading from the summit downward and along the flank of the cañon into which the riders were descending. A single glance determined me that a few minutes of hard and rather rough riding would permit me to gain the cañon ahead of the riders and unseen by them, unless the brush proved heavier than it appeared or some impassable ravine intervened.

At last the venture was worth essaying, and so, not waiting

for a longer inspection of the enemy, I wheeled and rode along the summit and out onto the ridge which I hoped would prove an avenue to such a position as I wished to attain, where I might carry out a species of warfare for which we are justly famous, in that we are adepts at it.

I found along the ridge a faint game trail and this I followed at reckless speed, putting Red Lightning down steep declivities in a manner that must have caused him to think me mad, so careful am I ordinarily of his legs, but to-day I was as inconsiderate of them as I was of my own life.

At one place the thing I most feared occurred—a deep ravine cut directly through the ridge, the side nearer me dropping almost sheer to the bottom. There was some slight footing, however part way down, and Red Lightning never hesitated as I put him over the brink. Squatting on his haunches, his front legs stiff before him, he slid and stumbled downward, gaining momentum as he went, until, about twenty feet from the bottom, we went over a perpendicular dirt cliff together, landing in the soft sand at the foot of it a bit shaken, but unhurt.

There was no time even for an instant's breathing spell. Before us was the steep acclivity of the opposite side, and like a cat Red Lightning pawed and scrambled his way up, clinging motionless at times for an instant, his toes dug deep into the yielding earth, while I held my breath as fate decided whether he should hold his own or slip back into the ravine; but at last we made it and once more were upon the summit of the ridge.

Now I had to go more carefully, for my trail and the trail of the enemy were converging and constantly the danger increased. I rode now slightly below the brow of the ridge, hidden from whoever might be riding the trail along the opposite side, and presently I saw the mouth of the cañon to my right and below me and across it the trail along which the Kalkars must pass—that they had not already done so I was confident, for I had ridden hard and almost in a straight line, while they had been riding slowly when I saw them and the trail they were following wound back and forth down the cañon side at an easy grade.

Where the ridge ended in a steep declivity to the bottom of the cañon I drew rein and dismounted and, leaving Red Lightning hidden in the brush, made my way to the summit where, below me, the trail lay in full view for a distance of a hundred yards up the cañon and for half a mile below. In my left hand I carried the heavy Kalkar bow and in my right a bundle of arrows, while a score or more others protruded from my right boot. Fitting an arrow to my bow I waited.

Nor did I have long to wait. I heard the clank of accouterments, the thud of horses' hoofs, the voices of men, and a moment later the head of the little column appeared about the shoulder of a hill.

I had tried my Kalkar bow this morning upon the bucks, and I was surer of it now. It is a good bow, the principal objection to it being that it is too cumbersome for a mounted warrior. It is very powerful, though, and carries its heavy arrows accurately to a great distance. I knew now what I could do with it.

I waited until half a dozen riders had come into view, covering the spot at which they appeared, and as the next one presented himself I loosed my shaft. I caught the fellow in the groin and, coming from above, as it did, passed through and into his horse. The stricken animal reared and threw itself backward upon its rider; but that I only caught with the tail of my eye, for I was loosing another shaft at the man in front of him. He dropped with an arrow through his neck.

By now all was pandemonium. Yelling and cursing, the balance of the troop galloped into sight and with them I saw such a man as mortal eye may never have rested upon before this time and, let us pray, never may again. He sat on a huge horse, which I instantly recognized as the animal that had made the great imprints in the trail I had been following to the summit, and was himself a creature of such mighty size that he dwarfed the big Kalkars about him.

Instantly I saw in him the giant Raban, whom I had thought but the figment of Saku's imagination or superstition. On a horse at Raban's side rode Bethelda. For an instant I was so astonished by the size of Raban that I forgot my business upon the ridge, but only for an instant. I could not let drive at the giant for fear of hitting Bethelda, but I brought down in quick succession the man directly in front of him and one behind.

By now the Kalkars were riding around in circles looking for the foe, and they presented admirable targets, as I had known they would. By the blood of my fathers! but there is no greater sport than this form of warfare. Always outnumbered by the Kalkars, we have been forced to adopt tactics aimed to harass the enemy and wear him down a little at a time. By clinging constantly to his flanks, by giving him no rest, by cutting off detachments from his main body and annihilating them, by swooping down unexpectedly upon his isolated settlements, by roving the country about him and giving battle to every individual we met upon the trails we have driven him two thousand miles across the world to his last stand beside the sea.

As the Kalkars milled about in the cañon bottom I drove shaft after shaft among them, but never could I get a fair shot at Raban the giant, for always he kept Bethelda between us after he had located me, guessing, evidently, that it was because of her that I had attacked his party. He roared like a bull as he sought to urge his men up the ridge to attack me, and some did make the attempt, half-heartedly, prompted no doubt by the fear of their master—a fear that must have been a little greater than fear of the unknown enemy above them; but those who started up after me never came far, for they soon discovered that with my heavy bow I could drive arrows through their iron vests as if they had been wool.

Raban, seeing that the battle was going against him, suddenly put spurs to his great mount and went lumbering off down the cañon, dragging Bethelda's horse after him, while those of his men who remained covered his retreat.

This did not suit me at all. I was not particularly interested in the Kalkars he was leaving behind, but in him and his captive, and so I ran to Red Lightning and mounted. As I reined down the flank of the ridge toward the cañon bottom I saw the Kalkars drawing off after Raban. There were but six of them left, and they were strung out along the trail.

As they rode they cast backward glances in my direction as if they were expecting to see a great force of warriors appear in pursuit. When they saw me they did not return to engage me, but continued after Raban.

I had reslung my bow beneath my right stirrup leather and replaced the few arrows in my quiver as Red Lightning descended the side of the ridge, and now I prepared my lance. Once upon the level trail of the cañon bottom I whispered a word into the pointed ear before me, couched my lance, and crouched in the saddle as the splendid animal flattened in swift charge.

The last Kalkar in the retreating column, rather than receive my spear through the small of his unprotected back, wheeled his horse, unslung his spear and awaited me in the middle of the trail. It was his undoing.

No man can meet the subtle tricks of a charging lancer from the back of a standing horse, for he cannot swerve to one side or the other with the celerity oft necessary to elude the point of his foe's lance, or take advantage of what opening the other may inadvertently leave him, and doubly true was this of the Kalkar upon his clumsy, splay-footed mount.

So awkward were the twain that they could scarcely have gotten out of their own way, much less mine, and so I took him where I would as I crashed into him, which was the chest, and my heavy lance passed through him, carrying him over his horse's rump, splintering the wood as he fell to earth. I cast the useless stump aside as I reined Red Lightning in and wheeled him about.

I saw the nearer Kalkar halted in the trail to watch the outcome of the battle, and now that he saw his companion go down to death and me without a lance he bore down upon me, and, I assume, he thought that he had me on the run, for Red Lightning was indeed racing away from him, back toward the fallen foe, but with a purpose in mind that one better versed in the niceties of combat might have sensed.

As I passed the dead Kalkar I swung low from my saddle and picked his lance from where it lay in the dust beside him, and then, never reducing our speed, I circled and came back to meet the rash one riding to his doom.

We came together at terrific speed, and as we approached each other I saw the tactics that this new adversary was bent upon using to my destruction, and I may say that he used judgment far beyond the seeming capacity of his low fore-head, for he kept his horse's head ever straight for Red Lightning's front with the intention of riding me down and overthrowing my mount, which, considering the disparity in their weights, he would certainly have accomplished had we met full on, but we did not.

My reins lay on Red Lightning's withers. With a touch of my left knee I swung the red stallion to the right and passed my spear to my left hand, all in a fraction of the time it takes to tell it, and as we met I had the Kalkar helpless, for he was not expecting me upon his left hand, his heavy horse could not swerve with the agility of Red Lightning, and so I had but to pick my target and put the fellow out of his misery—for it must be misery to be a low creature of a Kalkar.

In the throat my point caught him, for I had no mind to break another lance since I saw two more of the enemy riding toward me, and, being of tough wood, the weapon tore out through the flesh as the fellow tumbled backward into the dust of the trail.

There were four Kalkars remaining between me and the giant who, somewhere down the cañon and out of sight now, was bearing Bethelda off, I knew not where or to what fate. The four were strung out at intervals along the trail and ap-peared undecided as to whether to follow Raban or wait and argue matters out with me. Perhaps they hoped that I would realize the futility of pitting myself against their superior numbers, but when I lowered my lance and charged the nearer of them they must have realized that I was without discretion and must be ridden down and dispatched.

Fortunately for me they were separated by considerable intervals and I did not have to receive them all at once. The nearer, fortified by the sound of his companions' galloping approach, couched his lance and came halfway to meet me, but I think much of his enthusiasm must have been lost in contemplation of the fate that he had seen overtake the others that had pitted their crude skill against me, for certainly there was neither fire nor inspiration in his attack, which more closely resembled a huge senseless bowlder rolling down a mountainside than a sentient creature of nerves and brain driven by lofty purpose of patriotism and honor.

Poor clod! An instant later the world was a better place in which to live, by at least one less Kalkar; but he cost me another lance and a flesh wound in the upper arm, and left me facing his three fellows, who were now so close upon me that there was no time in which to retrieve the lance fallen from his nerveless fingers.

There was recourse only to the sword, and, drawing, I met the next of them with only a blade against his long lance; but I eluded his point, closed with him and, while he sought to draw, clove him open from his shoulder to the center of his chest.

It took but an instant, yet that instant was my undoing, for the remaining two were already upon me. I turned in time to partly dodge the lance point of the foremost, but it caught me a glancing blow upon the head and that is the last that I remember of immediately ensuing events.

When next I opened my eyes I was jouncing along, lashed to a saddle, belly down across a horse. Within the circumscribed limits of my vision lay a constantly renewed circle of dusty trail and four monotonously moving, gray, shaggy legs. At least I was not on Red Lightning.

I had scarcely regained consciousness when the horse bearing me was brought to a stop and the two accompanying Kalkars dismounted and approached me. Removing the bonds that held me to the saddle they dragged me unceremoniously to the ground, and when I stood erect they were surprised to see that I was conscious.

''Dirty Yank!'' cried one and struck me in the face with his open palm.

His companion laid a hand upon his arm. "Hold, Tav," he expostulated, "he put up a good fight against great odds." The speaker was a man of about my own height and might have passed as a full-blood Yank, though, as I thought at the time, doubtless he was a half-breed.

The other gestured his disgust. "A dirty Yank," he repeated. "Keep him here, Okonnor, while I find Raban and ask what to do with him." He turned and left us.

We had halted at the foot of a low hill upon which grew tremendous old trees and of such infinite variety that I marveled at them. There were pine, cypress, hemlock, sycamore and acacia that I recognized, and many others the like of which I never before had seen, and between the trees grew flowering shrubs. Where the ground was open it was carpeted with flowers—great masses of color; and there were little pools choked with lilies and countless birds and butterflies. Never had I looked upon a place of such wondrous beauty.

Through the trees I could see the outlines of the ruins of one of the stone tents of the ancients sitting upon the summit of the low hill. It was toward this ruined structure that he who was called Tav was departing from us.

"What place is this?" I asked the fellow guarding me, my curiosity overcoming my natural aversion to conversation with his kind.

"It is the tent of Raban," he replied. "Until recently it was the home of Or-tis the Jemadar—the true Or-tis. The false Or-tis dwells in the great tents of the Capitol. He would not last long in this valley."

"What is this Raban?" I asked.

"He is a great robber. He preys upon all and to such an extent has he struck terror to the hearts of all who have heard of him that he takes toll as he will, and easily. They say that he eats the flesh of humans, but that I do not know—I have been with him but a short time. After the assassination of the true Or-tis I joined him because he preys upon the Kalkars.

"He lived long in the eastern end of the valley, where he could prey upon the outskirts of the Capitol, and then he did not rob or murder the people of the valley; but with the death of Or-tis he came and took this place and now he preys upon my people as well as upon the Kalkars, but I remain with him since I must serve either him or the Kalkars."

"You are not a Kalkar?" I asked, and I could believe it because of his good old American name, Okonnor.

"I am a Yank, and you?"

"I am Julian 20th, The Red Hawk," I replied.

He raised his brows. "I have heard of you in the last few days," he said. "Your people are fighting mightily at the edge of The Capitol, but they will be driven back—the Kalkars are too many. Raban will be glad of you if the stories they tell of him are true. One is that he eats the hearts of brave warriors that are unfortunate enough to fall into his hands."

I smiled. "What is the creature?" I asked again. "Where originates such a breed?"

"He is only a Kalkar," replied Okonnor, "but even a greater monstrosity than his fellows. He was born in the Capitol of ordinary Kalkar parents, they say, and early developed a lust for blood that has increased with the passing years. He boasts yet of his first murder—he killed his mother when he was ten."

I shuddered. "And it is into the hands of such that a daughter of the Or-tis has fallen," I said, "and you, an American, aided in her capture."

He looked at me in startled surprise. "The daughter of an Or-tis?" he cried.

"Of *the* Or-tis," I repeated.

"I did not know," he said. "I was not close to her at any time and thought that she was but a Kalkar woman. Some of them are small, you know—the half-breeds."

"What are you going to do? Can you save her?" I demanded.

A white flame seemed to illumine his face. He drew his knife and cut the bonds that held my arms behind me.

"Hide here among the trees," he said, "and watch for Raban until I return. It will be after dark, but I will bring help. This valley is almost exclusively peopled by those who have refused to intermarry with the Kalkars and have brought down their strain unsullied from ancient times. There are almost a thousand fighting men of pure Yank blood within its confines. I should be able to gather enough to put an end to Raban for all time, and if the danger of a daughter of Or-tis cannot move them from their shame and cowardice they are hopeless indeed.''

He mounted his horse. "Quick!" he cried. "Get among the trees."

"Where is my horse?" I called as he was riding away. "He was not killed?"

"No," he called back, "he ran off when you fell. We did not try to catch him." A moment later he disappeared around the west end of the hill and I entered the miniature forest that clothed it. Through the gloom of my sorrow broke one ray of happiness—Red Lightning lived.

About me grew ancient trees of enormous size with boles of five to six feet in diameter and their upper foliage waving a hundred and more feet above my head. Their branches excluded the sun where they grew thickest and beneath them baby trees struggled for existence in the wan light, or hoary monsters, long fallen, lay embedded in leaf mould marking the spot where some long dead ancient set out a tiny seedling that was to outlive all his kind.

It was a wonderful place in which to hide, although hiding is an accomplishment that we Julians have little training in and less stomach for. However, in this instance it was in a worthy cause—a Julian hiding from a Kalkar in the hope of aiding an Or-tis! Ghosts of nineteen Julians! to what had I, Julian 20th, brought my proud name?

And yet I could not be ashamed. There was something stubbornly waging war against all my inherited scruples and I knew that it was going to win—had already won. I would have sold my soul for this daughter of my enemy.

I made my way up the hill toward the ruined tent, but at the summit the shrubbery was so dense that I could see nothing. Rose bushes fifteen feet high and growing as thickly together as a wall hid everything from my sight. I could not even penetrate them.

Near me was a mighty tree with a strange, feathery foliage. It was such a tree as I had never seen before, but that fact did not interest me so much as the discovery that it might be climbed to a point that would permit me to see above the tops of the rose bushes.

What I saw included two stone tents, not so badly ruined as most of those one comes across, and between them a pool of water—an artificial pool of straight lines. Some fallen columns of stone lay about it and the vines and creepers fell over its edge into the water, almost concealing the stone rim.

As I watched a group of men came from the ruin to the east through a great archway, the coping of which had fallen away. They were all Kalkars, and among them was Raban. I had my first opportunity to view him closely.

He was a most repulsive appearing creature. His great size might easily have struck with awe the boldest heart, for he stood a full nine feet in height and was very large in proportion about the shoulders, chest and limbs. His forehead was so retreating that one might with truth say he had none, his thick thatch of stiffly erect hair almost meeting his shaggy eyebrows.

His eyes were small and set close to a coarse nose, and all his countenance was bestial. I had not dreamed that a man's face could be so repulsive. His whiskers appeared to grow in all directions and proclaimed, at best, but hearsay evidence of combing.

He was speaking to that one of my captors who had left me at the foot of the hill to apprise Raban of my taking—that fellow who struck me in the face while my hands were bound and whose name was Tav. The giant spoke in a roaring, bull-like voice which I thought at the time was, like his swaggering walk and his braggadocio, but a pose to strike terror in those about him.

I could not look at the creature and believe that real courage lay within so vile a carcass. I have known many fearless men—The Vulture, The Wolf, The Rock and hundreds like them—and in each courageousness was reflected in some outward physical attribute of dignity and majesty.

"Fetch him!" he roared at Tav. "Fetch him! I will have his heart for my supper," and after Tav had gone to fetch me the giant stood there with his other followers, roaring and bellowing, and it always was about himself and what he had done and what he would do. He seemed to me an exaggeration of a type I had seen before, wherein gestures simulate action, noise counterfeits courage, and craft passes for brains.

The only impressive thing about him was his tremendous bulk, and yet even that did not impress me greatly—I have known smaller men, whom I respected, that filled me with far greater awe. I did not fear him.

I think only the ignorant could have feared him at all, and I did not believe all the pother about his eating human flesh. I am of the opinion that a man who really intended eating the heart of another would say nothing about it.

Presently Tav came running back up the hill. He was much excited, as I had known he would be.

"He is gone!" he cried to Raban. "They are both gone—Okonnor and the Yank. Look!" He held out the thongs that had fastened my wrists. "They have been cut. How could he cut them with his hands bound behind him? That is what I want to know. How could he have done it? He could not unless—"

"There must have been others with him," roared Raban. "They followed and set him free, taking Okonnor captive."

"There were no others," insisted Tav.

"Perhaps Okonnor freed him," suggested another.

So obvious an explanation could not have originated in the pea girth brain of Raban and so he said: "I knew it from the first—it was Okonnor. With my own hands I shall tear out his liver and eat it for breakfast."

Certain insects, toads and men make a lot of unnecessary noise, but the vast majority of other animals pass through life in dignified silence. It is our respect for these other animals that causes us to take their names. Whoever heard a red hawk screeching his intentions to the world? Silently he soars above the treetops and as silently he swoops and strikes.

9

Reunion

THROUGH THE CONVERSATION that I overheard between Raban and his minions I learned that Bethelda was imprisoned in the westerly ruin, but as Raban did not go thither during the afternoon I waited in the hope that fortune would favor me with a better opportunity after dark to attempt her liberation with less likelihood of interruption or discovery than would have been possible during the day, when men and women were constantly passing in and out of the easterly tent. There was the chance, too, that Okonnor might return with help and I did not want to do anything, while that hope remained, that might jeopardize Bethelda's chances for escape.

Night fell and yet there was no sign of Okonnor. Sounds of coarse laughter came from the main ruin, and I could imagine that Raban and his followers were at meal, washing down their food with the fiery liquor of the Kalkars. There was no one in sight and so I determined to come out of my concealment and investigate the structure in which I believed Bethelda was imprisoned. If I could release her, well and good; if not I could but wait for the return of Okonnor.

As I was about to descend from the tree there came down with the wind from out of the cañon to the south a familiar sound—the nicker of my red stallion. It was music to my ears. I must answer it even though I chanced arousing the suspicions of the Kalkars.

Just once my answering whistle arose sharp and clear above

the noises of the night. I do not think the Kalkars heard it—
they were making too much noise of their own within doors—
but the eager whinny that came thinly down the night wind
told me that two fine, slim ears had caught the familiar sum-
mons.

Instead of going at once to the westerly ruin I made my
way down the hill to meet Red Lightning, for I knew that he
might mean, in the end, success or failure for me—freedom
or death for Bethelda. Already, when I reached the foot of
the declivity, I faintly heard the pounding of his hoofs and,
steadily increasing in volume, the loved sound rolled swiftly
out of the darkness toward me. The hoof beats of running
horses, the rolling of the war drums! What sweeter music in
all the world?

He saw me, of course, before I saw him, but he stopped
in a cloud of dust a few yards from me and sniffed the air.
I whispered his name and called him to me. Mincingly
he came, stopping often, stretching his long neck forward,
poised, always, ready for instant flight.

A horse depends much upon his eyes and ears and nostrils,
but he is never so fully satisfied as when his soft, inquisitive
muzzle has nosed an object of suspicion. He snorted now,
and then he touched my cheek with his velvet lip and gave a
great sigh and rubbed his head against me, satisfied. I hid
him beneath the trees at the foot of the hill and bade him
wait there in silence.

From the saddle I took the bow and some arrows and,
following the route that Tav had taken to the top of the hill,
I avoided the hedge of roses and came presently before the
south archway of the ruin. Beyond was a small central court
with windows and doors opening upon it. Light from flares
burning in some of the rooms partly illuminated the court,
but most of it was in shadow.

I passed beneath the arch and to the far end of the inclo-
sure, where, at my right, I saw a window and a door opening
into two rooms in which a number of Kalkars were eating
and drinking at two long tables. I could not see them all. If
Raban was there he was not within range of my vision.

It is always well to reconnoiter thoroughly before carrying out any plan of action, and with this idea in mind I left the court by the way I had entered and made my way to the east end of the structure, intending to pass entirely around it and along the north side to the westerly ruin, where I hoped to find Bethelda and devise means for her rescue.

At the southeast corner of the ruin are three gigantic cypress trees, growing so closely together as almost to resemble a single huge tree, and as I paused an instant behind them to see what lay before me, I saw a single Kalkar warrior come from the building and walk out into the rank grass that grew knee high on a level space before the structure.

I fitted an arrow to my bow. The fellow had that which I craved—a sword. Could I drop him noiselessly? If he would turn I was sure of it, and turn he did, as though impelled to it by my insistent wish. His back was toward me.

I drew the shaft far back. The cord twanged as I released it, but there was no other sound, except the muffled thud as the arrow entered its victim's spine at the base of the brain. Mute, he died. No other was around. I ran forward and removed his sword belt, to which were attached both sword and knife.

As I arose and buckled the weapons about me I glanced into the lighted room from which he had just come. It was the same that I had seen from the court upon the other side and directly adjoining it was the other room that I had seen. Now I could see all of them that I had not seen before.

Raban was not there. Where was he? A cold terror ran suddenly through me. Could it be that in the brief interval that had elapsed while I went down to meet Red Lightning he had left the feast and gone to the westerly ruin! I shuddered as I ran swiftly across the front of the house and along the north side toward the other structure.

I stopped before it and listened. I heard the sound of voices! From whence came they? This was a peculiar structure, built upon a downward sloping hill, with one floor on a level with the hilltop, another above that level and a third below and behind the others. Where the various entrances were and how to find the right one I did not know.

From my hiding place in the tree I had seen that the front chamber at the hilltop level was a single apartment with a cavernous entrance that stretched the full width of the ruin, while upon the south side and to the rear of this apartment were two doors, but where they led to I could not guess.

It seemed best, however, to try these first and so I ran immediately to them, and here the sounds of voices came more distinctly to me, and now I recognized the roaring, bull-tones of Raban.

I tried the nearer door. It swung open, and before me a flight of stairs descended and at the same time the voices came more loudly to my ears—I had opened the right door. A dim light flickered below as if coming from a chamber near the foot of the stairs.

These were but instantaneous impressions to which I gave no conscious heed at the time, for almost as they flashed upon me I was at the foot of the stairs looking into a large, high ceiled chamber in which burned a single flare that but diffused the gloom sufficiently for me to see the figure of Raban towering above that of Bethelda whom he was dragging toward the doorway by her hair.

''An Or-tis!'' he was bellowing. ''An Or-tis! Who would have thought that Raban would ever take the daughter of a Jemadar to be his woman? Ah, you do not like the idea, eh? You might do worse, if you had a choice, but you have none, for who is there to say no to Raban the Giant?''

''The Red Hawk!'' I said, stepping into the chamber.

The fellow wheeled and in the flickering light of the dim flare I saw his red face go purple and from purple to white, or rather a blotchy semblance of dirty yellow. Blood of my Fathers! How he towered above me, a perfect mountain of flesh. I am six feet in height and Raban must have been half again as tall, a good nine feet; but I swear he appeared all of twenty and broad in proportion!

For a moment he stood in silence glaring at me as if overcome by surprise, and then he thrust Bethelda aside and drawing his sword advanced upon me, bellowing and roaring as was his wont for the purpose, I presume, of terrifying me and, also, I could not help but think, to attract the attention and the aid of his fellows.

I came to meet him then and he appeared a mountain, so high he loomed; but with all his size I did not feel the concern that I have when meeting men of my own stature whose honor and courage merited my respect. It is well that I had this attitude of mind to fortify me in the impending duel, for, by the Flag, I needed whatever encouragement I might find in it.

The fellow's height and weight were sufficient to overcome a mighty warrior had Raban been entirely wanting in skill, which he by no means was. He wielded his great sword with a master hand, and because of the very cowardice which I attributed to him, he fought with a frenzy wrought by fear, as a cornered beast fights.

I needed all my skill and I doubt that that alone would have availed me had it not been upborne and multiplied by love and the necessity for protecting the object of my love. Ever was the presence of Bethelda the Or-tis a spur and an inspiration. What blows I struck I struck for her, what I parried it was as though I parried from her soft skin.

As we closed he swung mightily at me a cut that would have severed me in twain, but I parried and stooped beneath it at once. I found his great legs unguarded before me and ran my sword through a thigh. With a howl of pain, Raban leaped back, but I followed him with a jab of my point that caught him just beneath the bottom of his iron vest and punctured his belly.

At that he gave forth a horrible shriek, and although sorely wounded began to wield his blade with a skill I had not dreamed lay in him. It was with the utmost difficulty that I turned his heavy sword and I saved myself as many times by the quickness of my feet as by the facility of my blade.

And much do I owe, too, to the cleverness of Bethelda, who, shortly after we crossed swords, had run to the great fireplace and seized the flare from where it had reposed upon the stone shelf above, and ever after had kept just behind my shoulder with it, so that whatever advantage of light there might be lay with me. Her position was a dangerous one and I begged her to put herself at a safe distance, but she would not, and no more would she take advantage of this opportunity to escape, although that, too, I urged upon her.

Momentarily, I had expected to see Raban's men rushing into the chamber, for I could not understand that his yells had not reached every ear within a mile or more, and so I fought the more desperately to be rid of him and on our way before they came. Raban, now panting for breath, had none left with which to yell and I could see that from exertion, terror and loss of blood he was weakening.

It was now that I heard the loud voices of men without and the tramp of running feet. They were coming! I redoubled my efforts and Raban his—I to kill, he to escape death until succor came. From a score of wounds was he bleeding and I was sure that the thrust in his abdomen alone must prove fatal; but still he clung to life tenaciously, and fought with a froth of blood upon his lips from a punctured throat.

He stumbled and went to one knee, and as he staggered to arise I thought that I had him, but then we heard the hurrying feet of men descending the stairs. Instantly Bethelda hurled the flare to the floor, leaving us in utter darkness.

"Come!" she whispered, laying a hand upon my arm. "There will be too many now—we must escape as they enter or we are both indeed lost."

The warriors were cursing at the doorway now and calling for lights.

"Who hides within?" shouted one. "Stand forth, prisoner! We are a hundred blades."

Bethelda and I edged nearer the doorway, hoping to pass out among them before a light was made. From the center of the room came a deep groan from where I had left Raban, followed by a scuffling noise upon the floor and a strange gurgling. I came to the doorway, leading Bethelda by the hand. I found it impassable, choked with men.

"Aside!" I said. "I will fetch a light."

A sword point was shoved against my belly. "Back!" warned a voice behind the point. "We will have a look at you before you pass—another is bringing a light."

I stepped back and crossed my sword with his. Perhaps I could hew my way to freedom with Bethelda in the confusion of the darkness. It seemed our only hope, for to be caught by Raban's minions now after the hurts I had inflicted upon him would mean sure death for me and worse for Bethelda.

By the feel of our steel we fenced in the dark, but I could not reach him, nor he me, although I felt that he was a master swordsman. I thought that I was gaining an advantage when I saw the flicker of a light coming from the doorway at the head of the stairs. Some one was coming with a flare. I redoubled my efforts, but to no avail.

And then the light came and as it fell upon the warriors in the doorway I stepped back, astounded, and dropped my point. The light that revealed them illumined my own face and at sight of it my antagonist voiced a cry of joy.

"Red Hawk!" he cried; and seized me by the shoulder. It was the Vulture, my brother, and with him were the Rattlesnake and a hundred warriors of our own beloved clans. Other lights were brought and I saw Okonnor and a host of strange warriors in Kalkar trappings pushing down the stairway with my own, nor did they raise swords against one another.

Okonnor pointed toward the center of the chamber and we looked, and there lay Raban the Giant, dead.

"The Red Hawk, Julian 20th," he said, turning to those

crowding into the chamber behind him. "Great Chief of the Tribe of Julians—our chief!"

"And Jemadar of all America!" cried another voice, and the warriors, crowding into the room, raised their swords and their hoarse voices in acclamation. And he who had named me thus pushed past them and faced me, and I saw that he was no other than the true Or-tis with whom I had been imprisoned in The Capitol and with whom I had escaped. He saw Bethelda and rushed forward and took her in his arms, and for a moment I was jealous, forgetting that he was her brother.

"And how has all this happened," I asked, "that Or-tis and Julian come here together in peace?"

"Listen," said my brother, "before you pass judgment upon us. Long has run the feud between Julian and Or-tis for the crime of a man dead now hundreds of years. Few enough are the Americans of pure blood that they should be separated by hate when they would come together in friendship.

"Came the Or-tis to us after escaping the Kalkars and told of your escape and of the wish of his father that peace be made between us, and he offered to lead us against the Kalkars by ways that we did not know, and the Wolf took council with me and there was also the Rock, the Rattlesnake and the Coyote, with every other chief who was at the front, and in your absence I dissolved the feud that has lain between us and the chiefs applauded my decision.

"Then, guided by the Or-tis, we entered The Capitol and drove the Kalkars before us. Great are their numbers, but they have not the Flag with them and eventually they must fall.

"Then," he continued, "came word, brought by the little Nipons of the hills, that you were in the mountains near the tent of Raban the Giant and we came to find you, and on the way we met Okonnor with many warriors and glad were they of the peace that had been made and we joined with them who were also riding against Raban to rescue the sister of the Or-tis. And we are here awaiting the word of the Great Chief. If it is for peace between the Julian and the Or-tis, we are glad; if it is for war our swords are ready."

"It is for peace, ever," I replied, and the Or-tis came and knelt at my feet and took my hand in his.

"Before my people," he said very simply, "I swear allegiance to Julian 20th, the Red Hawk, Jemadar of America."

10

Peace

THERE WAS STILL much fighting to be done, for although we had driven the Kalkars from the Capitol they held the country to the south and west and we could not be satisfied until we had driven them into the sea, and so we prepared to ride to the front again that very night, but before we left I wanted a word with Bethelda who was to remain here with a proper retinue and a sufficient guard in the home of her people.

Leading Red Lightning, I searched about the grounds around the ruins and at last I came upon her beneath a great oak tree that grew at the northwest corner of the structure, its mighty limbs outspreading above the ruin. She was alone and I came and stood beside her.

"I am going now," I said, "to drive your enemies and mine into the sea. I have come to say good-by."

"Good-by, Julian." She held out her hand to me.

I had come full of brave words and a mighty resolve, but when I took that slim and tender hand in mine I could but stand there mute and trembling. I, Julian 20th, the Red Hawk, for the first time in all my life knew fear. A Julian quailed before an Or-tis!

For a full minute I stood there trying to speak and could not, and then I dropped to my knees at the feet of my enemy and with my lips against her fair hand I murmured what I had been too great a coward to look into her eyes and say: "I love you!"

She raised me to my feet then and lifted her lips to mine

and I took her into my arms and covered her mouth with kisses; and thus ended the ancient feud between Julian and Or-tis, that had endured four hundred years and wrecked a world.

Two years later and we had driven the Kalkars into the sea, the remnants of them flying westward in great canoes which they had built and launched upon a beauteous bay a hundred miles or more south of the Capitol.

The Rain Cloud said that if they were not overcome by storms and waves they might sail on and on around the world and come again to the eastern shores of America, but the rest of us knew that they would sail to the edge of the earth and tumble off and that would be the end of them.

We live in such peace now that it is difficult to find an enemy upon whom to try one's lance, but I do not mind much, since my time is taken with the care of my flocks and herds, the business of my people and the training of Julian 21st, the son of a Julian and an Or-tis, who will one day be Jemadar of all America over which, once more, there flies but a single flag—the Flag.

A NOTE TO ERB ENTHUSIASTS

For readers interested in learning more about the life and work of Edgar Rice Burroughs, Del Rey includes the following list of ERB fan clubs and their magazines. Write to the address below for information on memberships and subscriptions.

British Edgar Rice Burroughs Society
77 Pembroke Road
Seven Kings
Ilford, Essex
IG3 8PQ England

Burroughs Bibliophiles
Burroughs Memorial Collection
University of Louisville
Louisville, Kentucky 40292

Erbania
8001 Fernview Lane
Tampa, Florida 33615

ERB Collector
7315 Livingston Road
Oxon Hill, Maryland 20745

ERB-Fan
Eschenweg 5
8070 Ingolstadt
West Germany

ERB News Dateline
1990 Pine Grove Drive
Jenison, Michigan 49428

Tarzine
914 Country Club Drive
Midland, Texas 79701

ABOUT THE AUTHOR

Edgar Rice Burroughs is one of the world's most popular authors. With no previous experience as an author, he wrote and sold his first novel—*A Princess of Mars*—in 1912. In the ensuing thirty-eight years until his death in 1950, Burroughs wrote ninety-one books and a host of short stories and articles. Although best known as the creator of the classic *Tarzan of the Apes* and *John Carter of Mars*, his restless imagination knew few bounds. Burroughs's prolific pen ranged from the American West to primitive Africa and on to romantic adventures on the moon, the planets, and even beyond the farthest star.

No one knows how many copies of ERB books have been published throughout the world. It is conservative to say, however, that with the translations into thirty-two known languages, including Braille, the number must run into the hundreds of millions. When one considers the additional worldwide following of the Tarzan newspaper feature, radio programs, comic magazines, motion pictures, and television, Burroughs must have been known and loved by literally a thousand million or more.